ONCE AN ALIEN

Book Three of
The Alien Chronicles

Robin Martin

Published by Bennett Lane Press 2019
Copyright © 2019 Robin Martin

www.robinmartinthomas.com

The characters and events portrayed in this book are fictitious. Any similarity to real persons, living or dead, is coincidental and not intended by the author.

A catalogue record for this book is available from the National Library of Australia.

Book cover design and formatting services by Self-publishingLab.com

ISBN:
978-0-9946465-7-6 (pbk)
978-0-9946465-8-3 (e-bk)

To my sister, Judy

Far in distance, close in heart

Chapter One

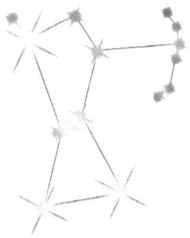

Mist, like a spectre, curled on the cool pavement of a Brisbane suburban street and gathered in a dense cloud. The night sky was clear, and there was no meteorological reason for its formation. But it was the quiet time when everyone was asleep, and the only witness to this phenomenon was a grey tabby sitting on a nearby fence post. Tired after the night's exploits, it took no notice at first. Then its sleepy gaze intensified, and its ears pricked. The mist stilled and, slowly dissolving, revealed a tall, angular shape. The cat arched its back, fur bristling and tail twitching. The shape began to look human in form, female. She shook her head, sending long hair cascading over a shoulder. A soft, low laugh shattered the silence of the night. The cat hissed and showed its sharp teeth. Its claws extended and dug into the splintered wood of the fence.

'Hey kitty cat,' the figure said in a soft voice. Her fingers clicked, sending an arc of light toward the feline.

The cat's emerald eyes dilated, but only for a moment. Retracting its claws, it jumped off the fence and trotted over to this strange female, who bent down and gave a pat to the little feline. The tabby raised its head to her touch and purred loudly. Then standing again, the woman said, 'Let's hope humans are as easy to control as you are,' and blew on her long fingers. Putting her hands on her hips, she looked around the quiet street and breathed in deeply. Then she said, 'Really, Orion, how could you have kept all this fun of being an organic for yourself? Time to share, I think.'

With another laugh, this time a little louder and not quite so soft, she strode down the street, the sound of her footsteps disappearing into the night.

'Seriously, Rion, I can't believe you of all people are going to make me late for school on the first day back after the Easter break.' I looked at him, feeling only a little irritated, because I wasn't exactly known for being anywhere on time. I closed the front door behind me.

He pushed the dark hair from his face and smiled. So unfair that smile. It made something inside me melt every time. 'I know. I'm sorry, but I had a good reason,' he said.

'What?' I asked, looking up at him.

'First things first.' He dropped his bag, pulled me into his arms, and kissed me with his warm, firm lips. Aliens really knew how to kiss—well, this one did anyway.

After a moment or two, I pulled away, curious about what made Rion late. He was anally conscientious about time usually.

'I guess that was worth waiting for,' I said, 'but what's this good reason?'

Rion looked at me sheepishly. 'This.' He bent down and pulled a small square box out of his school bag. It was covered in crinkled blue paper and on the top was a red bow slightly askew. 'I'm sorry, I'm not very good at wrapping presents. It took me five attempts to get it right.'

'You got me a present?' I looked at him and wanted to kiss him again. 'What is it?'

'Open it and see.'

I unwrapped it and took out a small blue jeweller's box. Taking off the lid, I saw a thin silver chain with a heart. Lifting it out, I stared at the delicate necklace.

'Turn the heart over and see what's there,' he said, anxiously.

On the other side of the heart was engraved 'Zoe and Rion' and underneath in small italic numbers was a date.

'It's beautiful, Rion. Thank you so much.' Holding the necklace and box tightly, I put my arms around his neck and this time I kissed him.

After a moment, or maybe two, he lifted his head. 'Do you like it?'

'I love it! But what's the date?'

'That's the day you finally remembered who I was again. The happiest day of my life. I got the necklace so you would never forget our connection again, or what you mean to me.'

'Oh, Rion,' I said, tears welling in my eyes.

Most of last term had sucked. Rion hadn't been there at the beginning, and when he did come back, things were... tricky between us. I had lost my memories of the close bond between us, due to Rion's guardian, Archimedes, removing them. It was only when Rion finally kissed me, that I remembered how much I cared about him, and then everything that had happened between us came flooding back to me. Now we were together again, and nothing was going to change that.

"I'm not going to forget you ever again, but I love this necklace. Wearing it will always make me feel closer to you. Will you help me put it on?'

I turned around, and he put it around my neck, fastened it, and kissed the back of my head.

'I did get something else too, but it's more practical.'

I turned to face him again as he reached down in his bag once more and pulled out a purple book. 'It's a diary, and I put something in it to help you this year.'

Curious, I took it from his hand and opened it. Inside was a printed sheet that he had glued to the first page. It looked like a schedule of some sort. I gave him a puzzled glance.

He rushed to explain. 'I made out a study timetable for you to follow, along with an exercise program slotted in and also time for recreation, sleep, and of course…' — he blushed — 'time for us to be together. It will take all the stress out of this year. I've planned it all out. If you follow it, it will make your life so much easier. I was just putting the finishing touches on it this morning. That's when I thought it might be a little inflexible, so I factored in a spontaneity portion of time for those small unexpected events that happen. It threw the whole thing off at first, but I managed to work it out in the end. What do you think?' His dark eyes widened in excitement.

I tried hard not to smile. 'I'm sure that will be very useful.'

'I know senior year is supposed to be stressful, and now that we're together, I didn't want that to make it harder for you. I wanted to make everything as easy as possible for you this year.'

This time I did laugh. He looked at me puzzled. 'Only you could think of such an original gift. Thank you.' I reached up and gave him a quick kiss. He had come a long way as a human, but there were still times that he was my fact-obsessed, yet surprisingly thoughtful alien. And it was one of the quirky things I loved about him.

He beamed at me.

'And, speaking of schedules, we'd better get a move on if we have any hope of getting to school on time,' I added.

At school, it seemed as if we hadn't even had that two-week break. Assignments were due or set and group projects, reading lists, and presentations pelted down on us like hail from a thunderstorm. When were we supposed to sleep? Perhaps that schedule Rion made for me might come in handy after all.

At lunch I collapsed on the grass next to Harry, my long-time best friend and almost boyfriend. I say almost because for a while last term, it could have gone that way if it weren't for Rion. But in the end, though I really liked Harry and we knew each other so well we could almost finish each other's sentences, I knew my heart belonged to Rion. Harry knew it too. At least I thought he did. We hadn't really talked much since Rion had become my boyfriend.

'I am so over this term already,' I complained as I opened my lunch box and looked in distaste at the limp lettuce leaves and slightly brown avocado in it. Salad had seemed such a healthy option this morning, but after having been in my bag for four hours in nearly thirty-degree heat, it had suffered. Right now, even a peanut butter sandwich was looking more appealing.

Harry handed me one of his crispbreads and cheese. 'Here, have this. I'm not very hungry.'

I looked at it, tempted, but I shook my head. 'Nah, I'm good.'

The laughter lines crinkled around his hazel eyes as he grinned. 'I saw that look on your face. Go on. I'm really not hungry. I had a high-protein breakfast, and that keeps me going nearly all day. It's just Mum insists I take something.'

I caved and took it. 'Thanks. Don't know why I bother sometimes to be healthy, but jeez, Harry, you're doing well.' Up until this year, health and Harry had never occupied the same sentence. He ate junk food, didn't exercise, and was perfectly happy. Then, in term four last year, he caught glandular fever and was sick for months. His uncle helped him build up his strength with an exercise and diet regime, and Harry got really into it. Now, with a superhero physique, he turned girls' heads wherever he went. But the good thing about it was, he was still Harry, a really nice guy, and that hadn't changed at all.

He shrugged and said, 'Yeah well, it's just become part of my routine now. If I don't exercise, I feel really off, and I don't crave junk food nearly as much as I used to. I only think about a Big Mac and a double choc milkshake once a day now instead of every half hour.' He laughed. There was a pause, and I knew he was trying to sound casual when he asked, 'Where's Rion?'

'Today is one of the days he helps Mr Hasan clean up in the lab. He'll probably just eat his lunch there.'

'So, I guess you saw a lot of each other during the holidays.'

I felt the heat come to my face. 'Yeah. I guess you could say we're official now.'

He nodded. 'I thought as much. You're good together.' That was generous of him.

'Thanks, Harry.' Awkward silence.

To both our relief, Kerri walked towards us, laden with several books and her lunch on top. Her glasses had fallen halfway down her freckled nose, but her arms were too full to be able to fix them. She dropped her lunch and books on the grass and sat next to me. 'You know we really should be sitting in the shade. The UV rays at this time of the day are at their strongest.'

'How was your holiday?' I asked to change the subject before she insisted we move. I hadn't seen her since the end of last term, or anyone, except Rion as everybody seemed to have gone away for the break.

Kerri pushed her hat off her face and tucked a strand of red hair behind her ear. Then she gave me an actual smile, a rare occurrence. 'It was very productive. I got such a lot of work done. Finished all the assignments that were due and did a bit of advance reading for this term. I'm almost ready for term two, although another few days would have been nice. I haven't quite finished the extra reading list for English.'

'Did you do anything that was fun?' I asked, although I was pretty sure what the answer would be.

'Fun?' She took her ham salad wrap out and gave me a puzzled look. 'Well, getting most of the studying done that I'd planned was very satisfactory, but I did watch a few episodes of *Hospital Emergency*. I know it's commercial TV, but sometimes they have some interesting operations to perform. Oh yes, and my parents insisted we go to the Gold Coast for a few days. It was awfully hot, and I was always getting sand in my swimsuit. Still, they have a good library there.'

I sighed. Why did I bother?

I finished eating the crispbread Harry had given me.

Lou was the last to join us. She rushed over from the shade shelter that led to the entrance where our school lockers were. Her pale face was flushed, and her blue eyes were round with excitement. It flashed through my mind that she looked a little different from last term, but I wasn't sure how. And anyway, two weeks couldn't make that much difference. It must be my imagination.

She flounced down on the other side of Harry, dropping her lunch box on the ground. Crossing her legs under the skirt of her uniform, she leaned forward and said, 'Have you heard the news?'

Kerri looked up from the book she had opened and took a bite of her wrap. I shook my head, and Harry said, 'Go on, Lou, tell us.'

'There's a new girl, and she's in our year.'

That was mildly interesting but not exactly earth-shattering. From time to time, we got new students during the year. But Lou obviously thought this was a big deal. 'Have you met her?' I asked. 'Does she seem nice?'

'I haven't actually spoken to her, but I have seen her...' Lou looked as if she were bursting.

'And?' I said, wishing she would get on with it.

She seemed to search for words. Lou had always had trouble expressing herself. Then she said, 'She... she's amazing, so different. She came into our art class, and we were doing a still life of some fruit and a bunch of flowers. Within a few minutes, she'd done a sketch that was better than anyone in the class, even Mr Bouchard's. And she was so nice. She helped a couple students who didn't get it, and she even spoke French to Mr Bouchard, so she completely won him over.'

'Impressive,' Harry said.

Kerri took another bite of her sandwich and went back to her book, clearly finding it more interesting.

'What else can you tell us about her?' I asked, just a little intrigued. Someone who was good at art and spoke French had to be cool. 'Where's she from?'

'No idea,' Lou said. 'I wanted to talk to her, but when the bell went, there were too many other students crowded around her.'

The thing that impressed me most about this was that Lou would actually want to speak to someone she didn't know.

'So, what's she look like?' I asked, wanting details.

'Amazing,' Lou enthused.

'Yeah, you said that.'

'What's her name?' Harry asked a more practical question.

'Pandora,' a voice interrupted us.

We all looked up.

A tall girl with jet-black hair that fell like a curtain over her shoulders looked back at us with her cobalt blue eyes and an eyebrow slightly raised. She was standing with one hand on her hip and her head at an angle, an amused expression on her face, as if she not only heard every word we said but also knew every thought in our brains. We had the dorkiest uniform in Brisbane, with a long grey skirt and a blouse that would not have been out of place in Victorian times. On this girl, however, it almost looked cool. Her skirt was hitched up shorter than normal, and the blouse was unbuttoned almost to her bra line. The school tie, which we all hated, was loose and pushed to the side, almost like a fashion statement. I wondered how long the teachers would let her get away with that. I saw what Lou meant immediately. This girl was different and was sure to stir things up at school. In a word, I sensed trouble.

Lou turned a deep shade of red. 'Pandora, we didn't see you there.'

Even Harry looked impressed. 'Do you want to join us?'

'Sure.' She sat down and turned to me. 'So, you must be Zoe.'

I was surprised. 'How did you know?'

'I just figured. I've heard about you, and as I soon as I saw you, it was obvious.'

I wasn't sure how to respond to that. I wondered if what she'd heard about me in the brief time she'd been here was good or bad. I just hoped she hadn't been talking to Jas, who wasn't exactly in my fan club.

Her eyes focussed on me with an intent look that left me feeling uncomfortable. She smiled and said,

12

'We're going to be friends.' Then she sat back, and her glance took in the rest of the group. Even Kerri looked up from her reading and was watching Pandora with some curiosity.

'I saw you in art class, though you probably didn't notice me,' Lou said, the second part of her sentence disappearing into a mumble.

'Sure I did. You were sitting in the corner. You have such an interesting face, Lou, sometime I'd like to sketch your portrait. There's so much more going on there than most people see, isn't there?'

Lou turned even redder, if that was possible. 'Oh gee, thanks.'

'Do you need lunch or anything?' Harry asked, and I realised Pandora didn't have anything with her, not a drink, lunch box, or books. 'If you want, I can show you where the tuckshop is.'

She laughed and flicked her hair over her shoulders, and I could see my best friend looking as awestruck as Lou. 'I forgot about lunch, but anyway, I'm not very hungry right now. It's too hot. Though I would really love some water, cold preferably.'

'I'll get you a bottle,' Harry said, jumping up. 'Back in a few minutes.' He rushed away with all the eagerness of a Labrador puppy.

13

Pandora looked at me and said, 'He's so nice, isn't he? And not hard to look at either.'

She turned to Kerri. 'What are you reading?'

Kerri turned up the cover of her book.

'Oh, *The Elegant Universe* by Greene,' Pandora said. 'String theory is interesting, isn't it? But you know it's so passé now. Smolin's *The Trouble with Physics* has raised a lot of questions about string theory.'

I tried not to let my jaw hit the ground.

Kerri's eyes lit up with enthusiasm. 'Yes, I know. But I thought I would review the basics so that I would understand Smolin's ideas better.'

'Wise move. It's always good to know both the arguments and the counterarguments.'

'That's what I think too.' Kerri sat up straight and actually closed her book. 'So, what did you think of Smolin's ideas?'

But Pandora's attention shifted to something else, or rather *someone* else. Mine too.

'Rion, you finished in the lab,' I said. I still felt those butterflies inside when I saw him.

But he wasn't looking at me. He was looking at Pandora. Those butterflies died a sudden death and sank to the pit of my stomach.

'What are you doing here?' he said, and he was looking anything but happy.

Chapter Two

Pandora stood and sauntered over to him. She laid a hand on his chest, a hand that was entirely too predatory for my liking, and said, 'It's good to see you too, Orion. And, I have to say, you've changed for the better.'

As they looked at each other, I could sense the intensity between them. I wasn't sure if the vibes were good or bad, but for a moment it seemed like the rest of us didn't exist.

'You two know each other?' Lou asked.

No one answered her.

'You shouldn't be here,' Rion said.

Her laughter sounded creepy, and a sense of unease filled me. Who was this person?

Then she leaned a little closer to him and said, 'Is that any way to greet me?'

I decided enough was enough. I hopped up and strode over to Rion. 'Hey,' I said, putting my hand on his arm.

He looked down at me, as if suddenly realising I was there. His arm snaked around my shoulders. 'Zoe,' was all he said, but it was enough. We were good.

Pandora glanced between us. 'I'll catch you up later, Orion. I've got to go. See you guys later.' She nodded to Lou and Kerri and then headed towards the school building, her long dark hair swaying.

'Isn't she just the nicest person?' Lou said.

'It's so unusual to find someone who can hold a decent conversation,' Kerri added, not realising she was insulting the only friends she had.

Harry came rushing towards us from the direction of the tuck shop, holding a bottle of water.

'The line was so long, I had to wait forever,' he said, looking around. 'Where is she?'

'She's gone,' I answered, taking in his disappointed face. 'Never mind. If you're lucky, she might be in one of your classes.' Harry, for once, totally missed the sarcasm in my voice.

'Yeah, you're right. I'll hang on to this, just in case.'

The first bell went, and everybody around us began picking up their lunches, throwing scrunched-up papers into the bin, and slowly moving towards class. A few guys who had just come off the oval were throwing a football back and forth and getting in everyone's way, some twerpy year eights were pushing and shoving each other, and a few girls were heading straight to the girls' loo where they would make themselves beautiful for the afternoon session. In other words, just a normal end of lunch. Except it wasn't. Pandora had changed everyone's behaviour in our group, including mine. Just what was she up to and why? Because it was clear, at least to me, she had some kind of agenda.

I tucked my hand through Rion's arm as we walked back to class. 'How do you know Pandora?'

For a moment he was quiet, and then he shrugged. 'I don't know her that well.'

Didn't seem that way to me. 'Did you meet her during those months when you were living in south Brisbane by yourself?' I hadn't seen or heard from Rion during those long, lonely months, so it was conceivable that he met her then.

He shook his head. We had nearly reached the school building, and there were a lot of people around us and zero privacy. Another thought struck me. 'Is she one of your people?'

He didn't reply, but I realised I'd hit upon what made her so different. Pandora wasn't human.

So, we had another alien here at East Valley High. Another super good-looking, brainy, and yet totally different being from a planet somewhere in the Orion constellation—which was why Rion choose his name. I wondered though how she got here and, more importantly, why. Had she been one of those bodiless bubbles of intelligent entities waiting to inhabit a human host or was there something else going on here? Rion had been one of those and had landed on me, which automatically had made me his host. That cold July day on the beach hadn't even been a year ago, and yet so much had happened in that time. At first, I had thought it the unluckiest day of my life, but now, well 180-degree turn. I had thought him the most annoying, egotistical creature I'd ever met. Then, to help me out at a party, he materialised into the most beautiful seventeen-year-old boy I'd ever seen. Even then, we didn't get on. But when we got to know each other, I realised he was also thoughtful, kind, and always had my back. Maybe I was being too hasty in having a not altogether positive opinion of Pandora. Maybe she too would improve in time.

But what was she doing here? Did she materialise, like Rion, to help out a host? Or was she sent from the mothercloud for some other reason? Obviously, Rion had known as soon as he set eyes on her that she wasn't human. I was hoping to find out more from him when we walked home from school this afternoon.

In the meantime, I'd just watch her and try to work out what she was up to.

'Oh, hi! We're in English together. How nice,' Pandora said as she slid into a seat next to me. I saw Jas shoot a glance in her direction. She'd been queen bee around here ever since grade seven, and she didn't like competition. I wondered what she'd think about this new chick.

It didn't surprise me that Pandora aced every question Ms D threw out at us or that she got ten out of ten in a pop quiz on Macbeth, the play we studied last term. The way Ms D beamed at Pandora, I could tell she was already on the way to becoming a favourite.

It didn't surprise me either that Jas slid up to us as we were leaving class. 'Pandora,' she said, pushing herself not so gently between us, 'I'm Jas. Welcome to East Valley High. A few of us are hanging out at Maccas this afternoon. Why don't you join us? It'll give you a chance to meet people.' Although she had her back to me, I could tell she had a fake sweet-as-pie expression on her face to match her syrupy voice. Pandora had already passed Jas's stringent first judgement. Not many students were invited to join her little posse on their first day.

19

'So sweet of you,' Pandora said in her soft voice as she gracefully slid past Jas to join me on the other side. 'What do you think, Zoe? Shall we pop by?'

A look of annoyance flitted across Jas's face. 'Oh, Zoe's probably too busy to join us, now that she has a boyfriend.'

'Orion? Well, he can come too. We're friends.'

I didn't often see Jas caught off guard, but now was one of those times. And since last term, she disliked Rion even more than she disliked me. For a moment, I was tempted to crash her little afternoon get-together just for the hell of it. But Rion wouldn't want to go, and, thinking about it, neither did I. 'Sorry, guys, we can't make it this afternoon. But you go ahead, Pandora. You might find it... interesting.'

Pandora gave me a slow smile as if she knew exactly what I was thinking.

'Yeah, sure. It'll be fun to meet some new people.'

Jas resumed her self-satisfied look, happy that I knew my place in the social order of high school. 'Great, see you soon. Byeee.' She moved through the crowd with the self-assurance of a pop star greeting her fans, smiling at this one, nodding at that one, and totally ignoring the ones that didn't count, which was most of us.

'So, Zoe...' Pandora turned to me. 'You and Jas, not so tight, eh?'

I shrugged. 'We were friends once, for a brief time. But stuff happened.'

'Stuff like Orion?' She looked at me sympathetically.

'Yeah, partly. But also because I found out maybe we weren't quite as compatible as I thought.' I was trying to be diplomatic here.

'In other words, she's a bitch,' Pandora said.

I looked at her in surprise, and then we both burst out laughing. Then, I asked, 'How do you know so much when you've just got here?'

'I'm just really observant.'

Of course she was. She was an alien and, along with the super good looks, had superpowers. I didn't remember either Rion or Archimedes being that observant, at least not about people, but she was a girl and maybe that was the difference.

'And you know what, Zoe? Sometimes bitches can be very useful.' She flicked her hair over her shoulder. 'Anyway, I'd better go if I'm going to meet this "in" crowd this afternoon. Say hello to Rion for me and tell him I'll catch up with him—and you too. I think you'll find we have a few things in common.'

As she moved away, I wondered if one of those things was Rion.

Later, as Rion and I walked home, he was quiet. I knew he didn't want to talk, but I wasn't going to let this slide. We didn't go far before I said, 'So, what about this Pandora? How do you know her?'

He hesitated and then said, 'You're right, she's from my planet.'

'So, what's she doing here? I thought you were the only one here, apart from Archimedes, who came to look after you.' And a fine job he did with that—not. But I didn't share that thought out loud.

'I'm not really sure. She was on the mothercloud when I was. I knew her, but it wasn't like we were friends or anything. That's not our way. We only communicated with each other when necessary. Our main purpose was, as you know, to find a host and to increase our knowledge of humanity. I don't know why she has materialised, or even if she has a host, though I suspect not. You haven't noticed her close to any one person all day, have you?'

I shook my head.

'Yeah, that's what I thought. I don't think she would have been sent to contact me either.'

'Why not?'

'Well, first of all, I was told all contact would be severed and I'd never hear from my people again. And, secondly, she's a newbie, too junior to be sent on an important mission.'

'A newbie?'

'Someone who is less than 1000 years old. She hasn't been on the mothercloud for long. She's practically a baby.'

'Rion, you do realise I'm sixteen years old, don't you?'

He looked at me and smiled. Then, he put an arm around me and kissed the top of my head.

'But, you're sixteen in *human* years and you know a lot of stuff my people don't. She was probably your age when she joined the space program, dematerialised and left our planet for the mothercloud. She hasn't had years of learning about humans and their ways. It would be easy for her to make a mistake.'

'So, what are you saying? You're worried, aren't you?'

'I am. I just hope she hasn't gone rogue.'

'Rogue?'

'Yes, rebelled against our teachings and decided to materialise to see what it is like to be human, without permission and certainly without guidance.' He wrinkled his forehead. 'I probably should have arranged to meet her this afternoon to see what she's up to.'

'Well, that wouldn't have done any good. Jas invited her to Maccas after school with her group.'

Rion frowned. 'Jas and Pandora—I don't think anything good can come from that.'

'I don't know, Pandora seems like she can hold her own. I don't think Jas will worry her too much.' I thought of how everyone was tripping over themselves to get to know Pandora. Even Harry seemed starstruck, and that wasn't like him.

'It's not Pandora I'm concerned about,' Rion said, his voice sounding grim.

'Oh,' was my only comment. Jas had had a thing for Rion, and they had even kissed—more than once. I wasn't jealous, really. I was just surprised Rion cared about what happened to Jas. I certainly didn't.

'Yes, there's no telling what mischief she can do here.' He turned to me. 'Zoe, I don't really trust her.'

'Well, you must be in the minority because everyone seems to love her. And she told me she thought we would become friends.' I wasn't totally over the moon about her myself, but she had been nice to me and included me in the invitation when Jas had invited her to Maccas this afternoon. I thought Rion was overreacting, which was unusual for him.

'See, that statement right there is not something any of my people would say. We are respectful of humans, but we never would imagine that we could become friends with them.'

'Or certainly not care about them,' I snapped.

He stopped and tried to take me in his arms, but I resisted. I'd thought Rion had got over all this superiority of his race over mine. Apparently not. Instead, I stood with my hands on my hips and gave him a not-very-friendly look.

'That's not what I mean, and you know it,' he said in an exasperated tone. 'You and I, we're different. I chose to be human to be with you. I don't think I'm any better than you, quite the reverse. You've taught me more in a few months than I ever learnt in my 4000 years as an alien. But I'm just trying to explain how my people think, not that I agree with it.'

'So, I've taught you stuff, eh?'

'You know you have. You were the first person I ever kissed.'

I frowned at him. 'That's not exactly true,' I said, thinking about Jas.

He looked embarrassed. 'She kissed me. You were the first person I ever *wanted* to kiss.' He took a tentative step towards me. We were under the shade of a poinciana tree and not too far from home. I let myself be drawn into his arms this time, and I didn't object when he gave me a kiss. When we pulled apart, I decided to cut him some slack.

'All right. So, what are we going to do about Pandora?' I asked.

'I'll have to talk to her first, see what she's up to,' Rion said as we started to walk again. My house was in view, and I was surprised to see Mum's car in the driveway. She wasn't usually home from school this early. As a primary school teacher, she always had a lot of work to do or meetings to attend after school. Sometimes she didn't get home till five thirty or six.

'Well, East Valley High is not so big that you won't run into her.'

'Yes, and if she causes trouble, everyone will find out about it sooner rather than later,' Rion said as we turned up my front path to the two-story wood and brick house I'd lived in all my life.

'Do you want to come in?' I asked.

'I do, but I'd better not. I've got some studying to do, and I also have to cut the grass.'

Rion lived on his own, something that wasn't known by many people, as his guardian Archimedes had returned to the mothercloud. It wasn't a problem for Rion, who was capable, but it did mean he had to do everything for himself as well as go to school. Luckily, his people had given him an allowance to live on.

I nodded. 'Okay, see you tomorrow.' He gave me a hug and a quick kiss and headed down the path again.

I turned to open the door. Rion had given me a few things to think about. I, too, now wondered what Pandora was up to and just how long before we found out.

Chapter Three

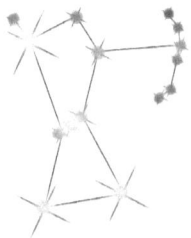

'Mum?' I called as I dropped my bag on the floor and walked through the lounge to the kitchen at the back. No answer. She was probably upstairs having a shower. I got a glass and filled it with juice from the fridge then headed upstairs to my bedroom. Maybe now might be a good time to look at that history assignment. Jeez, how I'd changed. Up until the second half of last year, I'd never been so conscientious about studying. I should have said, up until I'd met Rion. He was, of course, a brainiac and always had encouraged me to study. I resisted for as long as I could, but after he left in term four, there didn't seem to be much else to do, so I studied. And, to my surprise, I did okay, getting mostly As at the end of the year. So, this year the habit had stuck. And, if you were going to have a habit like that, then year twelve was the time to have it.

An hour later, when I decided to reward myself with a piece of that Sara Lee chocolate cake in the fridge, I went downstairs to find the kitchen, lounge, and study were still empty with no sign of Mum. Peeking out the window, I saw her car was still in the driveway, so I knew she hadn't gone out.

I headed back upstairs with my chocolate cake and ice cream—I mean who has chocolate cake *without* ice cream—stopping by my parents' bedroom door. I knocked softly and then, hearing no answer, opened the door and looked in. Mum was fast asleep on the bed. She must really have had a tough day with those grade sixes. I was backing out quietly again when she stirred and said, 'Zoe?'

'Hi, Mum, didn't mean to disturb you.'

'No, it's okay. I'm awake now. Come on in, especially if that's chocolate cake I see in your hand.'

I walked in and sat on the bed. 'You're actually expecting me to share this?'

'Didn't you say you wanted a driving lesson or two this week?'

My mother was crafty, no doubt about that. 'You drive a hard bargain, lady. Do you want me to go downstairs and get you a piece?'

'No, I'll make do with sharing,' Mum said as she sat up in the bed and reached for my plate. 'How was your first day of term, darling?'

'Okay, you know the usual—assignments, assignments, and then more assignments.' I settled myself next to her and rested my head on the pillow.

'How's Rion?'

As if she didn't see him every other day, but she took an interest in him because he had no parents, although she didn't know that was because he was an alien. She just thought his useless mother, whom we had invented, had skived off to Cairns with her even more useless boyfriend and his father wanted nothing to do with him. That, if anything was bound to touch Mum's soft heart, but she actually liked him too. As did my dad. I was such a rebellious teen—not. I had a boyfriend my parents approved of and was a model student. Still, I hadn't always been that way.

'He's fine too and, you know, perfect as usual.'

Mum smiled. I could have told her about Pandora, but I didn't want to go there at the moment, not with her being an alien and all that.

'What about you? It's not like you to have a nap after school. Those kids must have been rough today.'

She passed the plate back to me. 'No, I just really felt tired for some reason. And it's only the first day of term.' She gave a small laugh and said, 'Wonder what I'll be like on the last day? But it's nothing. I'm ready to get up and tackle dinner now.'

'I can get dinner if you like. I'm really excellent at frozen pizza, and I can whip up a salad if you're going to insist on something healthy.'

'No, it's okay. I'm fine now. And anyway, I have that leftover tuna fish casserole that I can reheat.' She slid her legs off the bed onto the floor.

'Oh,' I said, not feeling enthusiastic about that. Dad and I loved Mum, and she had many talents, but cooking wasn't one of them. Just as well I had this chocolate cake and ice cream—well, half of it anyway.

'But we might leave your driving lesson until tomorrow. I've got a few things to do tonight for school tomorrow, now that I've squandered my afternoon away sleeping.'

I got up too. 'Okay, but I'll hold you to that. We've got a deal, right?' I held up my plate as evidence. 'Half a piece of chocolate cake must be worth at least two driving lessons.'

As the cool water from the shower hit my skin, I thought how strange it was that one of my own people was here. Pandora could be a problem, especially if she was here without permission. The fact that she *was* here disturbed me even more than I'd let on to Zoe. I had been the first of my kind to materialise as an organic for any length of time, and that had been accidental. Archimedes was the second, but only for brief periods of a few hours, and he had only come to help me. That I really hadn't wanted his help was beside the point. He had come with official sanction from our supervisor. I couldn't see any reason why Pandora was here, unless it was due to her own agenda. And that's what worried me the most.

I dried off, pulled on a tee shirt and shorts, and then went downstairs to check what was in the fridge for dinner. I was just cracking the eggs in the bowl for an omelette when there was a knock on the front door of my townhouse. I wasn't expecting Zoe, but I couldn't stop the leap in my pulse that signalled an increased heartbeat. I could easily make that omelette stretch for two.

It wasn't Zoe.

'Pandora,' I said.

Wearing a sleeveless black shirt, tight jeans, and knee-high leather boots, she looked more like a bikie than the high school girl she was pretending to be. She didn't say anything at first but gave me an intense look that scanned my body from head to toe. I shifted the weight on my feet, uncomfortable under her gaze. I didn't know what she saw, but I had a feeling my night was about to get worse.

'Hey, Orion,' she said, pushing past me without an invitation. She stood in the small open-plan lounge, dining area and kitchen combined and looked around. My furnishings, which were bought by Archimedes when he first set up this place, were sparse, and I hadn't bothered to add to them. 'Cool place, but a little minimalist.' She flung herself on the leather couch and put her feet on the coffee table. 'Got any wine?'

I ignored her request and sat on the seat opposite her. 'What are you doing here?'

'Great way to greet one of your own,' she said as she got up and went to the kitchen, opening cupboard doors, drawers, and finally the fridge. 'Seriously, Orion, you're here living as an organic with all the senses, and you might as well be a monk in the eighteenth century. There's nothing but rabbit food and stuff that health nuts eat. What's the point of being here if you aren't going to enjoy it? I suppose it's too much to expect that you have any smokes?'

'If you mean cigarettes, no. In case you haven't realised it, we are technically underage here and therefore not supposed to drink or smoke.'

She laughed at me, shaking her head. 'I don't believe it. I've been around for centuries and you've been here for... how many millennia? The rules don't apply to us. We're not even human.'

'Maybe you aren't, Pandora, but I am. I gave up my former life as an alien to become human. I can't go back, and I don't want to. But I have to live as an organic, and I'm hoping not to cut my lifespan too dramatically by doing the wrong things both for my body and my mind.' I stood up, feeling that however she got here, it was time for her to go back and quickly.

'You're an idiot. You'll never be one of them, and you're kidding yourself if you think you are. But I'm not going to waste my time arguing with you. I'm here for a reason.' She grabbed a can of diet cola from the fridge, made a face at it, but popped it open and took a drink. Then she sauntered back to the couch and took up her former position.

I decided to ignore her insults and find out what she was really doing here. She was right in one regard, we did need to talk. I went back to sit opposite her. 'Do you have a host at the moment?' I asked.

'Hardly, there's no one within 100 metres of me, is there? No, my host died… last week, I think it was. He was fun while it lasted. He was a rock star you know, and we got on so well. He thought I was his muse. I wrote most of his best songs, but he never gave me credit for it.' She sighed and was quiet for a moment. Then she continued. 'Unfortunately, he had a tragic accident on his motorbike. I missed him for a while, almost an Earth day or so, which for us is an incredibly long time to mourn a human host. But... now I'm free. Wheee!' she said, lifting her feet up from the coffee table and then dropping them noisily. She downed another swallow of her drink. 'Which is why I'm here.'

I shook my head. 'I still don't follow. Are you here on a mission or something?'

She flashed a smile that was not particularly pleasant. 'Yeah, a mission, a mission to have fun. Why should you have it all to yourself?'

'Fun? Is that what you think this human existence is all about? Have you even got the permission of our supervisor to be here?'

'Well, if it isn't about enjoying yourself, then it should be. After all, they've only got about seventy or eighty Earth years here. That's too short to waste.' She finished the rest of her drink and gave a loud burp. 'I love being an organic.'

I noticed she didn't answer my question about permission. I decided to answer it for her. 'So, you've gone rogue. You just decided on your own to materialise after your host died. Not a good idea, Pandora. You have no idea what you're doing. You realise you may not be able to change back.'

She shrugged. 'They let you stay. Even gave you a chance to come back. I heard that guy who was supposed to be your guardian complaining…What did he call himself when he was here?'

'Archimedes,' I said, feeling my heart sink. We hadn't exactly parted on the best of terms.

'Yeah, him. Well, once I'd left my poor, deceased host and returned to the mothercloud, his complaining thought patterns were hard to ignore. He's not too happy with you. But I wouldn't worry, it'll only be a century or two before he stops.' She laughed and swung her feet down on the floor again, leaning forward, elbows on her knees. 'I thought this human life sounded amusing, for a while anyway. If you made the decision to stay, it must have something going for it. So, I decided to find out for myself and, poof, I materialised.'

I looked at this newbie of only a few centuries or so. She had no idea what she was getting into, and I really couldn't understand her attitude. Those of us who had been accepted into the space program on our planet had known what an immense privilege it was to be selected to serve our people. We lived for thousands of years in the pure pursuit of knowledge and the betterment of not only our own race, but humans as well. It had taken me some thought and meditation to reach the decision to become human. It had not been taken lightly.

'Why did you join the space program if you wanted to remain an organic?'

She flipped her long hair over a shoulder and shrugged. 'I was only sixteen when I joined. It seemed like a good idea at the time, and the thought of living forever was appealing. My hosts have been relatively harmless. Some of them have been good fun but... I just got bored. All that pursuit of knowledge and the greater good etc, was fine for the first few centuries, but after a while it got very monotonous. I wanted a change before I went to my next host.'

'It's not like an Earth job. We don't get holidays.'

She brightened. 'Yes, that's what I need, a holiday from being this pure intelligent entity. I will go back, eventually. After all, who wants to get old and die?' She shuddered. 'Think you made a big mistake there, Orion, in deciding to stay here forever. I agree with Archimedes on that point. But every century or so, a little break from the incessant yammering of a host would be good.'

'So, who knows you are here?'

'No one yet. They probably think I'm resting from my previous host and not yet ready for a new one. I've probably got a year or so before they notice. That'll be long enough. I can't wait to try out some of the things my rock star host got up too. I might even get a motorbike.' Her eyes shone.

The more she talked, the more worried I became. I could just imagine the damage she could do, not only to herself but to others. And she was right. It might be some time before our people noticed she was gone. Even though originally I'd materialised without permission, it was to help Zoe, who was at that time my host. And it hadn't been my intention to stay an organic. That came later, and I'd had permission to remain in my human form. I didn't think anyone had gone rogue like this before, at least not that I knew of. I tried again to reason with her. Maybe I could persuade her to go back.

'Listen, Pandora, by Earth's years, you are underage. That's going to cause you all sorts of complications. Do you even have a place to stay? Money? Clothes? Anything? And without the support of our people, where are you going to get those things?'

'Seriously, dude, chill. We are not a highly evolved, intelligent species for nothing. I use my powers to get what I need. I've found a respectable middle-aged woman, I think she's a secretary or a PA or something, and I mind controlled her to believe I was a long-lost second cousin whose parents had died. I knew she was lonely and had a big house, so it was a mutually beneficial situation. She even gives me an allowance. So, I'm fine for now. I'm also looking into ways to make some money. I have a good head for statistics, so I could try gambling, but I think I would do better with investing. The stock market is so interesting, don't you think? I hear cryptocurrency is on the rise again.'

'You mean you actually used your powers to manipulate a woman for your own gain? That is against every code we follow. How could you, Pandora?'

'How could you, Pandora?' she mimicked me. 'As for that woman—Maude Butterfield is her name by the way—she thinks I'm lovely. I'm like a ray of sunshine in her dull, colourless life.' Pandora smiled and twisted a lock of her hair around her finger. 'Not everyone is as judgy as you, Orion.'

'You need to go back, now,' I said, folding my arms across my chest. If I were still in contact with my people, I would have tried to reach them. But once I had made the decision to become permanently human, I had to sever all contact with them.

'Not a chance. Not yet anyway.'

'You don't know anything about living as a human. You'll only get yourself into trouble.'

'That's where you come in. That's why I decided to materialise here rather than somewhere more glamorous and interesting like Paris or even New York. I loved Paris. Did you know one of my hosts was a French ballerina. She ate like about once a week, but she was graceful. I've been trying to move like she did, and mostly I've been successful.'

'I can't say I've noticed.' I looked at her sprawled on my couch. 'I'm sure she didn't talk like you.'

Pandora rolled her eyes at me. 'I do speak French, fluently. However, that's not much use here except in French class. So, I decided to imitate the speech patterns as well as a few cool expressions from my rock star host. Since he's only just died, I thought they'd be relevant. At least I don't sound like I'm fifty years old and living in the last century like you do.'

'Then I can't imagine why you'd want to have anything to do with me or why you're even here.' I wondered why it was so difficult to get along with my own people. Archimedes and I hadn't exactly been best friends, and it looked unlikely that Pandora and I would be either.

'You're going to show me the ropes, dude. As you pointed out, I'm new at this being organic, and I might need a few pointers.'

'Will you even listen to anything I say, Pandora? There is no use wanting advice if you're never going to take it.'

She sat back and tucked her legs under her on the white leather sofa.

'Well, Orion, it's like this. Some things are non-negotiable. Don't try to persuade me to go back, because that's not going to happen and it's a waste of time. And try to remember, if you can, when we were organics on our own planet. We had our personalities then, and they weren't all the same. That's still the case. But, when we became intelligent, bodiless entities who inhabited humans for their lifespan, we didn't notice our individual differences so much. After all, we have very little to do with each other on the mothercloud other than communicate information and such. It's all very… cerebral.' She sighed. 'Now that we are organics again, we talk, we interact, and we do it differently. I'm not ever going to be like you, so don't try to change me. But there are things that you can teach me. You're right, it's all new to me, and I have to say it's kind of intoxicating. I'll settle down in time. Just help me not to do anything *too* disastrous.'

She smiled again, but this time it was more genuine. At least she had some understanding of her situation. I still thought she should return immediately to the mothercloud, but since that wasn't going to happen right away, I decided to make the best of the situation and at least meet her halfway.

'Okay, some of what you said made sense. If you want to fit in, you are going to have to stop using those special powers on people. It will only get you into trouble, and after a while people will notice you're different. They might get suspicious, and you don't want that.'

Pandora shrugged. 'Good point, I guess. But I really needed a place to stay, and Maude was very lonely. I actually like her, and she likes me, so unless you're going to let me stay here…' She raised her eyebrows and waited for my response.

'No way. I'm sorry, Pandora, that's totally out of the question. It would be so inappropriate.' I could just imagine Zoe's reaction to that, let alone everyone else's.

'We could say I was your sister.'

'Too late. You've already been to school and you haven't said a word about us being related. It would look too strange and unbelievable if you said that now.'

'Then I'll have to stay with Maude for now. But I will try not to use my mind-controlling and other powers, okay?'

I nodded. I didn't like the fact that she'd used her powers on a human—something I'd never done—but I couldn't see any way out of the situation for now. And, I remembered uncomfortably, that I'd had to lie to Zoe's parents when I first met them so that I could have a place to stay. Perhaps I shouldn't judge Pandora too severely.

'I've already tried to fit in. I've befriended your little ex-host, Zoe. The teachers already adore me. What could go wrong?'

I wasn't sure I wanted her to hang around Zoe too much, but that wasn't my decision to make. Zoe and I had already decided to respect each other's decisions, even when we didn't agree with them. It worried me that Pandora seemed so overconfident. But hey, that was the least of my worries. This whole situation seemed full of potential trouble. For now, I could see I wouldn't make much progress in persuading her to go back. It was better to remain friendly and help her out than let her be totally on her own—not a good idea.

She unfolded her legs and got up from the couch. 'Glad we had this chat, Orion. I'm off now. Doesn't look like there's much fun to be had here. I'll leave you to your rabbit food and books. I wonder where I can pick up a bottle of wine.'

She headed towards the front door.

'Pandora,' I said before she reached it.

'Yeah?' She turned around to face me.

'You're underage. You can't buy alcohol, and you certainly shouldn't be drinking it.'

'Killjoy.' She made a face. 'I guess I'll have to see what Maude has at home. Au revoir!' She turned away and went out the door.

As it clicked behind her, I sighed. Just what had I gotten myself into?

Chapter Four

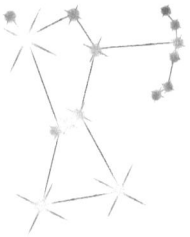

'Hey, Lou, I'm surprised to see you here,' I said as we almost collided in the mall. It was Saturday, and Rion said he had chores to do, so I decided to go shopping, hoping I'd see something fabulous that I could actually afford. My parents wouldn't let me take a part-time job other than the odd babysitting gig, so I had limited funds. I hadn't expected to see Lou because she was usually involved in a sport that her mother had pushed her into. She wasn't exactly the sportiest of types, but her mother believed it would help her make friends and help with her coordination. It hadn't helped either. She was still one of the shiest people I knew, but here she was in her candy pink shorts and white polo top, carrying so many bags you'd think it were Christmas and she was doing all her shopping in one hit.

'Hi, Zoe. I've quit tennis. Told Mum I didn't want to do it anymore.' She looked defiant. Another surprise. Lou rarely went against her mother.

'No point doing something you don't enjoy.'

Lou nodded. 'That's what I thought. Honestly, Mum treats me like such a child sometimes. Anyway, I decided to do some shopping.'

'So I see.'

'Hey, you want to grab a milkshake or a coffee or something?'

'Sure. You want some help with some of those bags?' Since I hadn't found any fantastic bargains yet, my hands were free.

'Thanks,' Lou said, passing me a couple of bags. 'Let's go to one of those new rooftop restaurants. I haven't been there yet, and I've been dying to go, but Mum always says it's too busy for her.'

We walked through the crowds and made our way to the rooftop where we found a totally cute, old-fashioned milkshake bar, perfect for a hot Saturday afternoon. After we ordered milk shakes, we sat in a booth with bright green seats. Lou seemed different. I'd felt that even from the beginning of term after the holidays. It wasn't so much how she looked, but more about the way she acted. Now I was seeing it even more. She seemed... resolute and cool even. Pushing her hair behind her ears, she folded her arms and rested them on the table between us.

'I'm really glad I ran into you, Zoe. You have such a great fashion sense. You really helped me last term when I was trying to decide what to wear for the play we went to.'

I remembered that disastrous evening. Chad Everett had punched Rion for kissing Jas, and that had set off a whole lot of other things too, particularly between Rion and me. But I also remembered that I'd made one or two suggestions to Lou about what to wear and how to do her hair. Everyone, including me, had been so surprised at how pretty she was when she wasn't wearing clothes for a twelve-year-old and put her hair back so you could actually see her face. I suddenly realised, since that time, Lou had continued to wear her hair back and show more confidence. I smiled at her, glad my friend was starting to sort of blossom and proud to have been a part of that process.

'Well, Lou, I only helped with what was already there. You were always pretty, you just didn't realise it.'

She returned my smile. 'Thanks, Zoe. It really opened my eyes, and I decided it was time to let Mum know I wasn't in middle school anymore, but in year twelve. So, I've quit tennis and used most of my savings today to buy some new clothes. I just hope I've made the right choices. You can have a look and let me know. I can always return anything I don't want.'

I wasn't sure I wanted to be responsible for Lou's whole new look, and I certainly wasn't any fashion guru. 'Just buy what you like, Lou. After all, you probably shouldn't go from your mum picking out your clothes to me. You need to work out your own taste.'

'I get what you're saying, but a second opinion doesn't hurt either, does it?'

'I guess not. So, what did you get?'

Her eyes lit up, and for the next few minutes, she showed me her purchases. It was hard to say if they suited her or not when she wasn't wearing them, but most of the things she bought seemed okay. You couldn't go wrong with skinny jeans, and there wasn't a frill or flounce in sight. One thing I did notice. 'There's a lot of black here, Lou.' It wasn't a colour I'd seen her wear before.

'I know. When you said black was good for evening wear last term, I realised I didn't have anything that was black, so I decided to change that. I think it'll make me seem older.'

I just nodded. Black was great in the winter or at night, but it was awfully hot during a Queensland summer. Still, I didn't want to say anything critical, not when Lou was so pleased about everything.

I asked the question that was on the tip of my tongue. 'So, what does your mum say about all this?'

Lou's lips tightened. 'She's not impressed, but I don't care.'

I decided this was one time to say nothing. Lou's mum could be kind of fierce at times, and I didn't want to get in-between her and Lou.

Our milkshakes came and Lou changed the subject. 'So how are things going with you and Rion?'

'Great,' I said, as a warm feeling came over me just thinking about him. The more we were together, the closer we seemed to get.

'I knew you two would eventually get together. You are so right for each other. It just took you a while to realise it.'

Last term had been a roller-coaster ride of emotions. But I couldn't tell Lou part of the reason it had taken so long for us to get together was because Archimedes had taken some of my memories of Rion away, and I certainly couldn't tell her he was an alien. That was a secret only Rion and I shared... and also Emerson, but he didn't count so much because he was only six years old, and besides, he was super loyal to Rion.

'I need to ask you a question, Zoe.' Lou stopped as if she didn't know how to continue.

'Go on.'

'I asked you last term, but things are different now.'

I knew immediately. 'It's about Harry, isn't it?' Lou had had a crush on him, and it seemed she still did.

She nodded and her cheeks turned pink. 'You know I liked him, but I thought you and he might have had a thing going. Now you're with Rion, you don't mind do you, that I'm kind of still interested in him?'

'No, of course not, Lou. Harry and I have been friends for a long time. And yes, for a very short period, like a couple of nanoseconds, I wondered if we might... you know. But it didn't happen, for lots of reasons. Now, we're just friends, that's all. So, if you want to go out with him, go for it, Lou.'

She beamed. 'You know something, I think I will.' She hesitated. 'Do you have any, like, tips?'

'Just be yourself.'

She shook her head. 'That hasn't worked so far. No, I mean real tips how to get him interested.'

I thought for a moment. Both Harry and Lou were two of the genuinely nicest people I knew. It made a lot of sense for them to be together. Lou would never hurt Harry like I had in the past. But Harry, because we'd been so close once and because he'd had a crush on me, never really saw how perfect Lou would be for him. Time to change that.

'Why don't you ask him to go to the movies with you?'

'I could never do that,' she said. 'I mean, I'd just never have the nerve. What if he said no? Besides, shouldn't I wait till he asks me out?'

'Lou, it's not the last century or something. Besides, you can make it like a friendship thing if you want, rather than a date.' I remembered that's what Harry did when he asked me out last term, and it wasn't an altogether unsuccessful evening, although the end of the night had been embarrassing—for me. I didn't want to think about that.

She looked at me, uncertainty written all over her face. 'It just seems so… No, I don't think I could do it.'

I suppressed a sigh.

'There must be some other way for Harry to notice me. That's one of the reasons I bought all these clothes.'

I thought again. 'Maybe we could go somewhere together, kind of like a group thing, but really a double date. You know Kerri will never go out anywhere because she always wants to study. And that just leaves you, me, Rion, and Harry. You'll get a chance to wear your new clothes and go out with Harry. Rion and I will head off after a little while, which will just leave the two of you. What do you think?'

'I think you're brilliant. I just knew you'd have some good ideas.' Lou leaned over the table and gave me a hug, nearly spilling our drinks. When she sat down again, she beamed at me. 'So, where will we go?'

I considered the possibilities. Going to the movies was an obvious option. It was low key and kind of suitable for a group thing. 'Movies. We could go for a snack either before or after to give you time to talk.'

'Great. We'll tell the boys on Monday and maybe go next Saturday, if everyone is free.' Now that she'd had some encouragement, Lou was full of determination.

I nodded, and we spent the next half hour planning and talking about our group "date." I started to get excited too. It would be fun to have a day off from all the studying and stress of year twelve.

When Rion came over that night, I told him about the idea. I left out the part that this was my plan to get Harry and Lou together. He had all these principles about never manipulating people and being totally honest about things—all very noble to a point... but I figured this was for a good cause. Harry just needed a little push in the right direction, and there was nothing wrong in that.

'I'd rather go just with you. We don't have a lot of time together. But sure, it might be fun to go with the group.'

Fun, that was a word I never thought I'd hear coming from his lips a few months ago. I smiled, thinking how far he'd come.

'What?' he said.

'Nothing.'

He took me into his arms. 'Come on, what is it? You know you can't hide anything from me.'

My smile increased. How wrong he was there. But just to keep him quiet, I said, 'I was just thinking how different your idea was about fun not that long ago, like maybe seven or eight months ago.'

He rolled his eyes. 'I don't know how you put up with me then.'

'When you were a bodiless, alien entity I didn't have much choice. I think this version of you is much better.' I kissed him to prove my point. His arms tightened around me, and for a moment I forgot all about my plans to help Lou.

When Rion lifted his lips from mine, he said, 'I can't argue with you on that point. There is nowhere I'd rather be than right here with you now.'

'Rion, I lo—' I stopped. I couldn't say it to him, not yet. Even though every day we were together I felt it more, and even though he'd given me that necklace. I wanted him to say it first, despite my brave words to Lou about taking the initiative and all that. So, instead I said, 'I love that you're here too.'

For a heartbeat, we looked at each other, and it seemed as if he knew what I was going to say. But it wasn't the right time, not yet.

He broke the silence by saying, 'We'll never persuade Kerri to come.'

'No, perhaps not.' Which was part of the plan, but I didn't tell him that.

He shrugged. 'I guess it doesn't matter. The four of us should have a good time, and Lou and Harry seem to get on well.'

'Yes, they do.' Everything was coming along perfectly.

Chapter Five

ey, Pan, over here,' Jas called, waving from her usual spot by the window in English. Pandora, pushing back her curtain of dark hair, gave a dazzling smile in Jas's direction and glided over to her.

'Sure, why not.' She slid into the seat across from Jas.

In that moment, I knew Pandora had joined the beautiful crowd.

Not that it bothered me. I had no desire to be "in" with Jas again. But I knew that Pandora's talk about being friends with me was just that, talk. Because no one could be friends with both Jas and me. It just wasn't possible—at least not in this universe.

'I just loved those cute boots you wore to Chelsea's on Saturday,' Jas said, leaning across to her. 'You'll have to tell me where you got them. As a matter of fact, we should go shopping together. There're a few parties coming up that won't be totally boring. You'll have to come.'

Pandora shrugged. 'Maybe.'

She obviously didn't realise the honour that Jas was bestowing. Not many people were that casual about invitations from her. Except Harry. I remembered how he had refused every attempt of Jas's to include him in her group last term. I looked over at him, surprised to see his eyes glued on Pandora. As I looked around, I noticed he wasn't the only one. She certainly knew how to attract attention.

Our English teacher, Ms D, swept into the room looking in a mood. She dropped a pile of papers on her desk with a thud and gave us a death stare. In general, she was pretty chilled, but when she wasn't, it was best to slink into your seat and hope you were invisible. The fact that she was only five foot two and about fifty kilos meant nothing when she was angry. She was like a cyclone that ripped through the class, leaving everyone in tatters and wishing they'd stayed home that day.

The talking instantly stopped. She looked at us for a long moment.

Finally, she spoke. 'I was under the impression,' she said slowly and in a deceptively quiet voice, 'that I was teaching a year twelve English class where most of my students were aspiring to get an OP that was somewhere in the realms of respectable. I thought some of you, indeed quite a few of you, had ambitions beyond occupying space, fogging up a mirror, and having a heartbeat. Apparently, I was wrong.'

Her voice started to rise. 'It seems that despite studying one of the greatest writers in the English language and even going to a play last term didn't help—although perhaps the less said about *that* occasion the better.' She tasered Rion and then Chad with her eyes. Rion turned bright pink, and Chad slunk further down in his chair. 'Despite being given every opportunity to learn about the great bard and one of his finest works, Macbeth, most of you have shown no more understanding of his work than a six-year-old child. And I'm insulting six-year olds here. We spent half a term going over this play. We watched videos of great actors, you were given copious notes, and I told you time and time again that this assignment would be worth 50 percent. Perhaps your maths is no better than your English. That means *half* of your *total* mark in English. You do understand that, don't you?' Her eyes bored into us. A few students gave hesitant nods, not sure if she wanted a response or not.

'Well, if that's the case I fail to understand why *this* is what was handed in.' She lifted the pile of papers and let them drop to the desk again. 'Let me give you some examples.' She picked up an assignment off the top. '"Shakespeare wrote lots of plays such as *Macbeth* and *Pride and Prejudice*." I wonder what Jane Austen thinks of co-authoring a book with Shakespeare? After all, they only lived several hundred years apart.' Then she took another paper and read, 'Lady Macbeth didn't like sex because she said, "unsex me now."' A couple of boys tittered until she glared at them. When silence fell again, she picked up another one. 'Ah, here's a gem. "Lady Macbeth was not very good at cleaning because she said, 'Out damned spot.' She swore a bit too." A temptation I can well understand at the moment.'

She dropped that paper on top of the others. 'I won't go on, though I could. These are just a smattering of year twelve's literary efforts I've had to read over the Easter holidays. I may as well give up now and not bother to try to illuminate your adolescent brains, which are obviously concerned with more important things than the inspirational works of some of the greatest writers in the English language. Perhaps I should teach Shopping 101, Miss Howard?' She looked at Jas. 'Or maybe Play Station 4, Mr Li.' She raised an eyebrow at Mike, who was a game addict. Then she turned her attention to Lou. 'And no doubt a course in day dreaming and doodling would suit you.' Lou actually looked as if she might burst into tears.

'There were one or two students who didn't totally disgrace themselves.' She looked at Rion. 'Your analysis of the inner conflict experienced by Macbeth had one or two insightful comments. And, Mr Crosby.' She shifted her glance to Harry. 'You showed some knowledge of the play, and *some* is better than *none*. But the person I was most surprised about, and not in a good way I might add, was you, Miss Nichols.'

Kerri's head shot up like it was on a spring.

'You may have the periodic table down pat, Miss Nichols, but you have no insight whatsoever in character analysis. Empathy and understanding of human nature, as expressed in the great literary works, seems something totally beyond your comprehension. I suggest you do something about it before the midterm exam.'

Kerri's face went deathly pale, and I honestly thought she was going to pass out. It seemed to me Mrs D wasn't displaying a lot of empathy herself at the moment. Though, of course, I didn't say that out loud.

It was a painfully long period. I got my mark back and saw it was a mediocre C, when I was used to As or at least Bs in English. It looked like I had some studying ahead of me.

When the bell went, no one lingered but got out of the classroom as quickly as possible.

I had an uneventful class in history next, and for once I didn't mind being bored. It certainly was better than being torn to shreds, though I got off better than most because Ms D didn't even mention me. Still, I wasn't happy with a C.

At lunch Lou had a blotchy face. 'I got a D,' she confessed to me. 'Mum's going to kill me. She's already cranky that I quit tennis.'

'Never mind, Lou. You'll do better in the next assignment. We're finished with Shakespeare now. We've got something more modern next.'

'At least I'll be able to understand the language,' she said with a sniff and took out a crumpled tissue to blow her nose.

'I suppose you got an A,' I said to Rion as he sat down beside me.

'Yes, though Ms Deveraux did make one of two critical remarks I didn't altogether agree with. But I didn't feel today was the right time to argue the point.'

'Ya think?' I said, though he completely missed my sarcasm.

'Wise choice,' said Lou.

Harry came over to join us, sitting down with a heavy sigh.

'Don't know why you're sighing,' I said. 'You were one of the stars in English today. One of the very few.'

Harry shrugged. 'I only got a B. I was aiming for an A. If I want to get into a veterinary course, I'm going to need to get straight As.'

'You'll get there. After all, you usually get good marks. Ms D was on the warpath today. I wonder what happened to put her in a cranky mood?'

'Who knows. I can never work teachers out,' Lou said. 'Sometimes I think they were born on another planet.'

I felt Rion stiffen next to me. I must have looked a bit weird because Lou rushed to say, 'Oh, sorry, Zoe.'

I felt my heart beat faster. Surely, she couldn't know about Rion. 'Why?' I asked in a strained voice.

'I forgot your mum was a teacher. But she's different. She's lovely.'

I let out a breath. 'Thanks, Lou.'

'I felt sorry for Kerri though,' Harry said. 'She looked in a state of shock.'

'I honestly thought she was going to have a heart attack or something,' I said.

'Well, maybe not that,' Rion said with a half-smile, 'but she certainly looked unhappy. I don't think she's used to getting a low grade in any subject.'

'Here's betting she stays up every night studying English. We probably won't see her at all until the finals are over,' I said.

But I was wrong. Not five minutes later, Kerri came towards us with her lunch box and without a book for once. But her face was glum.

'Hey, Kerri,' Harry said, making room for her.

She looked at us with tragic eyes. 'I was going to study, but then I thought, what's the use? I'm only going to fail anyway. I'll probably end up working at McDonalds for life.'

'I think you might be exaggerating,' Rion said. 'You're one of the smartest people I know.' This was a great concession from him as he thought most humans ranked only slightly higher than dogs when it came to intelligence. 'Anyway, it's only one assignment. You're bound to do much better on the next one.'

'What did you get?' I asked, fully expecting her to say a B, which was the equivalent of a fail in her eyes.

She gave a deep, shaky sigh and said in a low voice, 'C minus.'

We all looked at her in shock. No one ever thought Kerri could get a C in anything, let alone a C minus.

Finally, Rion asked, 'What did Ms D say was wrong?'

'You heard her in class,' Kerri snapped. 'Apparently I have no empathy. I looked at Macbeth's rise to power in objective terms, like any rational person would. I really couldn't see the point of his internal struggle once he had attained his objective of becoming king. I thought Shakespeare had really overdone the whole thing.'

'So, you criticised Shakespeare?' I looked at her in disbelief. She shrugged.

'The language *is* hard to understand,' Lou said.

The look Kerri gave her was withering. 'I had no difficulty with the language.'

'Maybe a tutor would help with understanding characters and their motivation and everything.' I'd never thought I would say those words to Kerri.

'If only English wasn't so necessary for getting a good grade point average for university.' Kerri looked totally deflated.

'I'll help you if you want,' Harry said.

'You only got a B.' Kerri was so diplomatic—not.

'What about me?' Rion asked.

She looked at him and then shook her head. 'You said Ms D made some critical remarks about your assignment. Besides, you're always so busy with Zoe, work, and everything.'

That much was true. Rion helped out in the school lab, and he had to do everything for himself at home. He was even talking about getting a job so that he would have extra money. The allowance he received only covered the essentials.

Kerri looked across the grass to where Pandora was sitting with Jas and her friends. 'I know. I'll ask Pandora.'

'Pandora? She didn't even do the assignment,' Lou said.

'Yes, but she's really smart. I think she's even smarter than you, Rion.'

Wow, Kerri didn't pull her punches. My sympathy for her was evaporating quickly. Sometimes, she was just too hard to deal with.

She got up and, without another word to us, walked over to Pandora. Jas looked at her in disbelief, but Kerri just ignored her. I had to give her kudos for that. Kerri, unlike most of the rest of the school population, was neither impressed nor intimidated by Jas. I couldn't hear what Kerri was saying, but Pandora nodded and smiled.

When she came back to us, Lou said, 'Well?'

'She said she'd be happy to help me in English.' Kerri took out her salad wrap from her lunch box. 'Perhaps I won't have to work at McDonalds after all when I leave school.'

Rion and I shared a smile, and I felt a warm, happy feeling. No matter what happened, it was good to know he was in my life, and after last term, I was never going to take that for granted again.

Chapter Six

'D amn,' Dad said as he dropped the sauce spoon on the floor. I bent to pick it up and drop it in the sink. His thin face creased into a smile of thanks as he pushed back a short brown curl that had stuck to his forehead.

'Thanks, hon.'

'Why are you making dinner? I thought it was Mum's turn?' I grabbed a paper towel and cleaned up the mess, while he took another wooden spoon from the drawer. Mum and Dad took turns making dinner during the week, and I usually cooked at least one night on the weekend. None of us would ever make it on *Master Chef* or *My Kitchen Rules*, but so far we hadn't starved or been malnourished or anything.

'Mum was feeling tired, so I offered,' he said as he stirred the sauce.

'Spaghetti bolognese, hey? Again.'

Dad gave me a look, his dark eyebrows rising. 'You're welcome to make something for yourself. Plenty of peanut butter in the cupboard.'

'Did I ever tell you how much I love spaghetti?'

'Good answer.'

'What's up with Mum? She was in bed the other day when I came home from school. Is everything okay?'

Dad stopped stirring. I saw a look of concern in his eyes, but after a moment it was gone and he smiled. 'Of course. You know, teaching and all. It's a tiring job.'

I went over to the fridge and opened it, taking out the orange juice. 'Tiresome, you mean. I can't imagine anything worse than teaching a bunch of bratty little kids all day.'

'So, you won't be doing a teaching degree next year when you finish high school?' He moved the sauce to the back of the stove and got out the big pan for the pasta. I put my juice down and got the spaghetti from the cupboard, putting it on the counter beside him.

'No chance. Don't forget to put a little salt in the water. And a touch of olive oil too—it helps to keep the spaghetti strands separate.'

'How many years have I been doing this?' he asked as he filled the pot.

'Just trying to be helpful,' I said. Dad was enthusiastic, but a bit slap dash.

'So, have you thought any more about what you want to do next year?'

I shook my head. 'I'm just going to try to do well in school this year so I'll have options.'

'Not a bad plan. But there must be some area you're interested in. Accounting maybe? Or business.'

'Kind of boring sitting in an office all day and adding up numbers. Oops, no offence, Dad.'

Dad threw the spaghetti into the water and turned to face me, leaning against the cupboard, arms folded and smiling. 'I'm sure accounting is not the most exciting job in the world, but it pays the bills.'

'I know you're great at your job, but it's not for me.'

'You're good at English. Maybe there's something you could do in that line. You don't have to teach little kids, you could teach at high school or even adults.'

Definitely not the time to tell him about my C in English. I shrugged. 'I'll figure something out.'

He nodded. 'I know. You still have plenty of time. Oops,' he said as the water boiled over on the stove.

As he turned it down, I said, 'I'll go and set the table.' I escaped into the dining room.

I thought about next year. I had the vague idea I would probably go to university somewhere, hopefully with Rion, but after that I drew a blank. As to what

I was going to *do*, I didn't have a clue. I was sixteen and a half, and seriously? I just wanted to be with my boyfriend and have fun with my friends. I suppose that made me shallow or something, but there it was.

Later that night, when I was talking to Rion on the phone, I asked him the same question. If anyone would have things figured out, it would be him. He was the most organised person I knew. So I was kind of surprised when he said, 'I don't know.'

'But you've lived all those years with hosts. You must have some idea of what you want to do.' I usually didn't like to think that Rion had once been a bodiless, conscious entity inside people for thousands of years. It was too weird.

'I have lots of ideas about what I want to do, Zoe, but most of them are things I want to do with you.'

I felt a warm glow inside.

'I'd like to visit Paris, kiss you on top of the Eiffel Tower, have gelato with you on a warm, crowded street in Rome, go ice skating with you in Central Park and catch you when you fall. One day, I'd even like to...'

'Go on,' I said, a little breathless. I wished he was here right now, because, Eiffel Tower or not, I really wanted to kiss him.

'One day I'd like to have a family with you. I want to grow old with you and watch our own kids grow up.'

I couldn't speak for a moment. My chest was all full of feelings, and my eyes leaked a stupid tear or two.

'Zoe? Are you still there? I haven't offended you or anything, have I?'

I took a breath and said, 'Of course, not. I was just… that's awesome, Rion. Actually, you're awesome. I…' I wanted to say it, but somehow the word just wouldn't form on my tongue.

'I wish I was with you now,' he said.

'Me too. Maybe you could come over and say you were helping me with homework.'

'I'm not sure your parents would be convinced,' he said with a laugh. My parents had this stupid idea that week nights were for studying and not seeing my boyfriend.

'Or we could meet in the boat shed.'

'I'm not going to do anything to deceive them.'

'Rion, sometimes you're a pain, a goody-two-shoes pain.'

'What? Is that supposed to be an insult or something?'

'Yes, I'm glad you realised it. Sometimes you don't. And, while all of the things you mentioned are lovely, none of them actually are a career.'

'I know, but I'm sure I'll work it out. The problem is there are so many interesting jobs I'd like to do that I can't quite make up my mind. I wouldn't mind being an astrophysicist or neuropsychologist. But then again, I'm also interested in environmental law, and aeronautical engineering sounds fascinating.'

'Jeez, Rion, right there is the difference between us. I don't even know what half those jobs are, let alone want to do them.'

'They're just words, Zoe. No big deal. We'll both figure it out, together.'

'Yeah, I guess.' I liked that he used the word together, because that was the way I felt too. Talking to him helped me turn the stress button off. Year twelve seemed to be all about expectations from everyone—teachers, parents, and even other kids—and choices that I wasn't ready to make. It was good to hear Rion say we'd work it out. When he said it, I realised I believed it.

'Rion, at the risk of inflating your already healthy ego, I think you might be good for me.'

'You only *think* it? Really, Zoe, considering all the advice I've given you this past year on healthy diet, exercise, time-management skills, and not to mention the importance of suitable companions, you should *know* it by now.'

'Are you *kidding* me! You sound just like that self-important, smart-ass bubble that landed on me when I was innocently walking on a beach last July. Have you learnt nothing?' I was just getting started and was about to erupt in another tirade, when I heard his burst of laughter over the phone. I wished he was near me right now, but not to kiss him. No way. I was thinking more of flying pillows and anything else I could get my hands on.

'That wasn't funny, Rion.'

'I disagree. It was most amusing.'

I decided a huffy silence was the best way to deal with this.

'Zoe?'

Silence.

'Zoe. Hey, you know I didn't mean it. It was just a joke.'

'Some joke.'

'You know I've learnt more from you than you ever did from me.'

'Hmmm. Such as what?'

'Well, I learnt a lot about kissing from you.'

He didn't seem to need much help there. In fact, he seemed to be pretty good at it right from the start. But I let that slide. 'Okay,' I said. 'Maybe.'

'And you taught me a lot about modern music. As a matter of fact, I got some tickets to that girl band you seem to like, Nebula.'

I sat up straight on the bed. 'You're kidding! They're coming here, to Brisbane? And you got tickets?'

'Yes and yes.'

'You mean we've been talking all night and you just thought to mention it now?'

'Well, you were talking about things that were important to you, so I thought I should listen.'

'Jeez, Rion, thanks but... you got tickets to Nebula!' I gave a squeal of delight.

'So, you're pleased?'

'Ya think?'

'Back in your good books?'

'If you were here, I'd show you just how much you're in my good books.'

'I'm not often tempted to break your parents' rules about not seeing you on weeknights, but...'

I laughed. 'Don't worry, I'm not going to put you to the test. I can wait until tomorrow, especially now I know we're going to see Nebula. But how did you get the tickets? They're so hot right now their concerts sell out in hours, if not minutes.'

'I don't know. Just lucky, I guess. I'd heard they were coming, and so as soon as their tickets went on sale, I went online and got them. I was going to surprise you, but I think you needed cheering up tonight.'

'You're right, I did. Thank you.'

'I'm glad. Sometimes, even now, I'm not sure I've got this boyfriend thing covered.'

'I think you're doing just fine.'

'It was Pandora who suggested it.'

'Oh.' Suddenly something inside me went cold.

'Yes, we were talking after class one day, and she said they were coming to Brisbane in a few months and that you'd probably like it if I got tickets.'

'So, you were talking about me to Pandora. I didn't know you two were so chummy.'

'We're not. She just mentioned it, that's all. Is something wrong?'

I didn't want to be one of those controlling kind of girlfriends. Rion could talk to whoever he wanted and, perhaps, because she was an alien and all, they had a lot in common. But there was just something about her I didn't trust, despite her friendliness.

'No, nothing wrong. It's just I didn't think you liked her much.'

He sighed. 'Not really. But now that she's here, I just want to make sure she doesn't get into trouble. She can be… impulsive.'

'Has she told you why she's here?' Rion and I hadn't really talked much about Pandora. I think both of us were trying to avoid it, but she was kind of like the elephant in the room. Sooner or later, we'd have to face the fact that there was another alien here, and not someone who was easy to overlook.

'She doesn't have a host anymore. He died recently.'

'She doesn't exactly look like she's in mourning.'

'In her own way, I think she cared about him, but now she's just interested in having a good time here for a while.'

'I didn't think your people believed in fun much. I thought you were all high-minded and stuff.'

'I told you she went rogue. Every now and then someone is selected for the space mission who isn't quite suited. It doesn't happen very often. I think even Pandora herself is starting to realise that she made a mistake in joining us.'

'Can she go back to your planet?'

'No, it's too late now. Our bodies are kept for a hundred years in a cryogenic state, in case someone changes his or her mind or doesn't work out, but after that it's allowed to wither naturally. She hasn't been an organic on our planet for nearly 1000 years.'

'Wow. I can't even begin to understand what that must be like. But both of you are organics now. How's that possible?' I'd never really understood it.

'Yes, here on this planet. There is a gene memory in our bodiless states that we can activate. But if we returned to our planet after a hundred years, because we would be technically dead there in the physical sense, we'd be unable to materialise. At least that's the theory. No one's ever tested it.'

'Your people seem to be able to do a lot though.'

'Yes, but only because we've evolved over time and have learnt how to use the natural forces around us.'

I thought for a moment. 'I noticed Pandora kind of uses her "power" to get what she wants. It's like she hypnotises everyone to like her or something. I never noticed you doing that.'

'It's just I choose never to use it. It wouldn't be fair. And anyway, I never wanted to control anyone—except Archimedes when he was here.' He and Archimedes had never got on.

'How long is she going to stay?'

'I don't know. Not long, I hope. She seems to think our people will zap her back whenever she's ready. I'm worried that won't be possible.'

'In other words, we might be stuck with her.'

'I hope not.'

We talked for a few more minutes and then said goodbye. The brief, happy feeling I'd had about going to see Nebula had vanished. In its place I had a nagging feeling that Pandora was about to become a big factor in my life, and not in a good way.

Chapter Seven

Hey, Lou, over here,' I called, waving to her as she threaded her way through the crowded food court. She smiled and waved back, heading towards us. We were finally on our movie date with Rion and Harry, although we were calling it a group thing. As Lou sat down with us, I noticed again how different she seemed from last term. Her black jeans were skinny with rips in them, and her black and white top had slipped fashionably down over one shoulder. She even had short boots with a slight heel. Her hair was held back on one side with a jewelled clip. If I didn't know her so well, I would hardly have recognised her.

Glancing over at Harry, I saw I wasn't the only one who noticed. There was a look in his eyes that I'd only seen once or twice before, and both times it had been directed at me. Now it was for Lou. It was what I wanted, and I was glad. Harry would always be my friend, and I wanted him to be happy, but there was a teensy part of me that felt sad he was over his crush on me.

Then I felt Rion's arm around me, and I looked up at him and smiled. If we were good, then nothing else mattered.

'Hey, Lou,' I said, 'that new top's cute.'

'Thanks. Mum went a bit nuts over how much of my savings I'd spent, but it was worth it. She'll get over it, and at least I have some things that don't make me look twelve.'

'You certainly don't look twelve,' Harry said.

The pink spread over Lou's cheeks.

'So, what's this movie we're going to see again?' I asked.

'The new sci fi movie,' Harry said. 'I've read the reviews and —,'

'Noo,' Lou and I said together.

'You're going to spoil it if you tell us what they said,' I added.

'I'm not going to spoil it. I was just going to say—'

Lou stopped him by leaning across the table and putting her hand across his mouth.

'Not one word,' she warned him.

His green eyes looked surprised but not unhappy or anything. Far from it. He took her hand down and held it for a few seconds. I could almost see that electricity buzz between them.

'Look, here comes Kerri,' Rion said.

'I didn't think she was coming,' I said as I watched Kerri, her red bob swinging, look around to find us. I raised a reluctant hand to wave at her. Of course, we'd invited her. She was our friend and we didn't want her to feel left out, but she always said she had to study, so I had thought Lou and Harry would have some time alone together. Kerri saw us, and then she turned around as if she were waiting for someone.

'And Pandora,' Rion said in a dead voice.

Sure enough, Pandora came from around the corner, long dark hair tumbling over her shoulders, skin-tight leather jeans, knee-high boots, and a sleeveless white crop top that rode above her navel. A few heads turned in her direction.

What she was doing here? We were, to put it bluntly, the nerds at school. No one wanted to hang out with us much, and we weren't the envy of anyone. That label was reserved for Jas's group, which was where Pandora had been hanging out lately. What was she up to?

They moved to our table, and Kerri sat next to Rion, while Pandora sat next to Harry.

'Hi guys,' Pandora said. 'Thought I'd join you. You don't mind, do you?' A totally rhetorical question. I got the feeling she couldn't care less if we minded or not.

'No, of course not,' Harry said, in his usual friendly manner. Sometimes I wished he wasn't quite so nice.

I looked over at Lou and saw the disappointment in her eyes. I hoped she and Harry would still have that vibe they had a few minutes ago, despite the extra company.

'I didn't think you were coming. Didn't you say you had some work to catch up on?' Lou said. Kerri was always freaking out that her marks wouldn't be straight As. Now that she'd got that C in English, we'd all thought she wouldn't go anywhere for the rest of year twelve.

'I did it this morning. Pandora helped me with the new English assignment, and she was just awesome,' Kerri said, her eyes shining. 'I think I really understand what Ms D said by empathy now.'

I wasn't totally convinced by that, but I said nothing.

'When I mentioned you were all going to the movies, Pandora said we should join you,' Kerri added.

'Watching a movie is a great way to analyse character and motives,' Pandora said. 'Fun too.' She smiled at Harry.

'We'd better get a move on. It's about to start,' I said.

'Oh, no need to rush. There's going to be at least twenty minutes of ads. My host nearly always rocked up half an hour late and he hardly ever missed the beginning of a movie,' Pandora said.

Rion looked at her sharply.

'What?' Lou said, looking puzzled.

'She means her host family when she was living in France,' Rion said quickly.

Pandora had told us one of the reasons she spoke French so well was that she lived there for a while. So it wasn't a hard stretch to believe she'd stayed with a host family there. It was quick thinking on Rion's part.

Pandora shrugged. 'Yeah, whatever.'

'Still, we probably should get going if we want to get snacks or anything,' Lou said.

As we headed towards the escalator leading up to the cinema, Pandora managed to position herself next to Harry, leaving Lou and Kerri to walk together.

'Hey, Harry, I'm looking for a good gym to join. Zoe tells me you work out all the time. Where do you go?' She linked her arm though his. And, before he had time to answer, she said, 'Why don't you take me there and show me around?'

'Sure,' said Mr Politeness. 'When do you want to go? It doesn't have a pool or anything like that, but the fees aren't too expensive.'

I looked up at Rion in exasperation. 'We've got to do something,' I whispered.

'What do you mean?' he looked at me blankly. 'I can't control where she goes. If I could, she wouldn't be here.'

I remembered I hadn't told him about my plan for Lou and Harry.

So, it was up to me. I left Rion's side and walked up to Harry and Pandora, just before they were about to get on the escalator. 'Hey, Pandora.' As she turned back, I managed to grab her arm and pull her towards me, smiling at her in what I hoped was a pals-y sort of way. 'Go on, Harry, I just wanted a quick word with Pan here.'

Tilting her head to one side, she looked at me with narrowed her eyes. 'Yeah?'

I had no idea what to say. All I knew was I wanted to separate her from Harry. I had to think fast. So, I said the first thing that came into my head. 'That's really cool you were helping Kerri.'

She shrugged and said, 'No biggie,' and was about to move off.

'Maybe you could help me too. I didn't do so well in that English assignment either.'

'I heard you were pretty good in English. Didn't think you'd need any help.'

'I'd hardly call a C in English pretty good.'

'You'll be fine. After all, it isn't a D, and it doesn't strike me that you have any trouble with understanding motivation at all.' Her tone was a little sarky, and I realised she knew exactly what I was trying to do.

I was about to level with her and ask her to give Harry and Lou a chance, when Rion moved up to us and touched my sleeve. 'Hey, we should catch up with the others.'

'Good idea, and if you need help with English, you should ask Rion. After all, he is your boyfriend, isn't he?' Pandora said and, flicking her hair over her shoulder, turned her back and headed for the escalator.

'What was that all about?' Rion asked as we followed.

'Nothing,' I said in a totally unconvincing way.

'Don't try to tangle with her, Zoe. She's unpredictable and probably not someone you should trust.'

'You mean because she's an alien? Or because she's gone rogue?'

'Both.'

'I think I can handle it. Besides, you're an alien, Rion, and you materialised without permission. Yet, we're together, so what does that say?'

He sighed and put an arm around me as we got off the escalator and moved into the foyer of the cinema. I could see Harry and the others were headed towards the ticket counter. 'I probably wasn't the greatest either when I first materialised into human form, but I wasn't quite so... rebellious. Besides, I'm not an alien anymore. I choose to be human.'

It struck me again what a sacrifice that must have been for him to give up his alien identity and his ties to his people. And part of the reason, I knew, was so that he could be with me. I gave him a hug. 'Let's not talk about it anymore. I don't think Pandora is interested in being friends with me now, which is fine. Come on, let's join the others.'

When we went inside the cinema, without seeming to lift a finger, Pandora managed to sit next to Harry. Lou was on the other side of him, next to me, so I had to hope for the best. Kerri was sitting on the other side of Pandora.

'Sorry, Lou, I didn't know she was coming,' I whispered.

Lou shrugged, but she didn't look happy.

The movie was totally lame too, and I couldn't help but notice that Pandora was giving her comments through the whole thing, mainly to Harry. Apparently, she didn't realise people were supposed to be quiet when they were at the movies.

Afterwards, as we were walking out, she said, 'Let's all go for a drink somewhere.'

'There's a coffee shop just outside,' Lou said.

'Coffee?' Pandora looked scornful. 'We can do better than that surely?'

'Well, you can also get milkshakes,' Lou added.

'Milkshakes. What are we, children?' She shook her head, sending her long, luxurious locks flying.

'Technically, yes. That's exactly what we are,' Rion said, giving her a warning look. She rolled her eyes.

'There's a really cool American-style snack bar upstairs where all the new cafes are. It's even got a jukebox. Zoe and I have been there a couple of times,' Lou suggested.

'That sounds like fun,' Harry said. 'Why don't we give it a go?'

'I should probably go home and read over my chemistry notes. We've got a test coming up,' Kerri said, but her tone was reluctant.

'Come on, Kerri. It won't hurt you to have a break,' I said. I may not have wanted her to come at first, and certainly not with Pandora, but now she was here I realised she was my friend too and sometimes needed support.

'You'll probably study better if you do. Think of it as a brain break,' Harry said.

'Do you think?' Kerri looked at us.

'I believe it's been scientifically proven that breaks at regular intervals improves the ability of the brain to retain information,' said my alien—I still called him that, even though he insisted he wasn't.

'Okay then, let's go,' Kerri said as if she were about to set out on a dangerous mission, like a trip to a *Survivor* set or something.

The Saturday crowds were heavy in the mall, and we had to almost push our way through them. Rion and I got separated from everyone. By the time we reached the cafe, the others had already found a booth. I noticed Pandora had managed to sit next to Harry, while Lou and Kerri were on the other side. I sighed inwardly. Pandora was almost as hard to deal with as Jas. Who was I kidding? She was much harder, and far more unpredictable.

The place was buzzing. The lime green booths and the seats at the chrome bar were all filled. We'd been lucky to get a place to sit. An old-fashioned jukebox was in the corner with real vinyl records, and an old Elvis Presley song was playing.

'It's just like a set from *Happy Days*,' Rion said, looking happy.

'Don't tell me you're still watching that,' I said. When Rion first materialised as a human, his favourite TV shows were *Happy Days* and *Star Trek*. I tried to tell him that Happy Days was set in the dark ages—like the 1950s—and had no resemblance to the way people were today. But, of course, he ignored me.

'Every time I watch it, I learn something new.'

I just shook my head. 'Trouble is it was new over fifty years ago. Never mind, let's join the others.'

I had to squeeze in next to Lou, while Rion sat on the other side next to Pandora. She gave him a bright smile. 'This is cosy, isn't it?'

A waitress with a pink dress and apron, looking like an extra in a movie, came over to take our order. After she left, I turned to Lou. 'This is cool. I'm glad you suggested it. It has a different vibe at night.'

'Yeah. When we were here last week, I thought it might be a good place for us all to go.'

'I'm going to try out that jukebox,' Pandora said.

'I'll come with you,' Rion said. 'I wonder if they have the *Happy Days'* theme song?'

As he and Pandora headed for the jukebox at the other end of the diner, I watched them. They looked so well matched, tall, dark haired and gorgeous— perfect in every way. Were all the people on his planet so beautiful? And a small voice inside me asked, what did he see in me?

He and Pandora seemed to get into a heavy conversation at the jukebox. I wondered what it was about. I could go over there, but I wouldn't. Our relationship rested on trust and the freedom to make our own decisions. I wasn't going to act like a clingy, insecure girlfriend, no matter what I felt like inside.

They must have selected a record, because suddenly a song exploded into the cafe and everybody, totally everybody, started to listen. I didn't know a lot about music from the fifties, but it was a time when Gran had been young and occasionally she had played some of her vinyl for me—which I thought had been way cool. This one sounded familiar, and I realised it was 'Jailhouse Rock' by Elvis. Without even thinking about it, I was tapping my feet. I looked over at Harry, who was beginning to click his fingers in time to the music. We weren't the only ones caught up in the beat. Looking around, I saw heads nodding and fingers drumming on tables. Then, Pandora started to dance to the music in the space near the jukebox. It looked like the jive, and like everything else she did, she was doing it extremely well. Our eyes were drawn to her as if she were a magnet and we were helpless little metal objects.

She held out her hand to Rion, pulling him closer to dance with her. I thought he might refuse at first, but no, he started to dance. He was every bit as good as her. I'd only ever seen people jive on old clips on YouTube or movies like *Grease*. I never realised Rion could dance like that. There wasn't a lot of space for them to move, but they used every square centimetre of it effectively. Rion swung her out then back into his arms, and she followed his every move. Soon, just about everyone in the small cafe was clapping in time. Even the staff had stopped to watch. Where had they learned to dance like that, these aliens who were once disembodied bubbles of consciousness?

When the song stopped, the clapping changed into applause and some people whistled, while a guy got up and slapped Rion on the back. A couple of people waved their phones. One called out, 'Do it again. I didn't quite get all that.' I'd lay bets that their dancing had already hit the internet via Instagram and Facebook.

The next song, "Rockin' Robin," was just as addictively catchy, but Rion seemed to remember where he was. Smiling, he shook his head at Pandora, who tried to persuade him to dance again. She shrugged at the people trying to cheer her on and followed him back to our table, where I'm pretty sure the rest of us just sat open mouthed, though I don't know for sure because I was too busy looking at Rion.

As he and Pandora slid back into their seats, I said, 'Where did you learn to dance like that?'

'Yeah, that was awesome,' Lou said.

'Pandora, you were amazing,' Harry added, his eyes bright with admiration.

'I picked it up from my host—'

Rion gave her a sharp look.

'—family. They were very into the fifties.'

I looked over at Rion. 'What about you?'

His face was flushed, and his hair was ruffled in a way that was not totally unattractive. He gave me his crooked smile and said, 'I told you I'm always learning new things from *Happy Days*.'

'All I can add to that is, wow,' I said.

'I can teach you if you want. It's not that hard,' he said, reaching over to hold my hand.

Considering I was almost as poorly coordinated as Lou, I didn't think that was going to happen, but I didn't say anything. The waitress came over with a tray of colas and hot chips.

'We didn't order this,' Rion said.

She smiled. 'It's on the house—for your performance. You two were great.'

And so it went on. A few people came over to our table and some even tried to get them to dance again. Pandora would have been game, but Rion kept shaking his head. I was glad. Seeing Pandora and Rion together only reinforced the feeling that they were well matched. And that didn't exactly make me feel comfortable—not that I was jealous or anything, although Rion seemed over his earlier annoyance that she had crashed our group outing.

Pandora divided her attention between Harry and Rion, throwing an occasional comment to Kerri, Lou, and me. She wasn't bitchy like Jas. She was just this colourful, attractive force that drew everyone to her, while the rest of us in comparison were just a little... colourless.

'Let's find somewhere we can really dance,' she said. 'Jas is having a party. You guys should come.

That was the last thing I felt like. Besides, we would not be welcome at any party Jas was throwing. 'I'm a bit tired. I'm going to head home.' I slid off the seat and stood.

'I've been out far too long as it is,' Kerri said. 'I think I'm getting a headache. I knew I shouldn't have had that second cola, all those chemicals and sugar.' She did look pale. Poor Kerri wasn't used to so much excitement.

Lou slid out of the booth. 'I'd better get home too. It's getting late, and Mum will wonder where I am.'

'Rion? Harry? Come on, guys, you can't really be ready to call it quits so soon.' Pandora spoke in a convincing voice.

But Rion was already on the other side of me and slid an arm around my waist. 'I'm going to take Zoe home.'

That only left Harry. Since Pandora had joined us, he seemed to only have eyes for her. Poor Lou. This afternoon and evening hadn't turned out like we planned at all.

But, to my surprise, he said, 'Thanks, but I should get going too. I've got Mum's car, and I need to get it back. It was certainly a fun day though. We should do it again sometime.' Whether or not he meant all of us or just Pandora and him wasn't clear.

'Seriously, you guys need to learn to live a little,' Pandora said as she followed us out. 'I'm just going to the taxi stand out front. See you later.'

She took out her phone and, swinging her hair over her shoulder, headed off into the Saturday evening crowd. Both Harry and Rion's eyes followed her until she disappeared around a corner.

I let out the breath I'd been holding. Now that she was gone, it seemed like everyone was normal again, if somewhat exhausted. Pandora was like a mini cyclone that swept into our lives sending everything helter-skelter and then sweeping out again, leaving us all to pick up the pieces. I just hoped it would be a cyclone that would soon blow itself out to sea—or at least back into space where she belonged.

Chapter Eight

After I dropped Zoe home, I had a decision to make. I'd originally intended just to go home and have an early night. But, when we'd been at the jukebox earlier, Pandora had said something to me that had me worried.

'I'm going to show those kids at Jas's how to party. It'll be a blast. You should come.'

'Pandora, that's not wise. You need to be careful.'

She'd just tossed her head, sending her hair flying, and laughed. Not reassuring.

So, I was considering going to the party just to keep an eye on her. She was what they called 'a loose cannon,' and there was no predicting when she might go off or what she might hit. She'd even affected me. It had been fun dancing with her, and for two minutes and forty-four seconds, I'd forgotten my agenda to persuade her to be more low key and not draw attention.

Then, when the music ended and I sat down, I realised how foolish I'd been. It was just dancing sure, but it was more than that. Pandora was on a mission to have fun, and she really didn't care about the consequences. Sometimes she didn't even see them. She was reckless. Bad enough in a human, but disastrous in one of my people. Our natural abilities were enhanced by millennia of scientific and technological advancements. We knew more, and so we could do more. I had always controlled that part of my abilities, for the most part, but even I'd made mistakes. Pandora showed no signs of even trying to control it, and that's what worried me most.

So, I was thinking I should follow her to this party and see what she was up to. I knew Jas and her friends would be far more susceptible to Pandora's influence than Zoe and the rest of our friends.

But, and this was what was bothering me, should I have told Zoe? I knew I should go on my own so I could judge the situation and intervene if I had to. Of course, Zoe would come if she realised why I wanted to go, but I didn't want to involve her. This was alien business, and no one would be able to deal with Pandora better than me if she got out of hand. I hoped it wouldn't be necessary, but I wasn't sure. Yet, Zoe and I had always been honest with each other, and trust was important. If I went without telling her, would she feel betrayed?

I had just reached my townhouse, a short walk from Zoe's, when I made a decision. I'd go. Zoe would understand. Wouldn't she?

The music was ear splitting, and the room was crowded with gyrating bodies, people drinking beer from plastic cups, and everyone talking at a roar. Chelsea, the host and Jas's best friend, was dancing with some guy in the corner. There wasn't a parent or adult to be seen—not that I was surprised. Chelsea's mum was known for her liberal views, and so a lot of parties were often held here.

Strange to think this was the place I'd first materialised into an organic form nearly a year ago. I did it to help Zoe win over a boy. No, who am I kidding? I did it to show off. But considering everything that had followed, I couldn't regret it. I had Zoe. I was human at last, and I was happy, except for this distraction of Pandora. Where was she? This party seemed much wilder than the one I had been to nearly a year ago. It wasn't hard to guess who was responsible for that.

I didn't have to look far. She was in the middle of the room, her arms in the air, and her head back, laughing as she danced to the music. There was a plastic cup in one of her hands and an admiring group, mainly boys, around her.

'Hey, Pandora, you're spilling your drink,' one of the guys said. I looked over and saw Chad Everett grinning at her. Without even meaning to, I felt my hand clench and my insides tighten. Last term we'd got into a fight, but we'd never finished it—not that I approved of violence… my people had eliminated it from our society a long time ago. But, somehow, whenever I saw Chad, I forgot that. Now was not the time to think about him.

Pandora laughed again and then drained her cup, spilling much of it because she was still dancing. She put one hand on the back of her head and stretched out the other with her now empty cup. 'Be a good boy and fill this up again, Chad.'

He stepped forward, pulling her into his arms. 'What will you give me if I do?'

Pandora put her arms around his neck and moved her swaying body even closer as she whispered in his ear. No one would have heard what she said, but because of my still enhanced hearing, I heard every word. 'More than you bargained for, Chad.'

I could see his eyes light up, and his hold on her tightened. Then, with a backward step and a swift push on his chest, she laughed as she moved back from him. 'Now, scoot and get that filled before I change my mind.'

He gave a deep breath and a last lingering look at Pandora before he 'scooted' through the crowd to do her bidding.

I'd seen enough. I pushed my way through the moving bodies till I reached her. Her eyes were slightly glazed, and her dancing was getting more unsteady. She saw me and smiled. 'Orion, you came after all.' And then, pulling me closer, she slid her arms around my neck. 'Got rid of the little girlfriend, have you? Nice enough, but you can do much better. After all, you are an al—'

'What are you doing?' I said, interrupting her before she said something we both regretted.

'Dancing with you, I think. Although, you're not as good at it as you were this afternoon.'

I moved us away into a quieter part of the room. 'Pandora, this is crazy. You're going to get yourself into trouble.'

'I sincerely hope so. What's the point of becoming human otherwise? I want to have fun, fun, fun!' She moved away from me and started twirling in a circle. In many ways, she reminded me of Archimedes at that embarrassing dinner at the Brennans'. He'd eaten and drunk far too much, made inappropriate comments, and generally disgraced himself. Were my people totally unable to cope with being in a human state?

I pulled her towards me again and said in a low voice that I hoped no one else near us would hear, 'You won't be having much fun if they find out you're an alien.'

'Why?' Her dark eyes looked into mine, and I realised she really didn't know. She still had so much to learn.

'They wouldn't let you live a normal life. You'd be taken away to some scientific institution where they would perform countless experiments on you. They'd want to know everything about our people, and it would ruin our entire space mission on this planet. Do you really want that?'

She swayed a little, and I caught her before she fell. 'Well then, I just won't tell them.'

'You may not be able to stop yourself, especially if you've been drinking.'

'Then I'll make them forget what I said. You know I can do it. Archimedes did it to Zoe when he took her memories of you as an alien away. Easy-peasy. You worry too much, Orion.' She laid her head on my shoulder. 'But I am getting tired. Can we go outside for a breath of fresh air?'

As I headed towards the front door with her, I heard Chad call out, 'Hey, Pandora, where are you going? I've got your drink?' He held it up in the air.

I wondered where Jas, his girlfriend, was. Where was she when we needed her? Ignoring him, we left. I breathed a sigh of relief. Now, all I had to do was to get her home.

But Pandora had other ideas. She sat down on the step and leaned her head against a slender column supporting the roof above it. 'Just need to take a breath or two, and then I'm going back inside. You should too. It's time you learned how to live.'

'This is crazy. You shouldn't even be here. And as for living, you haven't any idea of how to do that. You need to slow down, act more... human.'

She raised her head and looked at me. 'But that's just what I'm not. I'm an alien on this planet, and so are you. We aren't the same as they are. We know more. We can do more. We are... *more*.'

I sat down on the step beside her. Behind us inside the house, the music throbbed, mingled with laughter and the sound of voices. I could understand how all this must seem intoxicating, in more ways than one. I remembered when it happened nearly a year ago, I had felt it too. Unlike Pandora, instead of embracing it, I'd tried to fight it. But, *just* like her, I had felt superior to human beings—at first. I now knew how misguided that feeling was. I tried to explain it to her.

'You're wrong. We might know more facts than they do, even be able to conjure up a few tricks, but we certainly aren't better than them. Think, Pandora. We've been without bodies for so long that we've forgotten what it is to experience life through our senses, to see beauty, to smell a rose, to feel the touch of another person. That's so powerful, it changes you in ways you don't realise. Human beings only have a short time on Earth, and yet they have accomplished such amazing things; they have written great books, composed music that could move you to tears of joy, learned to love in ways we can only begin to understand. They are not less than us. In many ways, they are greater.'

Pandora tossed her head, sending her hair flying. 'Rubbish. That's not true, and you know it. They've also started wars, killed each other, shown incredible greed, and nearly brought the planet to the edge of extinction. They are stupid. I might have plans for a short time to enjoy myself here, but I won't forget for a moment who I am. And you shouldn't either. You're an alien, Orion, not a human.'

I shook my head. 'No, I'm not. Once I was an alien, but not anymore. Our supervisor told me that in making my decision to stay here, I would no longer be one of our people. I am now human and will live a normal lifespan, if all goes well. That's what I chose, Pandora. That's who I want to be.'

'Then you're a fool.'

I gave a half-smile and then said, 'I've been called that before, and worse.'

'You're also wrong. Once an alien, eh? Let me add to that to make it more truthful. Once an alien, *always* an alien. That's who you are and who you will always be. You need to remember it. I might play with these humans for a while—after all, being an organic again is fun—but I know who I really am. Do you?' She stood up and stretched. Her eyes were clearer, and she seemed to have lost the effects of whatever she was drinking. I suppose she would say that was evidence of her enhanced alien abilities. Although, I hadn't noticed a quick recovery in Archimedes when he indulged. Perhaps it was because he was so much older.

'I'm going back in. I think you should too. But it's up to you, of course.'

I put a hand on her arm. 'I don't think that's wise. You might say something, do something that you'll regret.'

She shook my hand off. 'Maybe, maybe not. But it's my choice. You can't control me, Orion. Don't even try. Besides—' She gave me a smile that showed me my words had no effect on her whatsoever. '—there's a beer waiting for me inside. And there's a rather cute guy who's holding it.'

She gave me a wink and then turned towards the front door, opening it and letting out the full roar of a party that was even noisier than when I first arrived. She went inside, closing the door, and the sounds were muffled again.

I turned away. There wasn't much more I could do. Pandora was right. I couldn't control her. I just hoped I wouldn't be called on to do some damage control.

As I walked into the night, my footsteps on the pavement soon became the only sound in the darkness, the noise of the party having faded into the distance. But Pandora's words stayed with me and gave me a sense of disquiet. Once an alien... would I always feel that it was still there inside me? And was I wrong to suppress who and what I had been?

Chapter Nine

Monday was weird, like I was in an alternate universe or something. First of all, Lou didn't sit with us for lunch, and it wasn't because she had something else to do, like choir practise or doing an assignment in the library. No, she was having lunch all right, just not with our group. She was sitting under the old fig tree in the corner near the bicycle rack, and she was with one of the guys from our English class, Mike Li. He was a tech head and into gaming and probably even quieter than Lou. What was going on there? What had I missed? They were the two most unlikely people to be talking to each other, let alone sitting down to lunch together. I was determined to find out from Lou as soon as I could get her on her own.

Then there was Harry, usually so easy and friendly. He hardly said a word at lunch, but I did notice him glancing over at Pandora, who was, of course, sitting with Jas's group. Even though she'd crashed our afternoon on Saturday, she seemed to show no desire to have much to do with us at school. Harry seemed down about that. It looked as if my plans to help Lou and him get together were hitting a few road blocks.

Kerri didn't bring a book to lunch, unusual for her, and told us she spent most of Sunday watching movies on Netflix. I was surprised the earth didn't stop in its orbit around the sun.

Even Rion was different. Like Harry, he was quiet, and though he still smiled at me and gave me a hug when he saw me, it seemed like his mind was elsewhere, like he was on autopilot.

So, it was up to me to inject some life and normalcy into this group. 'So, guys,' I said, trying to sound bright and chirpy, 'Rion and I are going to see Nebula when they come to Brisbane in August. Anyone want to join us? It should be awesome.'

Harry shook his head. 'I doubt we'd get tickets at this late date.'

'Pandora might be able to get some tickets,' Kerri said. 'She seems to be good at getting things. It might be fun to go together.'

'I don't think Pandora would be interested,' Harry said. 'She seems to have decided who she wants to hang out with.' He looked over at her sitting next to Jas. Pandora said something and everyone exploded into laughter.

'Yes, but, she's friends with us too,' Kerri persisted. 'She really helped me a lot with English, and she wanted to hang out with us on Saturday. It doesn't matter that she's sitting with her other friends. People don't have to be exclusive to one group.'

That was a very mature but not realistic view of high school life, I thought. Maybe in adult life it was different, but in high school, sadly, it was all about groups. I was just thankful I had friends I could trust and rely on. The same couldn't be said for some of the people in Jas's group, including Jas herself. I should know. I'd once been a part of them.

'They usually are, exclusive that is,' Harry said. 'But maybe Pandora is the exception.'

'Maybe we shouldn't worry about her at all,' Rion said, sounding annoyed. 'She'll always suit herself. I think we'd be wise to realise that.'

'It didn't seem to stop you from dancing with her on Saturday,' I said. I wasn't really jealous. I knew Rion wanted rid of her as soon as possible. But I didn't exactly love seeing how well they danced together.

'That was a mistake,' Rion said.

'And yet you danced together so well.' I couldn't help myself. I knew it was the wrong thing to say.

Rion's mouth tightened.

I didn't say anything else, but the vibe became tense and awkward.

Harry got up. 'I'll see you guys later.'

That just left Rion, Kerri, and me. Kerri didn't seem to notice anything and went on quietly eating her lunch, but then that was Kerri.

So, we sat in silence for a few minutes. I wanted to say something, I really did, but for once, I just couldn't think of anything.

Then, to my surprise, Pandora came over to us. Kerri looked up at her and smiled. 'Hey, Pandora, how are you?'

'Super.' She plonked herself down on the other side of Rion. 'Saturday was fun, eh?'

Kerri nodded enthusiastically. 'We should do it again, you know, the going out as a group thing.'

Rion was still quiet, but he was definitely looking uneasy. Nervous even.

'Great idea,' Pandora said, and then she turned to Rion. 'You should have stayed longer at Chelsea's party, though. You missed a good time.'

I felt a sickening feeling in the pit of my stomach. 'You went to Chelsea's party on Saturday night after you dropped me home? You didn't say anything about that. You told me you were going home.'

Rion's face had turned red. 'I can explain.'

Pandora gave an impression of looking surprised. 'Oh, you mean you didn't know? I just thought he told you, but you didn't want to go.'

I ignored her. She knew exactly what she was doing when she mentioned that little piece of news.

'So, explain,' I said, hoping my voice sounded as frosty as I was feeling.

'I will... later,' he said, looking as guilty and embarrassed as if he had just been caught stealing petty cash from the canteen or something. But it was worse, far worse. He had lied to me, and he had never done that before. I felt betrayed. No, worse than betrayed. I felt devastated. He left me to go to a party he knew Pandora would be at.

'You lied to me.'

'Yes, but...' He stopped and took a deep breath and said, 'I didn't mean to. Can we go somewhere and talk about it?'

I wanted to go with him, I wanted to understand why he would do such a thing, but the lump in my throat wouldn't go away and I felt my eyes moisten. I couldn't break down, not here in front of everyone, and especially not in front of Pandora. I had to get away fast. The bell rang, coming to my rescue. I did the only thing I could.

'I've got to go,' I said. As I scrambled to my feet, I felt his hand on my arm.

'No, wait.'

I shook my head and pushed his hand off. I needed to get out of there before the tears started to fall and the sob inside me escaped.

I watched Zoe move away, her head down and shoulders hunched. She was hurt, I knew it, and I was to blame. I jumped up to follow her. 'Thanks a lot, Pandora,' I said, looking down at her.

'You should have told her you were going to that party. Don't blame me. That's on you,' Pandora said and gave a shrug. Kerri just looked at us, slightly bewildered.

'I intended to,' I said, realising how lame my words sounded. I was at fault here. I knew I should have told Zoe about my plan, but it didn't stop me feeling annoyed with Pandora. 'Not that it's any of your business. Why did you even come here?' Before she had time to reply, I left to find Zoe.

I couldn't see her anywhere. She might have already gone to her class, but I had a feeling she'd disappeared into the girls' restrooms, probably to cry. That didn't make me feel good. There was no way I wanted to hurt her, and she certainly had nothing to worry about when it came to Pandora. I wished for about the hundredth time that Pandora hadn't materialised right here, right now. Why couldn't her host have lived a few more years?

She had come here without permission, and she couldn't care less it seemed. I had a sinking feeling that things were going to get a lot worse before I saw the last of Pandora.

Zoe wasn't in any of my classes for the rest of the day, and she didn't answer any of my texts to her. I waited by the school gate for her after school. She came out, arm in arm with Lou.

'Zoe,' I said, 'I need to talk to you.'

She looked at me, her face expressionless. Lou, on the other hand, frowned at me, and I knew Zoe had told her what had happened.

'I can't stop now, Rion. I'm going home with Lou, and her mum is waiting for us in the car.'

'Can't you give me a minute?'

'Sorry. Gotta go. But I'm sure Pandora would be delighted to talk to you.'

She and Lou walked away. Lou looked back and shook her head.

I tried to call and text, but Zoe just didn't answer. In all my years solving the problems of the universe and being with hosts whose IQs were among the highest on the planet, I had never felt so helpless and frustrated. How could a sixteen-year-old girl do that to me? And yet she did.

I could see how it looked. I'd told her I was staying home. I hadn't said anything about the party. Bad decision. I saw it now—too late. I hadn't wanted to involve her because I thought it was better for me to do it alone. Still, I wondered now if that was the only reason.

Pandora's words came back to haunt me. Once an alien... Did I want to reconnect with one of my own people? Was I missing that part of me that used to be alien, and probably still was? I didn't regret my decision to become human. Yet seeing Pandora reminded me again of what I had given up. Was there a small part of me that regretted that decision?

That night I turned off the light and looked out my bedroom window, gazing up at the night sky. I picked out the Orion constellation and found the star that was closest to my home, a home I hadn't seen in nearly 4000 years. If I had that choice again, would I have joined the space program on our planet, given up my organic body and life there to become a bodiless, intelligent entity that inhabited hosts in order to further our knowledge of the universe?

Once I wouldn't have hesitated to answer that question in the affirmative. But now... If I had stayed, I wouldn't be an alien because I would be home. I would have belonged. Now I wondered if I would ever belong here or anywhere else again.

I loved Zoe, but was it enough? Was I enough for her? She knew who I was, and she had, I thought, accepted it. But now that Pandora was here, maybe she was having second thoughts. Perhaps she saw me for what I was, an alien, and maybe she didn't like it.

I gave one last glance to the night sky and then went to lie down on my bed. I had a lot of questions, but tonight I didn't have the answers. And, for the first time, I wondered if I'd been right in my decision to stay here on this planet and give up all that I'd been.

Chapter Ten

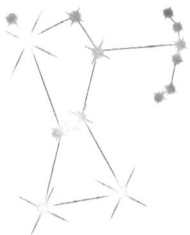

I can't believe Rion would lie to you,' Lou said again. 'It's just not like him.'

I leaned against her bed and put the bottle of nail polish next to me on the floor. In order to cheer me up, Lou suggested we paint each other's toe nails. But it hadn't helped. 'He admitted it, to my face. And Pandora looked so… ugh,' I let out an exclamation of anger and frustration. 'She wants every boy in year twelve to fall at her feet, and she's succeeding too. So much for her wanting to be my friend.'

Lou stretched out her legs and wiggled her scarlet toes to dry. Her forehead creased into a frown. 'I know. Harry never even gave me a second look once she arrived on the scene on Saturday. That's when I decided I'd just give up on him. He's had a massive crush on you for years, and finally now he's over that, I thought I might have a chance. But then Pandora came along, and now he has a crush on her. If he can't value me, I'm not going to wait around.'

'Good for you, Lou,' I said. 'Harry must be blind. You're worth ten of Pandora.'

'Thanks, but I don't care anymore. I've decided to move on. Mike's been talking to me off and on, so when he asked me to have lunch with him, I thought, why not? And you know what? He's actually really nice. We're going out on Friday.'

I sat up and smiled at her. 'That's great news, Lou. I'm so happy for you. I've never actually spoken much to Mike, but if you say he's okay, that's good enough for me.'

Lou had made a lot of progress this year. She had been one of the shyest people I'd ever known, and I'm sure, up till recently, Harry was the only boy she had ever spoken to. But now, she'd come out of her shell. We'd been friends, but not close. Then, last term, I'd helped her work out what to wear when our class went on an excursion to see *Macbeth*. I'd also given her a few tips on make-up and how to style her hair. I wasn't an expert or anything, but Lou was naturally pretty, and suddenly she realised it. Her increased self-confidence helped too.

Today, I realised she'd become a close friend. She'd been so kind to me when she heard what happened with Rion and said I should come home with her. I was glad to have an excuse not to deal with him. I needed time to process what had happened. Perhaps I'd be able to listen to him tomorrow, but just not tonight.

'Pass the bottle over here,' Lou said, 'and I'll do your toes now.'

I leaned over and handed the nail polish to her. The colour was Red Fire, an appropriate colour choice for the way I was feeling right now. But I was glad anger was starting to replace the hole Rion's betrayal left inside me. I stretched out my foot and closed my eyes as Lou started to paint my toes.

'I've never really been into video or computer games,' she said. I felt the soft touch of the brush and let myself relax. 'Or any games at all.'

'Me either.'

'But Mike makes it sound so interesting. He says it's like being in a movie, playing a part. And some of the storylines are really exciting. He's going to take me to a new retro gaming arcade and show me how to play some games on Friday.'

'That sounds like fun.' I remembered my first date with Rion when he took me to a bowling alley. At first,

I thought it was the lamest thing in the world, but we actually had a lot of fun. When we went home, we had our first kiss. I felt the moisture welling in my eyes again. I had to think of something else quickly. 'So, what sort of games does he play?'

'Everything just about. He showed me one on his phone today, and it was kind of awesome. I had a go, and he said I wasn't too bad for a beginner. He's really into *Fortnite* at the moment. Okay, next foot please.'

Opening my eyes, I transferred my other foot to her lap.

'I've only got one problem,' she said as she started to apply the polish.

'What's that?' It couldn't be what to wear anymore, since she had just bought a ton of clothes.

'Telling Mum. It wouldn't be such a problem if I was going out with Harry because she knows him and his mum. But Mike? She doesn't know him, and she's bound to ask a million questions.'

Lou's mum was nice, but she was strict, and she didn't seem to realise that Lou was sixteen.

'But won't she be glad you're making new friends? You know that's one of the reasons she put you into all those sports you used to do.' I tried to be positive.

'Girls maybe, but she's stricter when it comes to boys. She wouldn't let my sister date until she finished high school. There,' she put my foot down on the floor, 'you're done. Now you have to let them dry off.'

'You'll just have to think of all the good things about him. He's quiet, I think he does all right in school, and—' I searched for something else to say. '—I don't think he's ever been suspended.'

Lou laughed. 'I don't think that's much of a point in his favour. Mum probably wouldn't let any kid who's been suspended into the house, let alone allow me to go out with him.'

'You'll think of something.'

'And she'd have kittens if she knew we were going to a gaming arcade,' Lou added as she screwed the lid on the nail polish bottle.

'I suppose it wouldn't be right not to tell her where you were going?' I said, just a little hesitantly. Lou was mega honest.

She screwed up her nose as she thought for a moment. 'I don't know. Maybe I could say I'm going to watch a game or something. I don't have to tell her what game. Mike has his licence, so he's going to pick me up. Oh no. That's another thing she's not going to like. She'll be worried he's going to have an accident or something. She'll never let me go out. I'll be forty or something before she decides I can date.'

'Don't stress. You'll think of some way to persuade her.'

'I guess.' Lou seemed doubtful.

It was my turn to cheer her up. 'Come on. Let's make milkshakes. Did I tell you I'm the best milkshake maker in Brisbane—no, make that Australia—no, the world!'

'I think we can do better than that.' Lou's voice dropped.

'What do you mean?'

'Mum and Dad had a barbecue for Uncle Carl's fortieth birthday last weekend. There's still five or six bottles of bubbly left in the second fridge in the garage. Want to try some?'

'Won't they miss it?' Tempting as Lou's offer was, I didn't want her to get in trouble.

She shrugged. 'I don't think so. They won't miss one, because a lot of people brought stuff, and they didn't keep track.'

'Well…' It had been a while since I'd taken a sneaky glass of wine — Rion was just that good an influence on me. But now, I wasn't too fussed about what Rion thought at all. 'Sure, why not?'

A few minutes later, she was back with a bottle of bubbly. She took two plastic cups off the top of the bottle, and handed them to me. Then, she sat down next to me, and popped the cork. The wine bubbled over the top and onto the carpet. We started to laugh.

'Shhh,' Lou said, between giggles. 'Mum might hear.'

114

'You mean after that explosive cork pop?'

We started to laugh again. Lou filled our glasses to the very top.

I took a long swig and then looked down at my newly painted toes, admiring their fiery brightness.

'Boys,' I said, as I lowered my glass. 'Who needs them?'

Lou gave me a sympathetic look. 'So over-rated.'

'Sisters before misters,' I added.

We clinked our glasses together and more wine slopped onto the carpet.

We giggled again, and I thought that maybe this day wasn't turning out so badly after all.

Later, as I walked home, depression (not to mention the beginning of a headache) hit me again like a brick from a ten-storey building. Rion and I had had our ups and downs, but this was something else. Our relationship had been built on trust, and now that had suddenly been broken. I wondered if I would ever entirely trust him again.

Mum and Dad were sitting in the lounge when I got home, not ultra unusual except that Dad was home a little earlier than normal, and I couldn't smell dinner cooking. Maybe we were having takeaway? My spirits lifted. Not having to eat one of Mum's overcooked meals, or one of Dad's repertoire of three recipes was a relief.

'Zoe,' Mum called, 'come in and sit down.'

I plopped down on the saggy armchair, and looked over at my parents, sitting on the couch. As parents went, they were pretty good, and surprisingly, we got on well. I just hoped they wouldn't guess I'd had a glass or two of wine. That might test their good natures. I tried to sit up and look normal.

'So, are we going out to dinner then?' I said, just putting that idea in their minds in case they hadn't thought of it. 'After all, you have been a bit tired lately, Mum.'

Dad covered her hand with his, and Mum gave me a smile that was trying to be bright but somehow failed. Her eyes seemed less blue, and I suddenly noticed fine lines at the corners of them. When had that happened? But more than that, I was getting a weird vibe from them. Something was going on.

'What's up?'

Mum gave a small sigh, and Dad's hand tightened around hers. 'You're right, I have been feeling off lately, and so I decided to check it out, just to be sure. You see, I have a small lump in my breast.'

'What? Why didn't you tell me?' I felt a cold, creeping dread inside me.

'I didn't want to worry you. Quite often, it's nothing, and I just wanted to find out before I was sure.'

'Sure of what?' I could hardly get the words out.

'It seems the lump might be not just be a cyst,' Mum said. 'I have to get another test to be sure.'

I heard my mother's words, and yet they made no sense. Surely nothing could be wrong with Mum? This wasn't happening. Any moment now I would wake up and realise it wasn't real.

'Zoe, are you okay?' My mother's voice was anxious.

I looked at her face, her tired blue eyes staring into mine, and I realised she was more worried about me than herself. I made an effort to answer her. 'Could it be cancer?' The word itself was hard to say.

She bit her lips, then forced them into a smile. 'Probably not. No need to panic. I mean, I've been tired, but that's more a symptom of teaching, not breast cancer.' She tried to laugh. Then she added, 'I'm going to have a small op just to be sure.'

'An operation? Can't the doctor just do a test or something?' An operation sounded serious, as if Mum really had this horrible disease.

'He's done a biopsy, but it wasn't conclusive, and so now he wants to do an open biopsy just to make sure. It's just a day procedure. You know Gran had breast cancer a few years ago and so did my Aunt Hilda. So, it appears I'm in a high-risk group. But Gran survived. Look how healthy she is now.'

'And still bossing everyone around,' Dad said in a lame attempt to make a joke.

I forced the lump in my throat down and looked down at my hands, which I realised were clenched tightly in my lap. I forced myself to look back at Mum.

'You'll be all right, Mum, won't you?' Suddenly I felt like I was five years old again and still afraid of the dark, but this time it wasn't the dark I was scared about.

Mum came over to my chair and knelt down next to me, giving me a hug. 'Of course I will. It's just a precaution to make sure everything is all right. And you know what, I think a takeout is a great idea. Let's have Thai.'

Mum's news sobered me more quickly than a cold shower and a cup of coffee. Nothing would happen to her, I told myself. I wouldn't let it.

That night, while I was in bed, trying to sleep, Rion called. This time I picked up.

'Zoe,' his voice was relieved, 'at last. I'm so sorry about lying to you...'

Besides my parents, Rion was the person I felt closest to, and I didn't want to let go of any of the people I cared about because of a stupid misunderstanding. So I said,

'I should have listened to you, but I was too upset. So, tell me now.'

'I've been an idiot. I've been so worried about Pandora getting into trouble, that I decided to go to Jas's party to make sure she didn't do anything stupid.'

'And did she?'

'Don't get me started. She was reckless, drunk, and totally unconcerned about any consequences of her actions. Remember when Archimedes came to your place for dinner and how he acted? Well, times that by ten and that was Pandora.'

'Oh dear, that bad, huh? Well, at least you were there to step in.'

'Unfortunately, it didn't do any good. And, Zoe, I didn't tell you because I didn't want you to have to put up with her nonsense. I didn't want to involve you in our ridiculous alien business. But it was the wrong decision. I should have told you, and I'm sorry.'

'Yes, you should have, but it's over now.'

'So, we're good then?'

'Yeah, we're good.' Now that he explained it, I got it. I realised too that I had let my insecurities about Pandora get the better of me. I knew deep down that Rion would never betray me. 'But, Rion, you're wrong about something else too. I'm already involved in your "alien" business, because I'm involved with you.'

'Zoe?'

'Yeah.'

'I'd like to kiss you now. I wish I was there with you. I've missed you.'

'Since lunch?' I forced a laugh.

'Seemed much longer. I hated that you wouldn't talk to me. I'm not saying I didn't deserve it.'

'Yeah, well, as I said, it doesn't matter now.' My voice trailed off. Now there was something much more important to worry about.

'Is there something wrong?'

Rion must have picked up my vibe. We were so close he could almost read my thoughts. And in the beginning when we first met, he could, much to my annoyance. But that seemed so long ago. I wanted to tell him about Mum, but I couldn't talk about it on the phone. It was too important.

'I'm fine, especially now that things are okay between us again.'

'And are they? Okay, I mean?' His voice sounded anxious, as if he couldn't quite believe it.

'Yes, and they will be even better than okay when I see you again.'

'I could come over now.'

'No, it's too late. I'll see you in the morning.' I didn't want him waking up Mum.

'I'll come over early tomorrow, so we can walk to school.'

I said goodbye and hung up, putting the phone on my bedside table. Closing my eyes, I tried to quiet the thoughts that were playing tag in my mind. Shut up, I told my brain, but it didn't listen, and I spent the next few hours wrestling with my pillow and tangling my sheets. Finally, I must have fallen asleep, because when I heard the alarm the next morning, I had forgotten why I couldn't sleep. All I thought about was why weren't mornings banned and why couldn't this be a Saturday when I could sleep in. Then, as I reluctantly tossed the sheet aside and swung my feet to the floor, I remembered about Mum, and my world became an uncertain place again.

Chapter Eleven

Any doubts I'd had about my decision to remain human had fled last night as soon as I'd heard Zoe's voice. The distance that had opened between us had closed. She'd forgiven me for lying to her, and that was all that mattered to me now.

But when I saw her in the morning, there were dark shadows under her eyes and I knew there was something wrong, something that had nothing to do with us. Mr Brennan came out the door just behind her, and he had the same look, but he smiled when he saw me.

'Hi, Rion, you're early this morning.'

'Hi, Mr Brennan. Yes, Zoe and I are walking to school.'

'Nice morning for it,' he said and then bent down to give Zoe a kiss on her cheek. 'See you tonight, sweetheart. And don't forget, it's my turn to cook.'

I waited for her to make some light remark, as she usually did, about her father's zero cooking skills, but she just nodded. Something was definitely up.

As he got in the car and reversed down the driveway, I turned back to her. 'Okay, I know something isn't right. Tell me.'

'Hug first.' She put her arms around me. Feeling her need for comfort, I held her tightly. Her heartbeat kept time with mine, and I realised again how precious she was to me. What had happened to make her so unhappy? Whatever it was, I was determined to make it right for her.

After a few moments, she pulled away. 'Let's walk,' she said. 'I'll tell you on the way.'

The morning was bright with just a few clouds in the sky, and there was a tinge of coolness to the early autumn air. I matched my stride to hers as we headed down the street. I waited for when she was ready to talk, not wanting to rush her. Her dark hair was pulled back into a ponytail, showing her pale face.

We'd reached nearly the halfway point to school when she finally said, 'It's Mum.'

'Your mum? What's wrong?' Mrs Brennan was one of my favourite humans. I would never forget how kind she'd been to me when I first materialised. She had accepted my flimsy story of why I had turned up on her doorstep with no belongings, no clothes, and no family, and she had treated me like one of her own. I couldn't bear the thought that anything bad could happen to her, any more than I could bear it happening to Zoe.

'The doctor wants her to have a procedure. It could be...' Zoe's eyes filled with tears. I stopped and put a hand on her arm, turning her to face me.

'What is it? You know you can tell me.'

She bit her lip and then said in a shaky voice, ' She might have breast cancer. She's having an open biopsy to find out.'

I took one look into her worried eyes and then pulled her into my arms again. I'd never known disease or even, up to this point, ageing, and still found it hard to comprehend an existence where such things happened. Of course, the many hosts I'd had over the millennia had suffered illnesses, injuries, and all the calamities of an organic existence. But though I had been saddened, it had never affected me. Not until now. I felt the cold, clammy hand of mortality, not on me but on someone I cared about. And, worse still, I had no idea how to stop it.

I kissed the top of Zoe's head and said, 'But they still don't know for sure. Perhaps she will be all right.'

Zoe moved away from me, wiping her eyes and shifting the school bag on her back. She shook her head. 'My grandmother and my great aunt had it. It's in the family. And besides, she and Dad wouldn't have told me anything unless they thought it might be a possibility.'

'But they don't know for sure. She might be fine. And even if she does have it, they have excellent treatments for cancer now. There is so much they can do. And your grandmother is better, isn't she?'

'Yes, but my Aunt Hilda died of breast cancer when I was a little girl.'

I tried to reassure her. 'Your mum is still young, and she looks after herself. She has a really good chance of beating this.' I corrected myself. 'She *will* beat this.'

'Yes, she will. I know it. But it sucks that she might have to try.'

'You're right, it does suck. But let's wait and see first. They don't know for sure yet.' I took her hand. 'I'm here for you, Zoe. You know that, no matter what happens.' I bent down and kissed her softly. She kissed me back, and for just a moment, it seemed like we could conquer anything as long as we were together.

Then she moved away and gave me a sad smile. 'I know. That's why I couldn't stay mad at you anymore. You matter too much to me to argue over something that isn't really important.'

'You're right. Pandora means nothing to me. I was only worried about the trouble she might cause. But I don't care about that anymore. She can look after herself from now on. I only care about you.'

'I don't want to talk about her. It's in the past. Come on. We should get going, otherwise we might be late for school.'

We swung into step again, both quiet, both thoughtful. I knew it was possible Mrs Brennan might have cancer, but I also knew that I would do anything I could to help Zoe or her mother. Anything in my power.

'Seriously, Zoe, you're too good for him,' Pandora said, flicking her hair over her shoulder in a familiar gesture that was starting to annoy me. 'It's not that I care zip about him, and there's zero between us, but he should have told you where he was going.'

We were in history class, one of the classes Rion and I didn't share. Pandora had come over to me all friendly like and sat down in front of me, twisting around in her chair to talk. If we'd been anywhere else, I would have walked away. But I didn't want to get a detention for skipping class, as much as I wanted to leave.

'It's really none of your business, Pandora,' I said, trying to inject as much ice into my voice as possible.

She looked at me. 'I get it. You're annoyed with me. But you shouldn't be. Rion's the one who lied to you. I'm on your side. I'm all for girl power. Guys on this planet have it way too easy.'

I looked at her through narrowed eyes. She'd said, 'on this planet.' Did she realise I knew she was an alien or was it just a slip of the tongue? Hard to say, but I wasn't going to admit to knowing anything about her.

Jas came into the classroom looking like a thundercloud. Uh-oh, someone was in for it. She headed straight for Pandora and stopped in front of her, putting her hand on her hip. 'I thought we were friends, Pandora. You sure had me fooled.'

Pandora looked surprised. 'Of course we're friends.'

'Is that so? Well, friends don't try to make out with each other's boyfriends. Or don't they teach you that in France?'

By now everyone's attention was riveted to the scene playing out between them, especially the guys, and they looked like they were enjoying it.

Pandora still looked like she wasn't getting it. 'We were just having fun, no harm intended. Jeez, chill out, Jas. I don't want Chad. He could have been A, B, or C as far as I was concerned. He was just a guy, and I was just having fun.'

'Fun, eh? Is that what you call it? Or maybe it was mouth-to-mouth resuscitation? Were you trying to save his life or something?'

Pandora gave a light laugh and said, 'Good one, Jas. Yes, let's call it that. Anyway, it's not me you should be angry with, it's Chad. He was more than willing.'

Crack. Jas's hand slapped Pandora's cheek. I think there was a collective intake of breath in the class. Pandora's face reddened, and I was guessing it was more than because of the slap. She stood up next to Jas. Jas was tall, but Pandora was taller—and scarier. Her eyes were fiery, and she took a step closer to Jas. 'Try that again and it's you who'll need life support.' Somehow, I got the feeling she wasn't joking. 'Let's make this perfectly clear. There is nothing you have, no friend, no boy, no success—nothing—that I couldn't have if I wanted to with as much ease as snapping my fingers.' She put her fingers in front of Jas's face and clicked them together loudly. 'Push me again, Jas, and you'll find just how true that it.'

They stood for what seemed an eternity, breathing hard and glaring at each other. Jas, for once, had nothing to say.

Then Mr Parsons came into the class. 'Sit down, girls, and get your books out. You can gossip on your time, not mine.' He seemed oblivious to the drama that was going on, which just showed how clueless some teachers were.

'So much for girl power,' I said softly, and Pandora shot me a look that was far from friendly.

After class, she was first out the door, and I noticed everyone gave her plenty of space.

At break time, Rion and I went outside together. 'How are you holding up?' He grabbed my hand and gazed at me, concern in his eyes.

'I'm okay. It's hard not to worry, but you're right about one thing. We don't know anything for sure yet.'

He nodded and gave my hand a squeeze. Then we walked over to join our friends. Lou took one glance at us and gave a relieved smile. Kerri looked up and nodded as we sat down. I didn't think she had any idea that Rion and I had even fallen out yesterday. But that was Kerri. It was comforting in a way to know she was the same. Harry also smiled. I knew he cared about me as a friend, and he wanted to see me happy. I was lucky to have such good friends.

'Did you hear about the drama between Jas and Pandora?' Lou asked. She hadn't been in my history class, but it didn't surprise me that she knew about it. The news was spreading like wildfire.

I shrugged. I couldn't care less about those two girls and their fight over boys. Now that it was over, it seemed so trivial.

Rion and Harry started talking about their homework in physics class, clearly not caring either.

But, to my surprise, Kerri said, 'I heard about it, and I think Jas was clearly in the wrong. People, boys included, find it easy to like Pandora because she is nice to everyone. The same can't be said about Jas.'

'I'm no fan of Jas, but to be fair, it does seem like Pandora was flirting with Chad,' Lou said. 'And she knew he was Jas's boyfriend.'

'If that's true, then he isn't much of a boyfriend,' Kerri said, with irrefutable logic.

'Let's change the subject,' I said. 'How're your driving lessons going, Lou?'

She lifted her eyes and said, 'Terrible. I do everything wrong when Mum is with me. Dad is much more patient.'

I laughed and said, 'It's the opposite for me. Dad is the worst. I only went out for a lesson with him once, and that was enough for both of us. But Mum's good, and she took me out a lot over Easter. I'm nearly there with my hours.' I stopped as I realised Mum would probably not be taking me out on any more lessons soon. A lump formed in my throat.

'You okay, Zoe?' Lou asked.

I nodded. 'Of course.' But I put down the sandwich I was about to eat. I wasn't hungry anymore.

Kerri had retreated to her chemistry book, clearly uninterested in our conversation.

'Hey,' Harry said, 'you won't believe it, but I actually managed to get tickets to that concert you and Rion are going to.'

'Wow, really? I'm impressed. How did you do that?' I wondered if he'd asked Pandora to help him out. It wouldn't surprise me. Chad Everett wasn't the only one who seemed to have a crush on her.

But to my relief, he said, 'No, it was Uncle Adrian. He was going to go with his girlfriend, but her sister's engagement party is on the same night, and now they can't go. So, he gave me two tickets. Lou, Kerri, do either of you want the other ticket?' It was generous of him to offer and especially to ask Kerri as well, though no one seriously expected she would want to go. She confirmed that by saying, 'A loud, noisy concert with overpriced tickets and too many people who are far too close to you? No thanks.'

'Lou?' He was looking at her as if he wanted her to say yes.

She hesitated and said, 'That's a couple of months away. I'm not sure what's happening then. Can I let you know?'

Harry looked disappointed. 'Sure, but if you definitely don't want it, let me know soon so I can offer it to someone else.'

Lou looked uncomfortable, but she just nodded and said, 'Yeah, I will.'

I looked at her wondering. Even a week or so ago, she would have jumped at the chance to go to a concert with Harry. I hadn't really believed her when she said she was getting over him, despite the fact that she was going on a date with Mike. But I guess she'd meant what she said.

Rion stood up and brushed the crumbs off his trousers. 'See you guys later.'

'I'm going too,' I said, getting up.

As we walked past the old fig tree where Jas's group usually sat, I noticed something different. All the usual people were there, except for one—Jas. But even more unusual was the person who *was* there—Pandora, and sitting next to her was Chad Everett. I had no idea what she did or how she did it, but jeez, she was a fast mover. This day was beyond weird.

Chapter Twelve

Mum's procedure was scheduled for next week. We were all trying to act totally normally, but it was like everything was put on hold, until we found out. In the meantime, Mum still went to her teaching job, Dad still went to work, and I still went to school. Nothing changed, yet the days seemed to drag.

Rion and I had never been closer and yet… we loved each other but couldn't say the words. It was like there was this invisible barrier, and I wasn't sure why. For me, well, maybe I just needed for him to say it first. And as for Rion, he showed he cared in so many little ways, but he never said it. Maybe it was because he was an alien and aliens didn't do that. But I had to correct myself there, *once* he was an alien, and now he was… human. Anyway, that was another thing I put on hold. But I always wore my necklace.

School was a distraction, but one I needed. Jas and Pandora seemed to have come to an uneasy truce. I knew Jas could never win against Pandora, and maybe she knew it too. Also, there were just too many kids in her group that didn't want to choose between them. Pandora had obviously decided that fighting with Jas just wasn't worth her while. Chad seemed to have pulled his head in and had been forgiven. He was back with Jas. So, everything was back to normal, almost. But she and Pandora were still wary of each other. They were like two prize fighters circling each other in the ring, waiting to see who would make the first move.

So, when Pandora came up to me while I was getting some books from my locker, I wasn't totally surprised when she said, 'Hey, Zoe, I'm having a party at my place on Friday night. You and Rion should come.' She was leaning against the locker next to mine with her arms folded and looking mega confident. She had obviously decided to make the first move in this popularity battle.

'So, it's okay with Maude?' That was the lady Pandora had persuaded to 'adopt' her and give her a home. She was a quiet, ultra conservative woman, and I just couldn't imagine what she and Pandora had in common. It also seemed hard to believe that she would want a noisy party of teens at her house.

Pandora shrugged. 'I haven't asked her yet, but she'll be cool with it. I might even persuade her to go out for the night 'cause it would be so much more… convenient.'

Pandora must have greater powers of persuasion than I gave her credit for. I didn't doubt for a moment that she was using some of her alien 'powers.' But it wasn't of great interest to me, and going to a party with some of the people who would be there, wasn't my scene. Luckily, I had a good excuse.

'Sorry, I can't. I'm babysitting that night.'

'So? Blow them off. My party will be so much more fun than looking after someone's little kid.'

I shook my head. 'No, they're counting on me. Besides, I need the money. It's my only source of income.'

Pandora looked at me as if she couldn't quite believe my words. 'But your parents give you money, don't they? I mean, they're supposed to look after you?'

'Yeah, they look after me, but I need my own money for doing things. A lot of kids have jobs, but Mum and Dad won't let me because I'm still at school. So, babysitting gives me pocket money.'

Pandora still looked confused. Obviously, the thought that people actually had to work for money never even occurred to her. Maude must be more generous than I realised, or else Pandora had another source of income.

I didn't want to think about it. No wonder Rion was worried about her.

She shook her head. 'Whatever. But you know something, Zoe? You're sixteen, right? And you're only going to be sixteen once. You should make the most of it and have some fun. Sometimes, I wonder if you're quite normal.'

I nearly laughed out loud at that. She was one to talk. An alien telling me I wasn't normal. Go figure. And anyway, what did she care if I was there or not? Maybe she thought Rion wouldn't come if I didn't, especially after what happened last time. I got my books, then closed my locker. 'I'll see you round.' I left her still leaning against the locker and looking puzzled.

At lunch time I found that Pandora had asked just about everyone in our year level. I wondered how that little house she was living in would hold so many people.

'Are you going?' Lou asked as we left English class together and threaded our way through the crowded corridor.

I shook my head. 'Babysitting. You?'

'Maybe. If Mike goes.' Her cheeks turned pink.

'So, like, you're going together?'

'Maybe.' Lou gave a small smile.

'You like him.' It wasn't a question. 'You still haven't told me about your date to the games arcade last week. How did you persuade your mum to let you go?'

We exited the humanities block and were heading towards the spot where our group usually had lunch. Lou pulled me around the corner of the building where we couldn't be seen by the others. 'It was awesome,' she said. 'He's so nice, and we had such a lot of fun. He taught me to play a few games as well. You know, I can understand why people are into gaming now. And he's really smart, like a computer whizz.'

I smiled and said, 'Like the next Bill Gates or Steve Jobs?'

She laughed and said, 'Yeah.'

'But your mum? Does she like him?'

'Well, that's the weird thing. I thought I was going to have all sorts of trouble with her, and she did ask a lot of questions about him, but it turns out his Aunt Kwong is in Mum's bridge club, so she was totally cool with me going out with Mike.'

'Did she know you were going to a gaming arcade?'

Lou gave me a look. 'I'm not totally stupid, Zoe. I didn't actually lie, but I left a few details out. I said we were going for a meal, and we did have a hamburger while we were out. Anyway, I'm hoping we can go to this party together. I'll say we're going out with friends, and that's not a lie either.' She said the last sentence defiantly, as if she expected me to argue with her or something. But I remembered I hadn't been 100 percent

137

honest about some parties I went to last year, so I was in no position to judge.

I thought I might put in a word of caution. Lou was a total innocent about some things, and I really had no idea what Mike was like. 'It's a 'party', Lou. There will certainly be alcohol and other stuff too most likely, especially since Pandora's throwing it. You might not like it.'

'I've never been to a party, a real one I mean, and I want to see what it's like. You don't understand. It's like I've been in this bubble of protection for years, and I'm ready to break out. I'm nearly seventeen years old, Zoe, and I haven't done anything a ten-year-old hasn't. I'm sick of it. I want to experience being a teenager before it's too late. After all, we're only sixteen once.' Lou's cheeks went pink, and her tone was determined. Weirdly, I'd heard a similar line just a short time ago from Pandora. Yet, she was as different as possible from Lou.

'Have fun, then.'

Lou smiled and gave me a hug. 'You and Rion should come too. Let Mrs Stewart get someone else to babysit the boy genius.'

Again, the same advice Pandora gave. What was wrong with me? Was I becoming a recluse or something that I'd rather babysit Emerson than go to a party?

'Emerson's cool, and Mrs Stewart pays well,' was all I said. I hadn't told Lou about Mum. I wanted to wait until we knew for sure.

'Okay. Come on, let's join the others,' Lou said. 'Wonder if Kerri will go?'

I looked at her. 'Are you serious?'

Lou looked thoughtful and said, 'Well, she has been more sociable lately, especially since she got that C minus in English.'

'Maybe getting that C did her a favour and gave her more perspective on things,' I said as we strolled over to the grassy spot where our friends were sitting. 'But go to a party? No way? Earth'd have to stop in its orbit around the sun or something.' Lou nodded in agreement.

Rion looked up as we approached and gave me a wide smile. I never got tired of seeing that look in his eyes, which was just for me. For a second, or maybe two, it seemed like we were the only people in the universe. I sat down beside him, and he reached over to kiss my cheek. 'Hey, how are you?'

'What, since period 1?' I said.

He laughed and said, 'Yeah.'

Before I had a chance to answer, a voice cut through my thoughts.

'Mind if I join you guys?' I looked up and there was Mike standing next to Lou, who was looking all pink and pleased and just slightly embarrassed.

'Sure, no worries, mate.' Harry was the first to speak. He moved over to give Mike some room. Mike sat down, Lou on one side and Harry on the other.

'We're in physics class together, aren't we?' Rion said.

Mike nodded, adding, 'And IT.'

'That's right. You did that presentation last week on computer graphics. It was pretty cool.' For the next few minutes, they were chatting like they'd known each other forever. It seemed like we might have another nerd in the group, so no worries about him fitting in. He and Lou didn't talk much, but I knew it was a big step for him to come over and join us. There was only one reason for that—Lou.

I looked over at Harry to see how he was taking it. I could never work out if he liked Lou as a friend or if there could be something more. I knew, of course, that he had a bit of a crush on Pandora, as did every other male in our school, it seemed. But I didn't think anything serious was going to happen there, and I thought Harry knew it too. His face was a polite mask at the moment, not revealing anything at all. But that was Harry. Even if he felt things deeply, he didn't say much. I knew that better than anyone.

'So, who's going to Pandora's party?' Lou asked brightly.

'I might drop in for an hour or two,' Harry said, way too casually. 'And what about you, Lou?'

She hesitated, and then Mike said, 'Lou and I might go too, mightn't we?' He looked over at Lou who nodded shyly.

I saw a look of disappointment in Harry's hazel eyes that said more than words. So, maybe he did have feelings for Lou after all.

'I'm not going. I'm babysitting,' I said.

Rion shook his head. 'Me either. Not without you,' he said, looking at me, and this time, I knew he meant it.

'I've never been to a party before,' Kerri said. 'It might be interesting to observe the social interactions there. It might even help with my next English Lit assignment.'

Every single person in our group looked at her in surprise. Even though Lou had mentioned the possibility, I never really believed it would happen. Maybe the earth *had* stopped in its orbit around the sun after all. Kerri Kennedy was going to a party, and I was going to babysit. Just one year ago, I would have said that was in the realm of impossible. Though, as I looked over at Rion, an alien over 4000 years old, and now my boyfriend, I realised stranger things had happened in the last twelve months.

Chapter Thirteen

'Maybe you should go to Pandora's party after all,' I said
as Rion and I walked home from school later that day.

'What?' He stopped midstep, turning to look at me.
'That's what caused the problem between us last time.
And I don't want to go without you. Besides, I don't like
those sorts of parties, and I don't think you do either, at
least not anymore.'

He was right about that, though it had been at one
of those parties that Rion had materialised into the most
beautiful teenage boy I'd ever seen, and that was the
beginning of everything that had happened between us.

'It wasn't because you went to a party without me,
Rion. It was because you went without telling me. You
lied to me. That's what hurt. You should have trusted
me more. I would have said go.'

Rion hung his head, his dark fringe hanging over his eyes. 'I know, and I've regretted it ever since.'

'It's over and done with, but the reason you went is still there, isn't it? Pandora. She's wild and unpredictable. I don't think she has any idea of the trouble she can get herself into. And I'm pretty sure she's using some of her weird alien powers to get her own way. There's no way Ms Butterfield would let her have a party unless Pandora mind controlled her or something. And that's not right.'

'You're right. It's only a matter of time before she does something disastrous. She has no idea about consequences, especially of her own actions.'

'Isn't there any way you could contact your own people to let them know what's happening?'

He stared up at the white clouds that dotted the blue sky. 'I've tried, but when I made the choice to become human, my supervisor told me all contact with them would be severed. It was one of the conditions made. So, they can't hear me, and I can't hear them.'

I realised yet again what a sacrifice Rion had made in his decision to become human, a decision made so he could be with me. I took his hand and gave it a squeeze. 'I'm sorry, Rion.'

He bent down and kissed me, his warm lips just resting on mine for a moment. 'It's okay. It was worth it. Come on. Let's walk again.'

As we headed home, I knew I had to bring it up again. 'I still think you should go to Pandora's party. What if she lets everyone know she is an alien, or worse still, that you were too?'

'It's something I worry about all the time.'

'Then you should go. You can keep an eye on her, make sure she doesn't cause any trouble. I don't mind, really.'

He looked at me, his face anxious. 'Are you sure?'

'Yeah. Besides, you can fill me in on all the gossip afterwards—Lou and Mike, and Kerri. Who would have ever thought Kerri would go to a party like that?'

'You know, there's more to her than just an ultra-smart girl who studies all the time. But I think she's just finding that out.'

'That's perceptive of you. Last year you didn't always get normal stuff, especially when it came to people.'

He gave his crooked smile. 'I'm a fast learner, and I've had a good teacher.'

I gave a small self-satisfied grin. 'True that.'

I rang the doorbell of the up-market townhouse in the ultra-trendy neighbourhood that Mrs Stewart and her son, Emerson, lived in. I heard what sounded like the scampering of paws down the hall inside, but I discounted it right away. Mrs Stewart would never let Emerson have a pet budgie, much less a dog. Pets were unhygienic and made too much mess she'd said.

I was wrong. The door opened, and a brown and black bundle of fur threw itself at me. I dropped the bag I'd brought containing my school stuff and a couple of snacks for Emerson and me—Mrs Stewart didn't believe in snacks either, but I'd learnt long ago to ignore that one.

'Tiberius, get down.' Her voice was a couple of octaves above normal, but the dog took no notice of her.

'Hey, boy,' I said, crouching down to give him a pat as he jumped and wiggled with joy, his tongue trying to reach my face and his tail wagging.

'Come in, come in,' said a harassed Mrs Stewart, brushing a strand of hair back from her face and closing the door behind us as Tiberius—who gives a dog a name like that?—followed me into the hall.

A small, blond boy, the image of his mother, ran down the stairs towards us, his eyes bright and a smile on his face like a crescent moon. For once he looked like the six-year-old he actually was instead of a polite, intelligent robot.

'Do you like my new dog? Isn't he great!'

'Emerson, don't race down the stairs like that. You might trip and hurt yourself,' his mother scolded.

145

The dog left my side and skid across the polished floor to meet his small owner. Emerson bent down, and the dog put his paws on his shoulders, licking the little boy's face.

'No, no, no.' Mrs Stewart rushed over to the pull the dog away. 'Naughty dog. Don't let him lick you. Have you any idea how many germs are on a canine's tongue? I'm putting him in the garage for now.'

She dragged the dog over to the doorway at the foot of the steps, which led into the garage. Opening the door, she pushed him inside and shut the door, leaning against it and looking as exhausted as if she'd just run a marathon. Her hair was unusually ruffled, and there was dog hair on her black dress. I had never, ever seen her look like this before. I really had to stop myself from laughing.

'Oh, Mum, can't he just stay inside for a little while so I can introduce him to Zoe?'

Her lips thinned. 'No, he's staying there until your father comes to pick him up tomorrow. Why he let you have a dog in the first place, I'll never understand. Now go upstairs and wash your face and hands thoroughly with the disinfectant handwash in the second bathroom. And perhaps you'd better change your shorts while you're upstairs. You have dog hair all over them.'

Emerson gave a heavy sigh and went back upstairs.

'Come through, Zoe,' Mrs Stewart said as she led the way down the hall into the immaculately tidy, but boring family room that adjoined the stainless-steel kitchen, which looked like a proper meal had never been made in it.

'So, Emerson has a dog, cool,' I said, more than a little curious as to how this had come about.

Her face creased into a frown as she handed me the 'schedule' for Emerson's evening. She had done this from the first disastrous time I'd looked after him, and I knew I was going to ignore it tonight like I always did. Anyone who knew Mrs Stewart would understand why. She was one of those alpha mums that thought every minute of every waking hour should be filled with 'meaningful and educational' activities. It was a wonder Emerson hadn't had a nervous breakdown or something. And, while I didn't usually ignore the parents whose kids I babysat, I figured I was saving Emerson's sanity by throwing out the French grammar and bringing in the odd game of Snap or hide-and-seek. He loved it, and it was our secret, as were the snacks.

'As I mentioned, the dog was purchased by Emerson's father. Tiberius is only staying with us until Mr Stewart comes back from a business trip. Then it will go back to live with him.' Her lips thinned in disapproval. Emerson's parents had separated a few months ago, and

I got the feeling that Mr Stewart was probably letting him do all the things his mum never let him do when he visited every second weekend.

Mrs. Stewart smoothed her dress and picked off a brown hair, looking at it in disgust. She deposited it in the metal bin near the kitchen area, washed her hands, and then came back to me. 'You won't have to worry about Tiberius. I've fed him, and he has water.'

'What if he needs to go out, you know, to do his business?'

She wrinkled her nose in distaste. 'Then I suppose you may take him to the back garden. There is a box of plastic bags in the laundry. But under no circumstances is Emerson to handle him any more tonight, especially when he has his pyjamas on. I'm going upstairs to freshen up. I'll let you know when I'm leaving.'

Ten minutes later, she said goodbye to us and left us with a whiff of expensive perfume and the sound of high heels clicking down the hallway. When we heard the front door close behind her, Emerson and I looked at each other and grinned like two kids who'd just been let out of school.

'So, tell me about this new dog of yours,' I said.

'Isn't he great! Dad bought him for me. He's really smart and does nearly everything I tell him, or at least he will soon. He's just a puppy.'

'He's cute,' I said. 'Does he stay here much?'

'No, he's only here because Dad had to go to Sydney on business. Mummy suggested the boarding kennel, but Dad told her that dogs can pick up diseases from other dogs in a kennel and bring them home. She didn't want me exposed to germs, so she said he could stay here.'

I was beginning to have a new respect for how clever Emerson's dad was, but I said nothing.

'I only get to see him every second weekend when I go to Dad's, but that's okay. It's better than not having a pet at all. And besides, Dad lets him sleep on my bed.'

I wondered what Mrs S would say about that.

'Let's have a look at this schedule your mum left us,' I said, waving the piece of paper in my hand. I had to at least pay lip service to it.

'Aw, come on, Zoe, you know we don't bother about that.'

'We should probably look at it. You never know, there might be something fun on it.'

He gave me a withering look that had all the scepticism of the forty-year-old that I sometimes suspected was inside him. Grabbing it, he gave it a glance.

'*Practise French conversation.* Bonjour, au revoir, etc. Done. *Do relaxing yoga poses.* Here, hold this,' he said, handing me back the sheet. He put his hands on the floor and stuck his small butt in the air. 'Downward-facing dog,' he said and then collapsed onto his knees, looking up at me with a slightly red face and a mischievous look in his blue eyes. 'Done. There's also stuff about reading an *educational book*. Dad gave me a book on dog care, so we can look at that. And then there's *listen to classical music*, which I hate and gives me a headache, so we can skip that. Now, we can do the fun stuff.'

'Such as?' I tilted my head to one side, feeling that he had something in mind.

'Play with Tiberius.' He grinned at me.

I shook my head. 'Your mother gave me strict instructions that you weren't to touch him. I can bend the rules a little, Emerson, but I can't break them. That wouldn't be right.'

'Did you bring snacks, like you usually do?'

'Yes, of course. Muesli bars and chips, but they are low fat.'

'Well, that's breaking the rules, 'cause Mummy always says no snacks before bedtime.'

'Yes, but that's different.'

'How?'

'It's different because…'

'Go on.' He would make a great lawyer someday because he sure was good at cross-examining.

'Well, I don't want you to faint from hunger. You need to keep that blood sugar level up. Besides, aren't you hypoglycaemic or something?'

'Maybe, though I haven't been tested yet.' And that was a wonder, because his mother had had him tested for just about every disease known to man.

'I rest my case,' I said with just a touch of smugness.

'Yes, but…'

'Oh no!'

'What?' he looked at me suspiciously.

'I feel such a twitchiness in my fingers. I can't help it. I've just got to—'

'No way.' Emerson giggled and moved away from me.

'Yes, I just have to… tickle somebody.'

I reached out and grabbed him and started to tickle him. He laughed and squealed and tried, a little bit, to escape.

'Stop, stop,' he said between laughs.

'On one condition only.'

'What?'

'Only if you tame these terrible fingers with a game of Snap! Do you give up?' I tickled him under the arms for good measure.

'Okay, okay, you win. I give up!'

I let him go, and he rolled in a ball on the floor, still laughing.

'Great. Get the cards.'

A couple of games later and there was no mention of the dog. I was just congratulating myself on my excellent babysitting skills, when we heard a scratching on the door that led to the garage, accompanied by a howl.

Emerson put down his cards. 'It's Tiberius. He needs to go.'

'Let's just wait and see.'

But Tiberius howled again, and this time the scratching was even more frantic.

'Mummy won't be happy if he makes a mess in the garage,' Emerson said, and I knew he was right.

'You stay here, and I'll go and get him,' I said and got up to hurry down the hall.

Emerson ignored me and followed behind.

I cautiously opened the door, and the brown and black ball of fur hurtled out past my legs and bounded down the hall like an escaped prisoner. Emerson followed him, calling, 'Wait for me, Tiberius.'

I ran down the hall after them. The dog, thinking it was a great game, barked and ran into the white carpeted lounge with its uncomfortable but expensive chairs, antique looking vases on low tables and a baby grand piano. Tiberius ran under the tables and one of the vases wobbled. Emerson chased after him, almost as reckless as this crazy dog.

'Emerson, don't chase him. Tiberius, stop!' I may as well have saved my breath. The dog ran behind the sofa, Emerson following, and then both of them dived under the piano. Just as Emerson wiggled his small self under, the dog ran out again and jumped on a fancy brocaded chair. He started to scratch it frantically as if digging for a bone, and I could see the threads of the brocade coming loose.

I made a grab for Tiberius, but he was too quick for me and bounded down again, heading out the door of the lounge and up the stairs. I hit my knee on the sharp corner of the coffee table, and stifling a curse, I ran after that stupid dog. But Emerson was ahead of me. At the top of the stairs, he called out, 'Quick, he's gone into Mummy's room.'

I sprinted up those stairs like an Olympic athlete, just in time to see Tiberius exit the room with an expensive-looking red stiletto in his mouth.

'Uh oh, those are Mummy's Choo shoes,' Emerson said as he followed the dog into his own bedroom. The dog disappeared under the low, queen-sized bed.

'Tell me that isn't a Jimmy Choo,' I said, wondering if Mrs Stewart would ever let me babysit again.

'Yes, that's it.' He looked at me, wrinkling his nose just like his mother did. 'I think they're kinda expensive.'

'Just a little,' I said, hearing the despair in my own voice. 'We need to get that back off Tiberius before he damages it.'

But the bed was too low for me to get under, and even for Emerson, it would be a tight fit. 'I'll get the broom and maybe we can coax him out. You stay here and don't let him out of this room or we're both going to be in mega trouble.'

'Sure. I think he's calmed down now. I can hear him chewing.'

Either I'd never babysit again, or I'd have to do it for free until Emerson was grown up. And even then, I'd never be able to pay her back the cost of those shoes. I closed the bedroom door behind me and raced downstairs. As I passed the lounge room on my way to the kitchen, I noticed a little brown lump under the piano and a wet patch on the white carpet. Great. The only consolation was I didn't have to take Tiberius out anymore. I didn't think my nerves could handle that.

I got the broom from the closet and ran back upstairs. Emerson was lying on his tummy looking under the bed and speaking in a persuasive voice. 'Come on, boy. Come out and I'll give you a treat. Zoe has muesli bars. You'll love them. Come on.'

'Move to one side, Emerson, while I try to get him out. When he comes, grab him.'

'You won't hurt him, will you?' he said, anxiety in his voice.

'No, of course not,' I said, though at this point that was the least of my worries.

I wriggled the handle of the broom around until I found the sturdy body of a naughty puppy.

'Come on, Tiberius. Move.' But, of course, all he did was wriggle away from the broom handle. I kept moving it until the dog was up against the wall. I felt him bite the handle. Good. That meant he dropped the shoe. I wiggled the handle and felt him grab it again. He thought it was a game. He kept trying to grab the handle as I moved it further and further out. Finally, I saw a curly brown head emerge from under the bed. Dropping the broom, I grabbed the dog and dragged him out. He wriggled around in my lap, tail wagging and brown eyes looking at me with total affection. It was just like he was saying, 'Wasn't this fun!'

Sighing, I held him tightly. Emerson patted his head. 'You're a very naughty dog, Tiberius. But, never mind, you're only a puppy.' He planted a kiss on top of the dog's head. 'I wish I could keep him with me tonight. He was only lonely. That's why he went crazy.'

There might have been some truth in that, but I wasn't taking any more chances. 'It's your mother who'll go crazy if she finds him in your room. He needs to go back in the garage now and get some rest. And we need to clean up.'

I breathed a sigh of relief when we shut the door of the garage, with Tiberius safely inside. Then Emerson and I straightened cushions, cleaned up his 'mess' and rescued the red Jimmy Choo stiletto from under the bed. It was covered in drool, and there was a little dent on one side, which I pushed out so it looked almost normal. Other than that, it seemed miraculously unharmed. I wiped it down and returned it to the bedroom to sit beside the other shoe. They looked the same, more or less.

'I think we've earned those snacks,' I said as we both collapsed on the sofa in the family room.

'That was pretty exciting, wasn't it?'

'I guess that's one way of putting it.' I opened my bag and dug out two choc chip muesli bars and two small packets of salt and vinegar chips—they were Emerson's favourites. He got the water from the fridge and filled two glasses, bringing them over carefully.

Sitting on the floor, his legs crossed, he took the muesli bar I offered. 'I can't wait to tell Rion all about it. I wonder if they have dogs on his home planet.'

Emerson was the only other person, besides me, who knew that Rion was from another planet. It had happened accidentally when Rion was babysitting him and trying to console Emerson for being different because, as he said, he was different too. Emerson guessed the rest. But he wouldn't tell anybody. He knew how to keep a secret, even if he was only six. Besides, he loved Rion almost as much as I did.

Thinking about his question, I said, 'I don't know. We'll have to ask him. Maybe Pandora would know.'

'Who? Is she an alien too? Is there another alien here?' He sat up, eyes all wide.

Oops, hadn't meant to mention her. 'Oh, just a new girl at school.'

'A new girl, as from another planet? Has to be, because only someone from Rion's planet would know if there were dogs there.'

Unfortunately, Emerson was not a dumb kid.

'You can't tell anyone, right? She has to be a secret too.'

He nodded. 'But that's so awesome. I want to meet her. Please bring her 'round to see me. You can come to Dad's place next weekend. He doesn't mind visitors. He lets Rion come and play chess with me sometimes. I wonder if she's any good at chess?'

'She's good at most things. But, Emerson, not every alien is as nice as Rion,' I said, holding back a sigh. I wondered how Rion was getting on at her party.

I couldn't help feeling a little uneasy. Not because I didn't trust Rion. More like, I didn't trust Pandora.

Finally, I got Emerson into bed and I settled down on the sofa to try to study, but mostly to look at my phone. I sent a text to Rion, and he responded briefly to say that there was nothing too unusual about the party yet, except a few boys were drunk. So far, it seemed Pandora was being good. But expecting it to last was like expecting Tiberius to do what he was told. It looked like it was going to be a long night.

Chapter Fourteen

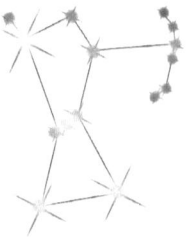

Did I think Chelsea's parties were a bit wild? They had nothing on Pandora's. The music blasting our eardrums was at least a hundred decibels, and that was only ten decibels fewer than a lawn mower and twenty decibels fewer than a jet engine. Much more of this and we'd be suffering hearing loss in the morning. There were approximately fifty people crowded into a small house that would comfortably accommodate six to ten people for a gathering of any sort. Many of those bodies were gyrating to the music, and any movement from one area to another was practically impossible. Hence, I was stuck in a corner between a bookcase and a lamp, which miraculously was still in one piece. When I texted Zoe an hour ago, I said nothing too unusual was happening, but since then a lot more people had arrived and the music was even louder. Pandora was right there in the middle of it all, laughing and dancing.

I couldn't see Lou and Mike. Maybe they'd decided not to come after all. Harry had been here for a while, but when things got more hectic, he'd said, 'I'm leaving. This just isn't my scene. I don't know why I ever let Pandora persuade me to come. It's not like she even knows I'm here.'

I felt I had to say something. After all, Harry was my friend, and I didn't want him to have false hopes. 'Pandora is all about Pandora. We're just here to make up the numbers so she can say her parties are bigger and better than anyone else's.'

'Yeah, you're right. Anyway, see you later.'

As he disappeared through the crowd, I wished I could leave too, but I knew I had to stay. Pandora was getting wilder and more reckless by the minute. I could hear her laughter above everyone else's. She was holding a glass of wine high in the air as she danced. I was hoping she was spilling more than she was drinking. A little went a long way on our alien physiology.

I considered moving closer and perhaps drawing her away. If I got her outside, maybe I could talk some sense into her. Then I saw Kerri not far from me, her head bobbing to the music and her red hair swinging. She was holding a plastic cup with some red liquid in it. Somehow I didn't think it was cherry cola or raspberry cordial. Maybe I should check to see if she was okay. This was so out of character for her. And I could only put it down to Pandora's influence.

The music changed from an Ariana Grande pop song to the opening chords of a much older Deep Purple song my previous host, who had been around in the 60s, had listened to. I was surprised because I didn't think many teens knew it today. Then I heard the thump of heels on wood, and I looked over to see Pandora on top of the coffee table, starting to dance and turn circles. Catching my eye, she stopped and lifted her glass. 'This one's for my favourite alien, Orion,—"Space Truckin'." Woohoo!'

I sensed rather than saw heads swivel in my direction. I felt dozens of pairs of eyes on me. How could she do that? How could she blurt out the one secret I'd tried so hard to hide? I felt the blood drain from my face, and I dropped the can of cola I was holding as the opening lines of the rock song blared out. Pandora downed her drink, threw her glass into the crowd, and started to dance again.

Then I heard laughter and someone, I think it was Chad Everett, say, 'Good one, Pandora. We always knew he was weird.' More laughter and everyone was dancing to the music, which was beating out as powerfully as my pulse was racing. No one was looking at me anymore. They thought it was a joke. Not for one moment did they think it was true. I stepped back, hitting the bookcase behind me. One of the books fell off the shelf, but I left it there while I tried to breathe normally again. Everyone thought it was a joke, this time. The next time she blurted it out, they might take her more seriously. But there couldn't be a next time. Somehow, I just had to persuade Pandora to return to the mothercloud. I just didn't know how—yet.

The music had everyone revved up. They loved it, and they loved Pandora. 'Go, Pandora!' I heard a familiar voice call out. Looking over the crowd, I saw it was Kerri, who also had her hands in the air and was dancing. I had obviously stepped into an alternate universe.

Closing my eyes, I took a deep breath, trying to centre myself and think. Should I just slip away and not draw any attention to myself in case Pandora decided to make another revelation?

But that would defeat the whole purpose of my being here. I had come to stop her from doing something foolish, something that might get her into trouble, and me too. I couldn't give up at the first hurdle.

Pushing my way through the closely packed swaying bodies wasn't easy. A girl, I think it was someone from my physics class, threw her arms around me and tried to kiss me. As gently as I could, I turned her around, and she immediately tried to do the same to the guy behind her. I pushed past some more people and knocked a guy's arm. Warm beer from the glass he was holding spilled over us both. 'Hey, watch it, mate.'

'Sorry, really sorry,' I said as I did my best to move away from him before he decided to take it further. A few pushes, bumps, and sorries later, I finally made it to where Pandora was still dancing on the table.

The music was so loud I doubted she would hear me, so I concentrated on a form of communication she might recognise. I hoped I was still able to do it. I closed my eyes again and ignored the jostling people around me. Telepathic communication had been more normal to me than speech not so long ago. I tried to find the quiet space in my mind where I could connect with Pandora. After all, she was one of my own people. Surely, I would be able to reach her. *Pandora,* my thoughts whispered.

Orion? I opened my eyes to see her looking down at me. The music had faded from my consciousness, and it was as if we were the only two beings in the room.

Come with me now. I want to talk to you.

She shook her head. *Later.*

No, now. Please.

This better be important.

It is.

She shrugged and said out loud, 'Well, here goes.' And turning with her back to me, she let herself fall from the table right into my arms. Everyone laughed and clapped and then began to dance again. I nearly fell over, and perhaps if I was a normal human, I would have. But my reflexes were quicker than a human's. I hadn't yet quite lost all my powers. I caught her and put her down on the floor. She looked up at me, laughing. 'Come on then, alien boy. Let's find somewhere quiet.'

Whether it was Pandora herself, not shy in using any resources she had, alien or human, or whether the crowd had thinned a little, somehow we made it across the floor and to the front door. I opened it and pulled her outside with me.

We nearly fell over Kerri, who was getting sick into Ms Butterfield's hydrangea bush. Pandora looked at her with sympathy. 'Poor Kerri,' she said, patting her gently on the back. 'After I've had a chat with Orion, I'll get him to take you home.'

Kerri couldn't talk but nodded before throwing up again.

Pandora grabbed my hand and led me down the path to a poinciana tree, whose branches hung over most of the footpath. It was quiet and cool out here, and I breathed in the fresh air, grateful to be away from the noise and the tangle of people inside. Pandora leaned against the tree, bending her leg to rest a booted foot against the trunk. Folding her arms across her black leather jacket, she raised her dark outlined eyes to mine. 'Okay, shoot. What's so important that you had to drag me away from some of the coolest music on the planet? I spent hours putting together a playlist of some of the greatest hits of the last fifty years. I didn't have a rock star host for nothing, you know.'

'Why did you tell everyone I was an alien, Pandora? You know we're not supposed to tell humans that. How could you do such a thing?'

'Nobody believed me, Orion. They all thought it was a joke.'

'Is that what you meant it to be? A joke? Because I didn't find it particularly funny.'

She rolled her eyes. 'Chill. It's not a big deal.' She stifled a yawn and said, 'I don't suppose you have a smoke on you? I'm dying for a cigarette.'

'What is wrong with you? You're smoking, you're drinking, you're spilling our secrets like you were spilling your drink. How long do you think you're going to last like this until you get yourself, or both of us, into trouble?'

'So, that's what you brought me out here for. To give me a lecture like some old grandfather who's forgotten

165

how to live. You might as well be eighty because you sure do act like it. Oh, I forgot, you're even older, 4000 years actually.' She tossed her head back and laughed.

I ignored her attempt to insult me. Instead, I tried to appeal to something she might understand, to reach that part of her that was still alien. 'You're jeopardising our whole space mission here, which relies on keeping our existence hidden. Our hosts might know us, but others don't know about our existence. And even our hosts often kid themselves that we're a delusion of the mind, but they put up with us because we do them a lot of good. We help them to be successful in their lives. They call us inspiration, or a muse or an inner voice, whatever comforting name they can find. But the others, the ones who aren't our hosts, they are the danger. If they really knew, if they guessed there were aliens here, we would have to leave this planet forever. Can you imagine what they would do to us? They would never let us live in peace. You gave up your life on our planet for a noble purpose. Have you forgotten that so easily? You need to go back to the mothercloud, Pandora, while you still can.'

'Oh blah, blah, blah. You do go on, Orion. And you worry too much. If anybody really does think we're aliens, I'll just wipe their mind of that memory. Archimedes did it once with Zoe, remember? And I'm not doing anything wrong. I'm just having fun. Something you could do with a little more. I'm only here for a little while. I'm not stupid. I don't want to be human, but I do want to be an organic for a little while. You know something? I've heard music through my hosts, but I'd never really *experienced* it. I'd seen dancing, but I never felt what it was like to move to its rhythms, with the adrenaline coursing through my veins as the music pumps. I'd never tasted food, drunk wine, or kissed a boy until now. I'm alive, Orion, and so are you.' She put her foot, which had been resting on the tree trunk, back down on the ground and took a step closer to me. 'We have such an opportunity here. We have the best of both worlds. We can enjoy the pleasures of being an organic, but we also have the powers of our race. We can have the time of our lives here, knowing we won't die and we can return to the cerebral existence for a little while more. After all, we came to this planet to learn about it. What better way than to experience it first-hand?' She looked at me, eyes shining and mouth curved into a smile.

'You sound like me when I was trying to persuade my supervisor to let me remain human, but there's a difference. Having the senses is intoxicating, but there's more to being human than that. It's the wisdom that comes from knowing you are mortal, that there are consequences for what you do, that your actions affect people. It's also caring about people. All you've done since you've been here is use people. Where is Ms Butterfield tonight? I'm sure she wouldn't have wanted this.' I spread my hand in the direction of the house where the music inside was still pumping.

She shrugged. 'She's gone away for the weekend to visit her sister. I told her I'd be okay on my own.'

'And I wonder where that idea came from?'

'I might have suggested it, but so what? We have a mutually beneficial relationship. She gets awesome company and a few tips on how to manage her superannuation so that she'll have more income to retire on, and I get room and board. I'd call that a win-win situation.'

'I'd call it a misuse of your powers to manipulate people. If her mind wasn't being controlled by you, this *situation* would never have happened. And what about this stupid power struggle with Jas? Jas doesn't have a chance, and you know it. You've used her. You've even used Chad Everett, though I don't have much sympathy there. In fact, you've used everyone in that house.'

'How? They are here of their own free will. Everyone loves a party. I'm actually giving them the time of their lives.'

I shook my head. 'If something goes wrong, if the police are called because of the noise and they come and find underage drinking here or worse, it's those kids who will pay the price, not you. You're using them for a good time, and if something goes wrong, you'll be out of here like a flash.'

She put her hands on her hips and leaned in closely. 'Nothing is going to go wrong. If someone was stupid enough to call the police, do you think I couldn't persuade them there was nothing going on as easily as I persuaded Ms Butterfield to go away for the weekend? Piece of cake. As I said, you worry too much, old man.'

'You need to go back to the mothercloud while you still can. If you stay much longer, you won't be able to go back. That's what happened to me. And then, you'll realise being human is not as much fun as you thought it was.'

'They gave you a choice, though, didn't they? As a matter of fact, they bent over backwards to help you sort yourself out. Do you think they won't do the same for me? You talk about humans so much, but you've forgotten about our people and the loyalty we owe each other. You gave all that up. I wouldn't make that same mistake. You aren't human, Orion, no matter how much you pretend.'

I shook my head, feeling exasperated.

She put her hand up. 'Here, put your hand against mine.'

Not sure what she was up to, but curious all the same, I slowly raised my hand to hers so that our palms and fingers were touching. I felt a jolt of energy surge through my body, and suddenly I could feel every cell in my body light up. Our hands formed a bridge that connected not just the energy of our bodies, but the energy of our beings. Light radiated from every part of us, and I felt my consciousness lift from my body and rise into the dark night sky. And Pandora was with me. We rose until we were above our bodies, above the house, the street, the city lights. Around us was the dark sky, punctuated by the stars above that seemed less distant than the world of humans below.

Do you remember the mountains of Xana at home and how they glowed under the moons at night? Remember the roar of the waterfalls that tumbled over their cliffs.

Her voice was a whisper in my mind. Suddenly the vision of their distant majesty came to me. They were an iconic symbol of our homeland. *Yes, they were beautiful.*

And the Lucian sea? How it glimmered in the bright light of our life-giving star? The water was always so warm against our skin, and the sea creatures that swam with us were so unafraid. We were one with the animals there on our planet. We swam, ran, and played with them as children. Do you remember?

It came back to me how free my childhood had been and how beautiful my planet was. *I remember.*

And the ones that gave you life? How they sacrificed being with you so that you could be something greater, something more wonderful than just an organic on our world. They let you go into the space program; they let you die to them so that you could live a better life. Do you remember, Orion?

Sadness infused my being, and I felt the tears on the cheek of my body below. *Yes*

You can't deny who you are. It's in you. Feel the power between us. That's the power of our race. You know it is a stronger tie than the one you have with these humans. And, Orion, you are only an alien on this planet. When you are with us on the mothercloud, it's the humans who are aliens.

Her words hit me with force, and I felt their truth. For a moment or an eon, I wasn't sure which, I felt the completeness of my identity and the connection with one of my own. Rainbows of light and energy surrounded me, and I heard the echoes of space from an infinity of time. I felt the multitude of beings from our mothercloud and the stream of pure thought and intelligence flow within and without my consciousness. It was joyful. It was noble. And it would always be part of me.

Then, like the softest whisper, I felt something else. But it was calling me back. I could let it go or I could listen to it. For an infinitesimal moment, I was uncertain. And then, I knew it was a call I couldn't ignore. I was alien, but something more too. I could no longer be one or the other; I was both. I moved my hand away from Pandora's, and my universe shrank.

I was standing on a Brisbane street on a cool autumn night, and in front of me was a teenage girl, looking like any other. Our connection was severed, and she too had shrunk back into her human form.

For a moment we just stood there looking at each other, earth bound again.

Words seemed heavy, unnecessary things, but I had to say them. 'Thank you, Pandora. I needed reminding of who I am. I am still an alien here. I realise that now. But I am also human. It wasn't an easy decision, but I don't regret it.'

She shook her head sadly. 'I don't understand you. How can you give all that up?'

I shrugged. How could I explain it to her, when I could hardly explain it to myself? So, I said, 'You choose to remain an alien. That's your right. But it isn't your right to come here and mess with these humans. They aren't your pets, and this is not your playground. You need to return to the mothercloud and return to your mission. That is your destiny, and this is mine.'

'No, it isn't. So, you have a thing for this human chick. What if she meets someone else? I can't tell you how many girlfriends and wives my bikie host had. What if she decides she doesn't want to be with a 4000-year-old alien? You can't say it hasn't crossed your mind. Are you going to give up everything you've worked for and believed in for some girl you might only spend a few human years with? And think about this. What if you could go back? You could still offer so much to our space program. Maybe being human isn't your destiny, and maybe choosing it is selfish. You're the one putting yourself before our cause, not me.'

Despite all her wildness, Pandora's questions unsettled me. I didn't want to go back. I wanted to be with Zoe. But I realised at the same time, I missed my alien life and being with my own kind. And not only that, the question that always had haunted me remained. Was I being fair to Zoe? Added to that was the most disturbing question of all. Had I betrayed our people and our cause by choosing to be human?

Pandora looked at me and said, 'Don't lie to yourself, Rion. And, especially, don't lie to me.' She was angry with me.

She moved away. 'And, since you're so concerned about these humans, take Kerri home. She's had more than enough tonight, and she might need someone to look after her.'

With a characteristic toss of her head, she turned to walk back towards the small house that was pulsating with music and the sounds of laughter.

Chapter Fifteen

I went back to where Kerri was sitting on the front step, shoulders slumped and her head in her lap. She looked up when she saw me. 'I need to go home.'

I nodded and sat down beside her. 'I don't have a car, Kerri, but I can walk you home if it isn't far, or I can call a taxi. Or your parents.'

She shook her head vigorously and then groaned, putting a hand on her forehead. 'Not my mother. She wouldn't be very happy seeing me like this. I don't know what I was thinking. Pandora gave me some punch to drink, and I didn't want to look stupid in front of her, so I took it. I think I had more than one. I was fine until a little while ago, and then I felt so sick.' She groaned again, and her head fell on my shoulder.

Sighing, I put my arm around her and said, 'I'll call a taxi, then. Where do you live?'

'Not far. We could walk, and then I could slip in the back. Mum might be asleep anyway, but she'd hear a taxi and wake up. She doesn't know I went to a party, and I don't want to see her till the morning. She knows I went to Pandora's house, but she thinks I went there to get some help with an English assignment. Pandora helped me once before.'

It seemed so out of character for Kerri to lie about going to a party and to end up sick because she was drinking. I could only blame Pandora. She seemed to influence people so easily, and not for the best either.

'Are you sure you can manage to walk?'

'Maybe it will do me good.'

'Okay, we're going to stand now.' I helped her up and gave her a minute to steady herself. 'How are you feeling?' I looked at her.

She took a couple of deep breaths. 'Yeah, better.' She moved away from me and took a few steps down the path. 'I'm good. I can probably manage on my own, Rion. You don't need to come with me.'

'That's okay, Kerri. I don't mind. It's late and better for you to walk with someone.'

'Thanks. Appreciate it.'

We sent off down the street, the noise of the party getting more and more distant. For a while, Kerri didn't say much, probably because it was an effort for her. But the more we walked, the better she seemed, and finally she said, 'I don't usually go to parties. But Pandora's been so good to me, helping me with English and everything, and I didn't want to disappoint her by not going.' Kerri sighed.

'I don't think she would have minded if you didn't go. There were a lot of people at that party.'

'I know. She hardly spoke to me all night, except to give me that drink. And then other people kept filling it up. But I don't blame her. She's so popular, and she had to talk to her other guests.'

We turned down a street where Kerri said she lived. 'And she asked you to bring me home. So she does care about me, as a friend.'

'Yes, but...' I tried to choose my words with care, 'Kerri, I wouldn't be too influenced by her. Sometimes, she can act impulsively and not always wisely. She does what she wants and doesn't always think of the consequences for others.'

Kerri turned to me, her eyes wide. 'You're wrong, Rion. Pandora is very considerate. She thinks I'm really smart and... she even said I was pretty. No one has ever said that to me before, except my mother once or twice. Pandora is wonderful.'

I could see I was fighting a losing battle here, yet I had to try one last time. 'But this isn't you, Kerri. You don't lie, or drink, and you aren't deceitful to your family. You need to make sure, if you do something, it's what you really want to do and not what someone else tells you to do. Even if that person is a friend.'

'No offence, Rion, but it's not really any of your business.'

We walked in silence for a little way.

'I live here,' she said, stopping in front of a modest brick low set with a manicured lawn and low-maintenance bushes along the front. There was a light in the front room, and I saw the curtain twitch. It didn't look as if Kerri's mum had gone to bed after all.

She made a face. 'I'd better go in. Thanks for walking me home, but you should go now too. The last thing I need is for Mum to think I'm with a boy.'

That, I thought, was the least of Kerri's worries. 'All right. Goodnight. I hope you feel better in the morning.'

I turned and headed back up the street, leaving Kerri to face her mum.

It had been an eventful night. I hadn't managed to convince Pandora of anything. She seemed determined to do what she wanted, no matter who she hurt. And I worried that the longer she stayed, the longer that list would be.

But her words stayed with me. When I'd touched her hand, I became connected not just with Pandora, but with everything we were and where we had come from. Remembering my home planet and my parents had affected me more than I'd wanted to admit. I'd also felt the energy and power that was still in me, that belonged to my race. My supervisor had said I would become completely human, but it wasn't true. I had become human, but I hadn't lost everything in me that was alien. I hadn't realised that until tonight. And it shook me.

I looked at my phone again. I didn't have a good feeling. Rion hadn't got back to me since about nine thirty, after I put Emerson to bed. I called him, but it went to his voice mail. I was home now from babysitting and getting ready for bed. For Rion not to have contacted me in a while probably meant he'd had to deal with something. I had no doubt that meant Pandora. I called him one more time.

'Zoe, sorry I haven't called before.'

I was just glad to hear his voice at last. 'What happened?'

'Pandora,' he said.

'Yeah, figured. What'd she do?'

'You mean besides the deafening music, the overcrowding of too many bodies in a space not meant to accommodate them, and underage drinking? Well, she told everyone I was an alien.' Rion's voice sounded heavy, tired.

'What?'

'Yes, but luckily everyone thought it was just a joke.'

Jeez, Pandora was a loose cannon. 'So, did you talk to her, tell her how stupid that was?'

'I tried to, but I don't think I'm ever going to get through to her. And I had to walk Kerri home because she got sick at the party.'

'Kerri? Our Kerri?' I couldn't believe my ears. 'How did that happen?'

'She had some punch, which she said was off.'

'Yeah, right. I can just imagine what went into it. And what about the others? Harry and Lou and Mike?'

'Harry went home early. I didn't see Lou and Mike. Maybe they didn't go. Or I missed them. There were a lot of people there.'

'How about you? How are you feeling?' I had rarely heard him sound so dejected and flat.

'I'm okay. I'm just not sure what to do about Pandora.'

'I think you're just going to have to leave it alone, Rion. There's nothing more you can do at the moment. You've tried.'

'She told everyone I was an alien. What if she decides to do it again? People might take her more seriously then. And she doesn't even have a guardian to keep her in line. I never thought I'd miss Archimedes, but I almost wish he were here now. He, at least, would have the power to do something.'

Archimedes had been a pain in the butt. However, Rion had a point. If anyone could bring Pandora into line, it was him. 'Maybe you should try to contact him. Perhaps, because he was your guardian and close to you, he might hear you.'

Rion gave a snort. 'There was nothing close between Archimedes and me. He was only too glad to be rid of me.'

I knew that was probably the truth. There was silence between us for a few moments. Then, he said, 'It's late. I should let you go. Maybe I'll think of something in the next few days.'

'Yes, I'm sure we will. I missed you tonight.'

'You should get some sleep. We'll talk later,' was his only reply.

As I lay in bed, I couldn't help feeling that Rion wasn't telling me everything. He seemed tired, almost defeated. And that wasn't like him. What else had gone on at that party?

Chapter Sixteen

'So how was last night?'

We were sitting in our favourite meeting place, the retro milkshake bar at the shopping centre.

'Mike and I didn't go. He said we'd have more fun at that games arcade we went to before, and even though I wanted to go to the party, I actually had fun. I'm really getting the hang of a few of the games there.' She looked at me. 'What's up? You seem down.'

'You know I had to babysit last night.'

'Yeah, that's too bad, but at least you earned money, right? And parties aren't really your deal either.'

'No, you're right. I really didn't want to go, especially with Jas and her groupies there.'

'So, what's the problem?'

'Rion went. It's okay,' I added as Lou gave me a surprised look. 'I was cool with it. He didn't go to have fun or anything. He just went to keep an eye on Pandora to see that she didn't get into trouble.' Even as I said the words, I realised how ridiculous they sounded. Lou had no idea that either Rion or Pandora were aliens, and it wasn't information I could share. I scrambled for an explanation. 'They knew each other from before, when Rion was travelling with his uncle. I think they met in France or something. Anyway, they're just friends, and Rion said she was a bit wild at times, so he wanted to go and make sure she was okay.'

Lou nodded, but I could see she wasn't convinced.

'And I was fine with it, really. It's just that…'

Lou looked at me sympathetically. 'Maybe you wished he missed you more?'

'He called me and everything, but he seemed, I don't know, just distant. And we're not even going to see each other this weekend. He's working today, mowing some neighbour's lawn. Tonight he said he had to write his physics assignment. You know he could pass physics with his eyes closed, and it's Saturday night! It's the one night of the week we can actually have off from all this craziness that is year twelve. Tomorrow Mum and Dad are driving to Gympie to visit Aunt Karen for her birthday.

I tried to get out of it, but you know what my parents are like about family time and stuff like that. Anyway, I won't see him until Monday, not that he seems to care.'

Lou squeezed my hand. 'Don't worry. I've never seen anyone so devoted as Rion. He doesn't even so much as look at another girl. He's totally into you.'

'I know. I'm overreacting. He is a freak about studying and all that. He even gave me a timetable at the beginning of the term, scheduling our studying, exercise, and dating time.'

'Well then, there's your answer. He's probably scheduled tonight as a study night. He's a bit... different at times. But he's a nice guy, Zoe, one of the good ones.'

'You're right. I'll go and check that schedule and probably find he's even put down "do physics assignment."'

I started to feel better just talking to Lou.

'So, you and Mike, you're becoming a thing, eh?'

Lou talked enthusiastically about how awesome Mike was and how great they were together. I listened to her, glad she had someone and was coming out of her shell at last. She was totally over Harry. I knew he'd gotten over his crush on me, but then I thought he might take up with Lou. Seemed unlikely to happen now.

We finished our milkshakes, and then I headed home. I couldn't help checking my phone every ten minutes.

Rion should be finished his lawn mowing job by now. But there was nothing from him. I could text him, but I didn't want to be one of those girlfriends who had to know where he was all the time. If he wanted space, I could do that. I had a life too. I wasn't going to wilt just because we weren't hanging out.

I kept up this positive self-talk while I made the pizza for dinner. It was my turn to cook tonight.

I was happy to do it because, with Mum not feeling the best at the moment, Dad had made a lot of meals. I was getting a little tired of Spaghetti Bolognese, even if it was his Italian grandmother's recipe.

I was grating the cheese when I had a thought. Maybe I could invite Rion over for dinner. He could go home early and study if he really wanted to. And after all, everyone has to eat.

Popping the pizza in the oven, I whipped my phone out of my pocket. It took four rings before he answered.

'Hey, how are you?' I said in a bright, perky voice.

'Hi, Zoe. I just got out of the shower.'

'Oh yeah, that's right, you were working today,' I said as if I'd completely forgotten it.

'So, how was your afternoon?'

'Okay. Lou and I went to the mall shopping and stuff. We had milkshakes at that cute retro place, the one that looks like a scene from *Happy Days*. I thought of you.'

'I'm glad you had a nice time.'

I waited for him to talk again, but awkward silence followed. It wasn't usually this hard to make conversation, even when I'd first known him, even when we were fighting.

I tried again. 'So, I'm making this ace pizza. You know I'm the best at pizza. It's pretty big, too much for Mum, Dad, and me, and I was wondering... would you like to come over for dinner? Save you having one of those awful nutritious meals you usually eat.' I laughed at my own lame joke.

'That's nice of you, but you know I have to do this physics assignment tonight.'

Nice? NICE? What was he playing at? 'You could go home early if you wanted to.'

'Thanks, Zoe, but I really should get stuck into this assignment. Besides, I've already eaten.'

'Before you had a shower? Like at five o'clock or something?' I was getting seriously annoyed. 'What's up, Rion?'

'Nothing. I'm just... a little tired.'

I wasn't convinced by that at all. 'If there's something wrong, you need to talk to me.'

I waited. There was silence for a moment. Then he said, his voice all cool and remote, 'Everything is fine, Zoe. I just need some time to... think.'

My stomach clenched. 'Think about what? Us? Pandora?'

'I meant meditate. It's really good for the mind and body, and I've been feeling a little off. Nothing to worry about. I'll have an early night.'

But he hadn't answered my questions. 'You are worrying me. Are you sick or something? What's going on?'

'I told you, nothing. Sorry I can't come over tonight. Have a nice time at your aunt's tomorrow. I'll see you on Monday.'

And before I could say anything else, he hung up. He had never done that before.

I waited for him to call again, but he didn't. And I had my pride. There was no way I was going to call him. When I checked that stupid schedule he'd given me at the start of the term, the activity he'd put down for tonight was 'date time.' He even had a smiley face next to it. Then this totally horrible thought popped into my brain. Maybe he was having 'date time' but just not with me. *Shut up*, I told myself. *Rion would never do that.*

I took the pizza out of the oven, which was burnt by the time I remembered it. But it didn't matter because I couldn't eat it. Excusing myself from the table, I headed to my room where I stared at my phone. He hadn't even texted. Crazy thoughts were running through my head, and unfortunately Pandora was in a lot of them. What had I been thinking to let Rion go to a party without me?

There was no way, no way in this world I was going to cry over a boy, especially an uptight, OCD, uptight, uncaring alien who hung up on me. I went downstairs again and grabbed some chocolate ice cream from the fridge and headed upstairs to watch back episodes of *Buffy*. Sometimes you just needed the classics to forget that life sucks.

Chapter Seventeen

I knew I was being a jerk, and I wanted to call her back right away. My finger went to press her number, and then I dropped my phone on the bed. I picked it up again. I did this at least three times until I made myself put it in the drawer of the bedside table.

Last night had been a revelation. When Pandora and I touched hands, I realised I was still an alien, even if I was living as a human. Through Pandora, I'd felt the power of our people, remembered my home, as well as the care and regard my parents had had for me. They had not been warm like Zoe's parents, but it hadn't made their feelings any less sincere. I had given up life as an organic on my planet long ago, and my parents had passed away. But even as a bodiless, intelligent entity, I'd felt a sense of belonging, a sense of oneness with my people, a unity of purpose. When I was with my human hosts, I had always felt my otherness from them. I had never confused the line between alien and human, until I met Zoe.

My feelings for her hadn't changed. I still cared about her more than any other being, alien or human, that I had ever met. But there were questions that had made sleep impossible last night. Was it wrong for me to be with her? I was an experiment. An alien who was trying to be human. Some might even call me a freak. What if that experiment failed? This organic body may not even last the normal course of human life. And there might be other complications later on. What if I couldn't have children? And if I did, what would those children be?

Zoe had said I had no right to make decisions for her. That I should never have deceived her when I stayed away all those months last year. In the normal course of things, she was right. But this wasn't the normal course of things, because I wasn't normal. That was a fact. My supervisor had been wrong when he said I would become completely human. Last night had shown me that. Pandora had shown me that.

And there was something else, something I didn't want to admit, even to myself. Had I betrayed our people's mission and the sacrifices made for me when I made the decision to be human and give up my alien existence? Was I being selfish when I could still contribute to our space program? No wonder Archimedes had been angry with me.

Would I go back if I had the chance again? Pandora had hinted it might be possible. It would free Zoe, let her be with someone who was really human. But it would also free me from this inner conflict of who I really was, alien or human. I would be what I was meant to be. It would be a sacrifice, but it would be *my* sacrifice. I had no doubt Zoe would get over me in time and live a normal life. I knew I'd never get over Zoe and the experience of being with her would stay with me forever, no matter what form I took. I was willing to accept that pain if it was the right thing to do.

I wrestled with these thoughts as the night hours gave way to dawn. But when early morning light finally lit the objects in my room, changing them from shadowy forms into the solid objects, the shadows in my mind also solidified into truth. I had no right to be with Zoe. I never had. And I had been selfish to reject my place in our space mission. It was not about choice anymore. It was about reality, the reality of who and what I was. Pandora said I might regret being with Zoe, but it was the opposite I feared. Zoe might regret being with me. I had to give her up. I had to break up with Zoe. For her sake.

Rion didn't turn up to school on Monday. What was going on? Confusion and depression hung over me like a black cloud.

It didn't help my mood that the whole senior school was buzzing about how great Pandora's party had been, especially since over half of year twelve had been there. When I got to my first class, people were surrounding Pandora like paparazzi around a movie star.

'Fab party,' gushed Ceci, one of Jas's friends.

'Best this year,' said Chelsea, Jas's *best* friend.

'How would you know? You spent most of it getting sick,' said Marco, with his usual bluntness.

'Did not,' Chelsea replied indignantly. 'And anyway, that was Kerri.'

'Who would have thought—Kerri?' Ceci rolled her eyes. 'She's such a dork.'

'Leave her alone,' Pandora said. 'Kerri's cool.' She shot Kerri a smile across the classroom, and Kerri turned bright pink.

Poor Kerri. I hadn't talked to her yet, but I was determined to find out from her everything that had happened. Interestingly, Jas said nothing, but she watched everyone through narrowed eyes. She wasn't too happy being eclipsed by the new star.

Mr McCurdy, our math teacher, walked into the room. 'All right you lot, settle down.'

There was sighing, eye rolling, and shrugging of shoulders, but everyone sat down and shut up. McCurdy wasn't a teacher you wanted to get on the wrong side of.

At first break, I cornered Kerri. 'Okay, what went on at that party, and don't leave anything out.'

If anyone could look guilty, pleased, and a little bit smug at the same time, Kerri did. 'It wasn't what I'm used to, but it was exciting.'

I said in my best casually innocent voice, 'Oh really. What do you mean?'

'Well, nearly everyone was there, so it was really crowded. And the music was pretty loud, but I didn't mind, surprisingly. And Pandora, of course, was great. She even got up on the table to dance. She's such a good dancer.' Kerri's eyes shone.

'What else? Did you see Rion?'

'Of course. He walked me home. Didn't he tell you?'

'Oh yeah. He said you weren't feeling too well.'

'It must have been something I ate,' she said, turning pink again. Kerri was one of the worst liars ever, but I let it slide. No point rubbing it in and saying, *more like something you drank*.

'Yeah, you've got to be careful about what you have at parties,' was my diplomatic answer.

'Pandora was so worried about me. She told Rion to take me home.'

'Oh, did she?' I hadn't realised that.

'Yes,' Kerri prattled on, 'when she and Rion went outside, she told him he should take me home, so he did later on after they finished talking.'

'So, they were talking outside, were they? Just them? In the dark?' I tried to stop my mind from racing to all sorts of wild thoughts.

Anyone but Kerri would have picked up on what I was saying, but she was totally unaware.

'Yeah. They seem good friends, but then didn't Rion say he knew her from when they were in France together? They kind of held hands, in a friendish way,' Kerri hastened to add, as if she suddenly realised that mightn't have been the best thing to say.

I couldn't talk. Rion and Pandora together talking and holding hands? I felt my heart sinking. I shouldn't jump to conclusions. But now he didn't want to see me, or talk to me or anything. Coincidence? I wondered if something more than just talking went on.

I caught up with Harry later on and gave him the third degree too. But he had nothing much to tell me as he'd left early. 'It was too crowded for me. I'm not really into parties.'

I nodded sympathetically. 'Not my thing either. But I had to babysit, so I told Rion he should go. No point in him missing out.'

Harry looked at me. 'That was pretty nice of you, considering he's your boyfriend. But I wouldn't have thought parties were his thing either.' Harry, unlike Kerri, was too perceptive at times, especially where I was concerned.

I shrugged. 'Maybe not. Did he look like he was having a good time?'

Harry raised an eyebrow. 'No, not really. He looked as bored as I was. Pandora might be cool, but she's a bit wild, and so was her party.'

I gave him a smile. 'So, over your crush on her yet?'

Harry gave an embarrassed laugh. 'Okay, I'll admit I did kind of like her when she first came. You have to admit, she's hard not to notice. But after a while, I realised she just wasn't my type. As you know, I don't really like Jas and all the people Pandora is hanging around with.'

'And just what is your type, Harry?' I knew I shouldn't have asked that. I shouldn't play games with my best friend, just because I was hoping for an ego boost.

'I think you already know the answer to that, Zoe,' he said quietly. 'I gotta go. I've got a class in five minutes.' He turned and walked away.

I deserved that, but it left me feeling even more dejected. I had made my choice, and it didn't help that the boy I'd rejected last term was also my oldest friend and such a totally decent guy that he didn't hold it against me. He would never have reminded me of how he felt, if I hadn't put him on the spot. There was just the smallest part of me that wondered, had I made a mistake? Harry would never, ever let me down. He would have been rock solid as a boyfriend. The thing was, I had thought that about Rion too, until now.

I went home feeling worse than when I set out for school that morning. Rion still hadn't texted or called or anything. When I got home, Mum wasn't home from school.

I decided to make dinner, even though it was Mum's turn. She would probably be tired when she got home, and somehow peeling vegetables and frying chicken seemed the best way to forget everything that had happened.

After dinner, I made up my mind. This silence from Rion just wasn't good enough. He was my boyfriend, and he owed me an explanation. This was no longer about being needy. This was about where we stood and what was going on and, more importantly, why. If he wanted to break up with me, I wanted to know why. I wasn't going to wait, all weepy, by the phone.

Telling Mum and Dad I needed to get a book from Rion, I hopped on my bike to make the short journey to his townhouse. It was just getting on dusk, but I had a light on my bike, and the streets in this suburban area were sleepy and quiet.

Everyone, especially adults, thought Rion was living with his guardian, Archimedes. At one time that had been true, but Archimedes had departed a few months ago, returning to his alien bodiless state. Rion still kept up the fiction though, because technically he was still underage—which itself was a joke as Rion had been around in one form or another for about 4000 years. Nobody knew he was on his own except me. Even Mum and Dad thought Rion's uncle was still around. They thought he was just keeping a low profile because he had disgraced himself when he came to our house for dinner a few months ago. He'd gotten drunk and been totally embarrassing. Dad, especially, was in no hurry to see him again.

So, I knew Rion would be home alone. As I pulled up in front of his place, I saw the light on downstairs. I got off my bike and wheeled it up the path, trying to steady my shaky nerves. Rion and I were usually so close. Once we had even shared our thoughts. Sometimes, even when we weren't touching, I could sense his heartbeat, and often it kept time with mine. I had never, ever been so connected to anyone in my life, and the thought of losing that, of losing him, was unbearable.

I raised my hand and knocked on the front door and waited. I knocked again. Finally, I heard steps and what sounded like muffled voices. Who would be visiting Rion at this hour? None of our friends even knew where he lived. It was probably the TV.

The door opened and Rion stared at me, surprised. His grey tee shirt was rumpled, and he had on his daggy track pants. His face was pale and tired looking, like he hadn't slept in ages. I wanted to ask what was wrong. I wanted to say it didn't matter what it was, we could fix it. For long seconds we looked at each other, making the connection that had seemed missing over the weekend. I thought he was going to reach out, pull me into his arms, and say everything was okay. I was wrong.

He stepped back a little, almost as if he was going to close the door. Our moment was over.

'Zoe, what are you doing here?'

'What's going on, Rion? You haven't texted or called. You don't even want to see me.'

'I… I was going to explain.'

'Well, I'm here now. Explain. And, for goodness sake, let me in. It's cold out here.' I started to move forward, but he blocked my way. I bumped into him, and his arms went around me automatically. It felt so good to feel the comforting strength of his arms holding me close that I put my arms around his waist and rested my head against his chest. I nearly lost it then. 'I've missed you so much,' I said in a voice that was close to tears. His arms tightened, and he breathed a heavy sigh as he bent his head to rest it on top of mine.

'Orion, who is it?' a familiar voice said, and I froze. I looked up as the door opened wider, and I saw Pandora behind him. I felt rather than saw Rion move away from me.

I tried to speak, but the words wouldn't come out.

'Zoe,' she said. It was only one word, but there seemed to be a lot of meaning in it. I was obviously the last person Pandora expected to see. 'You'd better come in,' she said, standing to one side.

Somehow my legs moved me forward, but I was still too stunned to speak. Even my mind seemed to have stopped working. All I could think of was one thing. Pandora was here with Rion.

I heard the door close behind me as I walked into the uncharacteristically cluttered lounge room. There were cushions on the floor and a pizza in a takeaway box. There was a bottle of red and two half full glasses next to it. Another thought pushed its way into my mind. Rion didn't drink. He wasn't even the slightest bit interested in it. Obviously, that had changed too. I collapsed into one of the lounge chairs, too shocked to stand any longer. Then I looked up at Rion, who was, if possible, paler than before. Pandora walked in and stood next to him, hand on her hip, her leather jacket open, revealing a tight black top. She wore jeans and knee-high black boots with heels that made her look at least six foot. Her jet-black hair hung in a straight curtain over her shoulders. Make-up enlarged her already large, dark eyes, and red lipstick made her lips seem even fuller. She was alpha and beautiful. No wonder guys fell at her feet. And I knew she was an alien too, with an intellect and a power that dwarfed everyone around her, except Rion. What chance did I have? None, it seemed.

His eyes on mine, Rion said, 'Pandora, I think you'd better leave now.'

But she shook her head. 'No, that wouldn't be wise.'

'I want to talk to Zoe alone.'

Anyone else would have done what he said, but Pandora wasn't anyone else. 'You need to talk to Zoe and tell her the truth. So no, I won't leave. She needs to hear this from us both. If I go, you won't tell her everything, and you'll make her think there's still a chance. You'll give her false hope. She deserves more than that. She deserves a clean break, so she can move on.'

Pandora's words chilled me to the bone. I didn't want to move on. I never wanted to move on.

The sadness in his eyes was replaced by anger. 'This isn't your concern. This is between Zoe and me. Go now before I'm forced to make you.'

She gave a mocking laugh. '*You'll* make me? Maybe once you might have been able to do that, but not anymore. Since your foolish attempt to pretend to be human, you've lost some of your strength and your powers. And that's the problem, isn't it? You've suddenly realised everything you've given up to be with this fragile human. And finally, on Friday night, you understood who you really are. You're an alien, Orion, and nothing will ever change that, and you could take back your powers if you really wanted to. You could be who you really are, but you suppress everything so you'll seem human.'

I couldn't take this anymore. I found my own strength, human and weaker perhaps, but it was still there. I stood up, put my hand on Rion's arm, and turned him to face me. 'Talk to me. Forget she's there. She isn't important. Tell me yourself. What's wrong, Rion?'

'Zoe,' he said softly, his eyes sad again, 'I can't be with you anymore. I realised that on Friday night. We are too different. Pandora is right about one thing. I will always be an alien, and nothing can ever change that.'

'We've been down that road before, Rion. You don't get to choose for me. And I choose you, alien or not. I want to be with you. I don't care what you call yourself. Have your little identity crisis if you must, but in the end, I know who you are. You are the person I love.' Finally, I'd said it. Put it out there in the universe. But it was the truth. I needed the truth back. 'You said you can't be with me. That's nonsense. Of course you can. What is more important is, do you *want* to be with me? Do you, Rion?'

He looked away. Finally, he said so quietly I might have missed it if I hadn't been so focussed on him, 'No. I'm sorry, Zoe.'

His words struck me like a blow to the chest. I'd told him I loved him, put it out there, making myself vulnerable. Not only did he not say it back, he said he didn't want to be with me anymore.

'It's because of Pandora, isn't it?' I said.

Pandora moved closer. 'Yes, that's right. You've got it. We're together now. It happened on Friday night. After all, we're the same kind. We're suited, and you know it.'

I looked at him. 'Rion?'

He closed his eyes. 'Yes.'

There was nothing more to say. But there was one thing I could do. I reached up and took the small silver chain off my neck and handed it to him.

He opened his eyes and pushed my hand away. 'No, Zoe. Please, don't give it back.'

'There isn't any reason to keep it anymore.' Since he wouldn't take it, I dropped it on the coffee table next to the wine glasses. I pushed past him, and this time he did nothing to stop me. Pandora followed me to the door. She put a hand on my arm as I went to open it. 'I'm sorry, Zoe, really I am. But it's for the best, and in your heart, you know I'm right.'

I couldn't let that one slide. 'No, it isn't. Not for me. The only person this is the best for is you. You want everything, don't you Pandora? Boys, popularity, fun times and, now, Rion. Who's the next conquest after you're tired of him? Because I have a feeling nothing lasts for you. You're playing with us all like we're puppets or something. Who will you hurt next? Because, Pandora, whoever is with you will always pay a price. But it won't be you.'

For once Pandora had nothing to say. Her expression went blank, and her lips tightened. I didn't care anymore. I just wanted out of there. I went out and closed the door behind me. Grabbing my bike, I headed home. How I got there, I couldn't remember, but finally I was in my bed. I was cold and wrapped the blankets around me tightly. But there were no tears. Only a hard little pebble inside me that had once been my heart.

Chapter Eighteen

Surprisingly, I slept. Maybe it was sheer exhaustion or maybe my body just shut down in protest. But when I woke up and touched my neck, finding it bare, it all came flooding back. I still couldn't cry. I felt numb. Everything seemed unreal. It was like I was looking at life, but not really part of it. I got ready for school automatically and even caught the bus on time. I didn't think of anything, but stared out the window, ignoring the noise all around me. When I got off at the school, I put one foot in front of the other. I kept breathing. I kept living. I just stopped thinking.

Rion was at school, but we might have been strangers. When I passed him in the hall, I looked over at him, but he avoided my eyes, and neither or us spoke. What was the point? There was nothing else to say. He didn't sit with us at lunch time. In fact, he never came out to lunch at all, so perhaps he was hiding from me in the library or the science lab where he had a job cleaning up and helping out. But Pandora was there, sitting with Jas's group, who were gathered around her hanging on to her every word. I wondered if it could even be called Jas's group anymore. The queen bee seemed to have been replaced. I almost felt sympathy for Jas.

I sat down next to Lou and Mike, who had joined our group now. He was actually okay, even if he was a computer and game nerd. Harry and Kerri were also there. Kerri had slipped back into her default mode of eating her ham and salad wrap and reading a book. It was good to know something was normal again.

'Where's Rion?' Lou asked.

I took a deep breath, knowing I had to tell them sooner or later. 'Rion and I have broken up.'

Lou looked at me with a shocked face. 'What? You can't be serious.'

'I am. It happened last night.' I slowly unwrapped the rye crispbreads and cheese that I'd grabbed for lunch this morning.

'That sucks,' Mike said. Understatement if ever there was.

Even Kerri looked up.

Harry said, 'I'm sorry to hear that, Zoe.' His eyes were sympathetic.

'But why?' Lou asked. 'You two were always so perfect together. Rion loved you so much.'

I almost cracked a smile at that remark. Lou said what Rion never had.

'I don't want to talk about it. I'd just rather forget and get on with things.' I couldn't tell them about Pandora yet, but they'd find out soon enough, and maybe it wouldn't be a total surprise. After all, who could compete with Pandora? Not any human, that's for sure.

'That's okay,' Lou said, placing a hand on mine. 'But we're here for you if you need us.'

The rest of the group nodded, and then no one said another word about it. It was as simple as that. One day we were Zoe and Rion, the couple everyone thought would last, including me. And the next day it was over, just like that.

But I had other things on my mind too. Tomorrow Mum was having her procedure, and so we were all carefully cheerful and upbeat at dinner. 'Everything will be fine. It's only day surgery,' Mum said brightly as she put the salad on the table.

'Yes,' Dad said, pouring some water into his glass. 'It'll be fine.'

I nodded. Concern for Mum overshadowed my unhappiness about Rion for the moment.

After dinner, Dad said, 'Why don't you go and do your homework, Zoe, and I'll clean up. And you have a rest,' he added, turning to Mum.

But she shook her head. 'I have a few things to sort out for school. I'll be away tomorrow, so I need to plan some work for the supply teacher.'

I looked at her incredulously. 'Really, Mum? You're going in for an operation tomorrow and you're going to do school work?'

'The world doesn't stop just because of that. Besides, it's only a day procedure.' She got up and bent down to kiss my head. 'Now scoot and get some of that homework done that you're always complaining about.'

I slowly climbed the stairs and went to my room, sitting on the bed. My first impulse was to call Rion and talk to him. I actually had the phone in my hand before I remembered. I hadn't thought about him in the last half hour or so. I'd pushed my breakup with Rion to the back of my mind. I couldn't stop thinking about what the results would be tomorrow.

The next day was long. I didn't tell anyone, not even Lou, that Mum was going in for a procedure and we would find out whether she had cancer or not. I was quiet, but I knew all my friends thought that was because of Rion. It was and it wasn't. It was everything. And talking wouldn't help.

Dad texted me later in the day to say the procedure was over and he was on his way to pick her up from the hospital.

When will she know the results? I texted back.

Not till tomorrow at the earliest. He replied.

When they got home in the evening, Mum was looking tired.

'Probably just the effects of the aesthetic,' she said, giving me a hug. Dad went out to get us some takeaway, and after dinner we all watched back episodes of *Star Trek Voyager* on Netflix. It was one of our favourite series and brought back memories, both good ones and painful ones. I remembered when Rion had been staying with us last year and we all watched it together. We'd had popcorn, or sometimes pizza or even some of those awful brownies Mum used to make. Now I sat next to Mum, leaning my head against her shoulder. I couldn't bear the thought of anything being wrong with her. In fact, I refused to believe it. She was just tired from teaching all those bratty little kids, and that lump was just a cyst. I'd lost Rion, but there was no way I was going to lose Mum. Everything was going to be all right.

The image of Zoe's face when I lied and told her I didn't want to be with her anymore was one I wouldn't forget. And what was worse, I told her I was with Pandora. That was the biggest lie of all.

Pandora had come over to my house uninvited that night. She'd brought pizza and wine and told me we had unfinished business. I told her we didn't. That I had already made up my mind to break up with Zoe, for her own sake. But that hadn't been enough for Pandora.

'We're both aliens in human bodies. We should stick together, Orion. As a team, we'd be unstoppable. Just think of what we could do, of where we could go, of the fun we could have. We could leave this boring place and travel the world. Why stay here in this small, limited town with these small, limited people? There is so much we could do and see. We shouldn't waste this opportunity.'

I wasn't tempted at all. In fact, it was the last thing I wanted. I had planned to see the world all right, but I had planned to see it with Zoe. I resented Pandora for opening my eyes and making me realise who I was. If she hadn't materialised in human form, Zoe and I would still be together. And maybe it wouldn't have been fair to Zoe, but I was selfish enough to want things back to the way they were. I had to keep reminding myself why I broke up with her.

'I don't want to go anywhere with you, Pandora,' I'd said. 'If I can't be with Zoe, I don't want to be with anyone. In fact, I'm going to try to get back to the mothercloud.'

Pandora had shrugged as she'd poured the wine. She handed me a glass. 'That's one of the most sensible things you've said. But you can have some fun here first, and then we'll both go back. You'll get over that little human in time. Here, have some of this. Wine is one of the better human inventions. This will help you forget for a while.'

I'd taken the glass and put it down. 'I don't want to forget, and I certainly don't want this. I think you'd better leave now.'

But then there'd been a knock on the door, and it was Zoe. The timing couldn't have been worse. Pandora was right about one thing. I don't know if I would have had the courage to leave Zoe, especially after she'd stumbled into my arms and I'd held her closely. But fate, or destiny or maybe just luck, bad luck, had taken it out of my hands. Pandora was there, a physical reminder of my alien identity. So, I'd lied and said I didn't want to be with her. And when she'd jumped to the conclusion Pandora and I were together, I'd realised that was probably the only way Zoe would accept our breakup. But one look at her face told me that not only had I broken up with her, I had broken her heart too. I would never forgive myself for that.

As to being with Pandora, that was never going to happen. She'd tried to persuade me to go along with the deception. 'She'll only try to get back with you if we aren't together,' Pandora had said after Zoe left.

'No, she won't. She's not like you. She doesn't try to get what she wants no matter what the cost,' I'd snapped. 'But you have what you want now. My life, my human life, is ruined. So now you can leave.' And finally, she did.

But now, facing long days at school and even longer nights at home, I wondered how I could get in touch with my people. Pandora had said it was possible, but I soon realised, too late, it was just talk. Despite all my efforts to communicate with my people, all I got back was silence. Perhaps I would go away by myself and leave Zoe to get on with her life. And this time I would stay away.

Chapter Nineteen

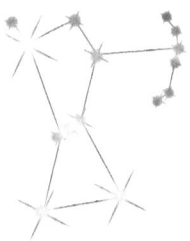

The next day, the only thing I wanted was to find out the results of Mum's procedure. I wasn't going to think about Rion at all. Easier said than done.

I was sitting between Lou and Kerri at lunch time, eating my sandwich, when I saw him come out of the library and head towards us. It was the year twelve area, and the groups were scattered under trees or out in the sun because it was getting cooler. Rion hadn't sat with us yesterday or even with Pandora. He hadn't come outside at all. If he and Pandora were together, they certainly didn't hang out much. But even if they weren't a couple, Rion had made it clear he didn't want to be with me. So, I was mega surprised when he came over to our group. He nodded to everyone. Harry said, 'Hey, man, how are you?'

Rion sat down next to me. I moved closer to Lou to give him room, and concentrated on eating my sandwich. There was an awkward silence for a few moments as everyone searched for something to say. Rion spoke first. 'So, um, Zoe, how are you?'

'Fine.' I wondered what he wanted. Did he suddenly have a change of heart?

'That's good. I'm fine too.'

Scintillating conversation—not.

Then he said, 'Mrs Stewart asked me to babysit Emerson tonight. I just thought, you usually do it. Do you want the job instead?'

'I can't do it tonight. Besides, Mrs Stewart asked you, not me.' Maybe she noticed that Jimmy Choo shoe didn't look so great after all. But anyway, I wanted to be home with Mum.

'I just wanted to check, to see if it was okay.'

I shrugged. 'I don't care. Do it if you want to. The money's good.' I finally looked over at him, and just for a microsecond our glances met. And then he looked away again.

'Okay then, I will. Thanks.'

Another awkward silence.

Harry finally said, 'How did you get on with that physics homework? It took me ages, and I'm still not sure I got the last question right.'

'Yeah, it was tricky. I'll look over it with you if you want.'

'I haven't got my book here, but maybe I'll give you a call tonight. It isn't due until tomorrow.'

'Yeah, sure, anytime.'

This time the silence was painful.

Then Rion finally said, 'I'd better be going.' He got up and brushed some grass from his trousers. 'I'll see you guys later.'

'Yeah, see you, Rion,' Lou said.

Harry nodded, and Kerri didn't as much as look up from her book. She'd hardly noticed he was here. I said nothing and didn't even look in his direction.

When he left, I let out the breath I hadn't realised I was holding. He hadn't come to reconcile or anything like it. He'd just come because he wanted to check if it was all right with me that he took the babysitting job with Emerson. I felt like a deflated balloon.

'So,' I said to everyone, 'as you can see, we are well and truly broken up.'

Lou looked at me sympathetically. 'I'm so sorry, Zoe. I don't know, and I'm not asking what happened, but I think he's an idiot to leave you. He doesn't deserve you.'

'Thanks, Lou. I'll survive. Really, the only thing I care about now is Mum and hoping she is okay.' I hadn't meant to say that, but it just slipped out.

'Your mum? What's wrong with her?' Lou asked.

And so, I told them we were waiting for the results of her procedure.

Harry said quietly, 'I heard about that from my mum, but I didn't bring it up because you never mentioned it, so I thought you probably didn't want to talk about it.'

I'd forgotten about Harry's mum, Eileen, who worked at the same school as my mother. Of course she would know and would have told Harry. 'Thanks, Harry. We're all trying to be positive.'

'When will your mum get the results?' Lou asked.

'I'm not sure, hopefully soon, today or tomorrow.'

'It'll be okay,' Harry said. 'Everything will turn out all right, you'll see.' He gave me a reassuring smile.

I nodded. 'Yeah, sure.' I knew he was trying to be supportive, but I also knew that saying things were going to be all right didn't necessarily make them so.

The bell went, and we gathered our stuff to go to class. As Harry and I walked to our English class, he said, 'You know you can call me anytime you want to talk. I'm here if you need me.'

'I know, Harry.'

'I'm not Rion, and I'm not trying to take his place or anything, but you, me, our families, we've known each other forever. We're still friends. Just don't forget that.' He gave my hand a squeeze.

I felt tears gather in my eyes, tears that I still hadn't been able to shed for Rion. 'I appreciate that, Harry, I really do.' And then I turned and went into class before I did anything foolish like break down. No doubt Pandora and Jas would love a scene like that.

When I got off the school bus, I sprinted home, burst through the door, and said, 'Mum?'

A familiar smell of something wafted towards me down the hall. 'I'm in the kitchen, dear. I thought I'd do a bit of baking before dinner.'

I smiled, dropped my bag, and headed down the hallway. Mum was taking something out of a baking pan, flour on her black top and her blonde hair coming out of her messy bun.

Mum baking, surely that was a good sign?

She finished putting the brownies on a plate.

'Has the hospital called yet?'

She shook her head. 'But I'm feeling optimistic and even more energetic today. Go on, spoil your supper,' she said, holding out the plate.

I looked at the small dark pieces on the white plate, and to please her took one and bit into it. As I chewed, I felt a little bit of sunshine creep through what had not been a great day. Burnt brownies had never tasted so good.

I was hoping looking after Emerson would distract me from the misery I felt about not being with Zoe.

Ringing the bell, I was surprised when the door opened and a dog leapt up to greet me. 'Down, boy,' I said to the panting, tail-wagging creature. He got down and gazed up at me with eager brown eyes. 'Sit,' I added, and he did, tail still thumping.

Mrs Stewart looked at me in surprise. 'Are you some sort of dog trainer, Rion? He never does anything we tell him. He is the most undisciplined dog.'

Emerson dropped to his knees and put his arms around the dog's neck. 'No, he isn't. He's just a puppy. He's still learning.'

'Emerson, get up immediately. You'll get dog hairs all over you, and that dog is bound to have germs.' Mrs Stewart looked at him in horror, but I had never seen Emerson look so happy.

He got up. 'Rion and me could bathe him if you want.'

'It's Rion and I, dear. Try to remember to use proper grammar. And no, you won't bathe him. That will make too much mess. Besides, that's your father's job.' Her lips thinned. 'He certainly seems to have a lot of business trips these days. I wonder if it was entirely wise of him to get you a dog, especially when he's away so much.'

'No, Mummy. He looks after Tiberius really well. He's a wonderful dog and such good company. Besides he's a guard dog too.' Emerson was really selling it hard.

Mrs. Stewart gave a heavy sigh and looked back at me. 'Well, it's out of my hands for the moment. Anyway, I have to get going or I'll be late for my book club meeting. You're familiar with the routine, Rion. The schedule for the evening is on the coffee table in the family room, and you have my phone number. Oh, and that dog is not to get up on the furniture and certainly not on Emerson's bed.'

I nodded, surprised that Mrs Stewart even let the dog into the house. Perhaps she was mellowing.

Then Emerson said, 'We used to keep him in the garage, but he cried and barked so much the neighbours complained.'

Mrs. Stewart's brow furrowed. 'Thank goodness he's not here very often.' Then she bent down, presenting Emerson with a smooth, white cheek. 'Give Mummy a kiss, dear.' He gave her a dutiful peck on the check. Then she straightened up, opened the front door, and closed it behind her with a click.

Emerson grabbed my hand. 'Come on, let's have some fun.'

The few times I'd babysat Emerson, I realised that everything was scheduled into Emerson's life except for fun. Apparently, Mrs Stewart didn't think that was important for a six-year-old. I always attempted to do most of the things on the written schedule she left for us, but Emerson and I also managed a few things that weren't on the schedule as well.

We went down the hallway to the family room and kitchen at the end, with Tiberius following us closely behind. Sitting down on the sofa, I had a look at the schedule with its usual activities of speaking French, reading educational books, and practising his flute. We could also play chess, which was fine by us because Emerson and I loved chess. Emerson sat beside me, and Tiberius attempted to jump up beside us.

'Down, Tiberius,' I said, and he immediately sat on the floor and placed his head on Emerson's little knees. Emerson placed his hand on the dog's head, stroking him.

'I think he likes you. Maybe it's because you're an alien,' Emerson said.

Emerson was the only human, aside from Zoe, who knew I was an alien. I had let it slip the first time I'd babysat him, but I knew I could trust him not to tell anyone, even though he was a child. He was highly intelligent, and we both knew what it was to be a little bit different from everyone else.

'I think it's more that my voice is the right pitch for him and has a tone of command. Dogs respond more to tone than what you actually say.'

'That's true. I'm reading a book about dogs at the moment, and it's really interesting. Dad gave it to me. Zoe and I read a little bit of it together. I wish you and Zoe could both come at the same time. Mother says you might distract each other and not notice me. We could have great games of Snap if she was here.' Zoe had taught him the simple game of Snap, and he loved it.

His words made me feel how empty my life had become since Zoe was no longer in it. I'd only made up the excuse of checking about the babysitting job because I wanted to talk to her. I couldn't seem to stay away from her. Then, when I got there, I acted like an idiot. I couldn't think of anything to say. If it hadn't been for Harry asking me about the physics homework, it would have been even more embarrassing.

Emerson looked at me. 'You look kind of sad, like Tiberius is when I have to leave him or say goodbye.'

I wasn't going to burden a six-year-old with my problems, not even a smart six-year-old. 'I'm fine. Let's play chess.'

'You never let me play chess until we've done some of the things on the schedule.' He looked at me closely with his wide blue eyes.

I ignored his question. 'Well, we can play chess and speak French. That way we can do two things on your schedule.'

'You're not very good at French.'

219

Sometimes I wished Emerson wasn't quite so clever. 'Do you want to play chess or not? Otherwise, we're are going to follow this schedule to the letter, and that includes the twenty minutes of yoga poses.' Emerson hated yoga and only did it when his mother insisted.

'Rion, you are very different tonight. I don't like it.' His eyes filled with moisture. I had upset him.

I had to tell him something. Besides, he would probably find out from Zoe.

'All right, Emerson, I didn't want to upset you with my problems, but since you are so determined to know, Zoe and I are no longer such close friends anymore. That makes me sad, but it's okay. Other than that, I'm fine.'

'Did she break up with you?'

That was a hard one to answer, but I wasn't going to lie. 'No, I broke up with her.'

Emerson's eyes opened wide, and a look of disapproval was on his face. 'Why would you do that? Zoe is the nicest person I know. I was going to ask her to wait for me until I grew up, and then she could be my girlfriend. But then you started going out with her, so I thought that my two best friends *in the world*, were dating, so that was okay.'

I felt myself smiling. 'I thought you were going to ask Giselle to marry you?' Giselle had been Emerson's au pair from Switzerland, and she had looked after him for a long while.

'Well, I did think that once, but she's decided to stay in Switzerland now and not come back. I missed her an awful lot at first, but then when Zoe started to babysit, I felt better. Now I really love Zoe. But,' he added seriously, 'I was willing to give her up for you.'

'I appreciate that, Emerson. But I felt that it wasn't fair for Zoe to be with me, since I was an alien. She should be with a human.'

Emerson tilted his head to the side. 'Did Zoe agree?'

'I think she probably understood, but it hasn't been easy for either of us.' There was no way I was going to tell him about Pandora.

'Does Zoe still love you?'

Emerson certainly knew how to ask hard questions. 'She used to, I think. I'm not sure now.'

'Do you love her?'

That question was easy. 'Yes, of course.'

'Then what's the problem?' I noticed Tiberius had snuck up on the sofa next to Emerson, but I let it go for now as I wrestled with Emerson's question.

'We are too different. I didn't realise how different until lately.'

221

'You and I are both different. You said being different was okay, remember?'

I did remember. Emerson had hated being the child genius, the odd one out at school and not accepted by any of his schoolmates. I had told him I was different too, and that was when the fact that I was an alien had slipped out.

'Yes, but...'

'Maybe Zoe likes you *because* you're different. Besides, if you can't have a girlfriend, it means when I grow up, I won't be able to have one either, because I'm different too.'

'It's not that simple, Emerson.'

'Yes, it is,' he said, folding his arms across his chest, looking at me like a lawyer who had just stated his case with irrefutable logic.

I sighed and wondered if it might have been easier not to babysit Emerson tonight. He was too young to understand all the implications of my difference. But he was too smart not to notice something was wrong.

I tried to explain. 'You are human, Emerson. I'm not.'

'So what?'

'Maybe I might not live as long as a human. Maybe I might get a strange disease. I might not be able to adjust to being human. Maybe...'

'Maybe you might want to be an alien again and leave here,' Emerson said, looking at me as if he could see my thoughts.

'No, no of course not.'

'Maybe you're sick of us humans. Maybe you'll change your mind about me too.' A tear rolled down his cheek.

I tried to reassure him. 'Emerson, you are one of my best friends here. I'll never get sick of you.' I gave him a hug, and he put his head on my chest. Tiberius tried to climb in my lap too.

'Get down, Tiberius,' I said, and all the dog did was to lick my face with his long, wet tongue. So much for him listening to me.

Emerson looked up and smiled. 'Tiberius doesn't want you to go either.' And then we both laughed as that ridiculous dog tried to jump even higher, putting his paws on my shoulders. We pushed him off.

'I think I've lost my dog-whispering abilities,' I said as I got up from the couch.

Emerson got up too and put his small hand in mine. 'I don't want you to go, but if you do, promise you won't go anywhere without saying goodbye first.'

'I promise,' I said. 'But,' I added, not wanting him to be sad any longer, 'I'm not intending on going anywhere.' It was the first lie I'd ever told him.

'Good. And now I think I'd better have something nice to eat as I need comfort food.'

Mrs Stewart didn't believe in eating between meals, but occasionally she let Emerson have a piece of fruit or some plain rice crackers if he was really hungry. 'I'll see if your mum has some fruit in the fridge,' I said, heading into the stainless-steel kitchen.

'We can do better than that. Dad gave me a secret supply of chocolate to have sometimes as a treat. It's in my room. Come on.'

'I'm not sure your mum would approve,' I said, feeling I had to put up a token protest.

'She can't approve or disapprove because she doesn't know anything about it. Besides, Dad is my parent too, and he said it was okay.'

'Someday, Emerson, you are going to make a very good lawyer.'

'I think I'd rather be a dog trainer because I'd have more fun.'

And again, I couldn't argue with that.

Chapter Twenty

I had one okay day. One day when I wasn't too worried about Mum or didn't think too much about Rion. Classes were boring but no worse than usual. After school, because it was late-night shopping, Lou and I decided to get a mani/pedi as they were on special.

'Midnight Blue Sparkle,' I chose my colour from the array of samples before me. My feet were in the gently bubbling water, and already I was beginning to feel relaxed.

Lou leaned over. 'That's cool. On your fingernails too?'

'Why not? At least they'll match my toes.' I wanted something different.

Lou studied the colours on the little sticks fanned out in my hands. 'I think I'll go for Vampire Kiss. I've got a lot of black stuff now, and that colour will match. Do you think Mike will like it?'

Lou seemed to want to run everything by him and made decisions based on what he liked or didn't like. He was a nice guy and everything, but I wished Lou would be more independent at times.

'I think he'd like anything you picked, Lou. Choose the colour you want.'

When we finished at the salon, we headed toward what was becoming our favourite place, the milkshake bar. As we threaded our way through the Saturday afternoon crowds, Lou's hand grabbed my arm.

'Hey, look over there, by the sushi place.'

I glanced towards the sushi bar near the exit to the car park and saw Kerri and Pandora, shopping bags in their hands and deep in conversation.

'Since when did those two become besties?' Lou asked.

I shrugged. 'Kerri's always liked Pandora, and they're both smart.' I was trying to be fair, but I was as surprised as Lou to see two such unlikely people together.

'We should go over and say hello.'

I followed her reluctantly. Pandora was the last person I wanted to say hello to.

Pandora noticed us first. 'Hey, girls, how are you?'

'Hi, what are you guys up to?' Lou asked.

Kerri gave us a wide smile. I'd never seen her look so happy. 'You'll never guess what we've just done. Look.'

She lifted the sleeve of her button-up top and showed the top of her arm where there was a plaster. Peeling it back, she revealed a tattoo of two small stars. 'Show them yours too, Pandora.'

Pandora lifted the sleeve of her black tee shirt, pulled back her plaster, and showed an identical tattoo in the same place.

When I recovered from my total amazement, I managed to say, 'Cool.'

Lou just looked, her mouth slightly open.

'They're binary stars, because we have so much in common.' Kerri sent a beaming smile in Pandora's direction. She smoothed the plaster down again.

Didn't quite know what to say to that one either.

Pandora's look, I thought, was kind. 'We're both really into science, and Kerri's one of the smartest humans I've met.'

I noticed the use of her word 'human,' but it seemed I was the only one.

Finally, Lou found her voice. 'Yeah, she is. They're awesome tattoos, girls.'

Pandora shook her hair over her shoulder. 'You should get one too. It's great fun and très cool.'

'My mum would kill me,' Lou said.

'Then, get one somewhere she won't see. After all, you only live once, Lou,' Pandora said.

'Yes,' Kerri added, 'and it only hurts a little.'

I couldn't imagine what Kerri's mum would say. She was even stricter than Lou's. But I decided not to comment. I was seeing a side of Kerri I never imagined, and maybe that was a good thing, though I was a tad worried Pandora had so much influence over her. I never entirely trusted her. Even less so now.

'We'd better get going,' Lou said. 'I've got to be home soon 'cause we've got company tonight and I've got to clean my room.'

Pandora lifted her eyes. 'Why? Are they going to have dinner in your room?'

Lou gave a little laugh. 'No, but you know what mothers are like.'

'I don't, thank goodness. Well, cool seeing you, girls. Chad's invited a few of us over to his place tonight.'

I couldn't imagine Jas allowing Chad to invite Pandora anywhere, let alone to his place, even if other people were going to be there. Just showed how powerful Pandora was. I wondered if Rion was going with her. I asked, even though I knew I shouldn't have, 'So, are you and Rion going together?'

Pandora gave me a smile. 'He might turn up.'

I felt my insides turn over. My hands clenched, but I said nothing.

Kerri looked downcast. 'Mum said I wasn't allowed to go out at night for a while, not after last time.'

That didn't surprise me in the least.

We said goodbye and headed off to the bus stop. As soon as we were out of earshot, Lou said, 'Can you believe it, Zoe? Kerri got a tattoo!'

'Never would have thought it if I hadn't seen it with my own eyes.'

'I know, right? Pandora really has a lot of influence over her.'

'Yeah.' I started to worry again. My first impression of her had been right. Pandora was trouble. And now she was with Rion. I felt a huge lump in my throat thinking about it. But we weren't together any more. It was time I accepted that. Unconsciously my hand went to my neck, but it was bare. Blinking back the tears, I followed Lou out of the shopping centre.

When I got home, Mum and Dad were in the kitchen. Dad was making the usual mess, but this time with lasagne, and Mum was sitting at the kitchen table with a glass of wine, which was unusual as she hadn't been drinking lately, because she was worried about her health. I was taking this as another good sign.

'Hi, darling,' Mum said, 'did you have a fun time with Lou?'

'Yeah, awesome. What do you think?' I spread out my hand to show her my indigo nails.

229

'Unusual, but interesting,' Mum said.

'Could be worse. At least they're not black,' Dad said, lifting a spoon from the sauce and spilling a drop on the floor.

I rolled my eyes at the expected response. Dad and cool—two words that never occupied the same sentence unless it included the word not.

I sat down next to Mum. 'I'll soon be seventeen. Perhaps I should join you in a glass of wine.'

'Sure,' Mum said, 'in sixteen months' time when you're legal.'

It was somewhat comforting to know that some things hadn't changed. My parents were as square as ever.

'So, what's up? I thought it was your turn to cook tonight, Mum.'

Mum and Dad shared a look. Something was up. My stomach immediately tensed.

'Zoe, I got a call from my doctor today. I have my results back.'

Great, that must be why Mum had a glass of wine. She was celebrating.

'The test was positive.'

Positive? That was good, wasn't it? Positive always meant something better then negative. But the next sentence proved the opposite.

'I have breast cancer.'

My chest tightened and felt like a steel band had suddenly been wrapped around it. Mum had breast cancer. Even knowing it had been a possibility, I never considered it could be a reality. Cancer was something that happened to other people, not to my still young mother.

Her hand found mine and covered it. 'It's okay, Zoe. I'm going to fight it. It'll be all right. I'm going to get better, I promise you.'

Dad put the spoon down and came over, putting his hand on Mum's shoulder. He spoke in a hearty voice that I knew was fake. 'Mum is strong, and if anyone can beat this, she can. And we're going to help her, right, Zoe?'

I nodded, finding it hard to speak.

'Don't cry, darling. It'll be all right.'

I didn't even know that I was, but now I felt the tears roll down my cheeks. I got up and put my arms around her, hugging her tightly.

'Oh, Mum.'

I had to call Rion. After all, he loved Mum too. Suddenly it didn't matter what had happened between us, or that we had broken up. I needed to hear his voice and to feel the connection between us. I pressed the screen and his number rang.

He picked up on the first ring. 'Zoe?' he said, as if he couldn't quite believe it was me.

'Rion...'

'What's wrong?'

'It's Mum. She's got cancer.' My voice broke.

'I'll be right over.'

'Wait. Don't come to the house, not yet anyway. It's just not the right time. Dad is acting like everything is going to be okay, and Mum's watching me like a hawk because she's worried I'm going to break down or something. I'll meet you in the boat shed.'

'I'm leaving now. I'll be there as soon as I can.'

I closed my eyes and put the phone to my chest when he hung up. Rion was coming. He was smart, he was an alien, he would have an answer. At the very least, he would make me feel better.

I slipped out of the house and ran across the cool grass to the shed where our old boat was kept. Reaching up on the ledge above the door, my shaking fingers found the key that opened the shed door. Why we even bothered to lock it, I didn't know. There wasn't anything in there worth stealing. The door creaked open, and my hand reached up to turn on the light, revealing our small cabin cruiser. It had been a meeting place for Rion and me several times. And all of those times seemed to be milestone moments, both good and not so good. Climbing up onto our boat, I went down the two shallow steps that led to the musty cabin. We hadn't used the boat in five months since the Christmas holidays. I sat on the cold vinyl seats of the cabin and waited, putting my arms around myself. I didn't have long to wait. I heard the creak of the shed door and footsteps heading towards the boat.

'Zoe?'

'I'm here, in the boat.'

The steps quickened, and the boat moved as he climbed aboard. Two steps down and he was there, his arms around me. I felt his familiar heartbeat and the warmth of his body, and it felt like coming home.

Chapter Twenty-One

I'm so glad you're here.'
His arms tightened around me.

'I've missed you so much.' I knew it sounded pathetic since we hadn't been apart for long, but it had seemed an eternity to me.

'I lied.' His eyes misted as he spoke. 'I was never with Pandora.'

I looked at him in confusion. 'But... why?'

'To make it easier for you to walk away. Pandora made me realise I'd always be an alien, and I was worried what that might mean for the future. Maybe I wouldn't live a normal lifespan. Maybe we wouldn't even be able to have a family. I know we've been through this before, but I thought I'd become human and we'd be okay. When I realised there was still a big part of me that would always be an alien, I owed it to you to set you free. I was being selfish to you and even to my own people. I turned my back on them. I was selected for the space program, and then I gave up my mission.'

'That's stupid, Rion. Nobody, human or alien, knows what the future will bring. You've got to take some things on faith and trust they'll work out. Besides, you being an alien is not a bad thing. It might help you, or us, in ways you don't know. As for letting your people down, your supervisor gave you a choice. He wouldn't have done that if he felt it was the wrong thing to do. That's like a gift. And rejecting it is pretty ungrateful. Also, I'm sure he knows a lot more than Pandora, whatever she said.'

Understanding crept into his eyes. 'You're right, Zoe. I never thought of it that way before. He did let me choose, and he never judged me for it. A gift? Yes, and it would be wrong to throw it back in his face.' He hugged me again. 'How come you've lived such a short time and yet you're so smart?'

'I'll remind you of that in the future, you know.'

He leaned forward and kissed me again. For a moment, I forgot about everything, even my worries about Mum. Then Rion lifted his head and said, 'I'm so sorry, Zoe. Once again, I've hurt you. I really thought I was doing the right thing. I never wanted to be apart from you. And, if it gives you any comfort, my heart was breaking too.'

'When I found out about Mum, you were the first person I wanted to talk to. And when you said you'd come over straightaway, I knew all that other stuff that went down between us didn't matter anymore.'

He stroked my cheek with his finger. 'Tell me about your mother.'

The words tumbled out. When I finished, he said, 'She'll be okay.' His voice was comforting and confident. I believed him, especially hearing him say it out loud. He would know what to do, how to fix things.

'I know. You'll help her, won't you?' I looked at him.

'I'll help in any way I can, of course,' he said, but he looked puzzled, as if he didn't quite understand my question. 'I'll always be there to support you and your family.'

It wasn't quite the response I'd expected, so I added, 'Yes, but I don't just mean support, like sympathy or cooking a meal or something. I mean cure her, help her get better. Use your super alien powers, like Pandora always seems to do. I told you, being an alien is not a bad thing. You can do stuff that ordinary humans can't.'

This time he didn't just look puzzled, he looked surprised. 'Zoe, you know I would do anything I could to help your mum. She's been like a mother to me too.

But I don't have the power to cure her. I'm sorry, that's beyond me.' He took my hands and squeezed them, his dark brown eyes full of sympathy.

'But Pandora said you have all these powers and that because you've chosen to be a human, you repress them.'

'She highly exaggerates what she thinks are our powers. We might be smart, and sure, sometimes we might be able to influence people to see things we want them to see by altering some of their perceptions, but we can't cure diseases.'

I wasn't convinced. 'Maybe you can, if you try. Look, just think. You were able to create this body out of nothing when you were just a bubble of consciousness. So was Archimedes, so was Pandora. Archimedes altered my memories so that I didn't know you were an alien. You guys can do stuff that ordinary humans can't. Also, you've been around over 4000 years, so you must have learnt something about medicine in all that time. You have more power than you realise, Rion. You just have to work out how to use it.' I pulled my hands away and put my arms around his neck, looking at him straight in the eyes. 'If ever there was a reason to try, it's this. You have to try to help Mum. We can't…' I felt a lump in my throat. 'We can't lose her.'

Rion's chest exploded with a deep sigh, and I saw the tears form in his eyes. 'You don't understand. Even if I did have those powers, which I don't, I wouldn't be allowed to use them. One of the highest oaths we make when entering the space mission is not to interfere in human affairs. Pandora is wrong in trying to influence that woman she is staying with. She breaks all the rules, and eventually, she will be disciplined for it by our people.'

I dropped my arms from around him and slid away. 'This isn't *Star Trek*, Rion, and I don't care about your damned prime directive. Are you telling me you're not going to help Mum because you're afraid your people will get mad at you?'

He closed his eyes for a moment and shook his head. Then he opened them again and said, 'I did that all wrong. I'm sorry. Let me try again. Because the people on my space mission have existed as conscious entities rather than organics, we haven't been very concerned about what happens to the physical body. We haven't had to. We were able to manifest as physical beings because we carried the imprint of our former organic bodies that we used to have on our planet, and even that has been attempted by very few of us. Now that I'm an organic, if I get sick, I can't heal myself, and I can't heal others. It doesn't work that way. If I could help your mother, I would, and no rules would stop me. You have to believe that. But I can't.'

My heart sank. I realised I'd been secretly hoping that Rion could do something to help Mum. Pandora seemed to be able to do so much with her alien abilities, and she was much younger and therefore less powerful than Rion. 'Surely there is something you can do.' My voice sounded shaky and pleading. 'You could at least try,'

'Zoe, believe me, I would do anything I could, but—'

'You can't. I get it.' I moved a step back from him.

'You know I care about you and your mum.'

I knew he did, yet I couldn't help feeling a crushing disappointment. Maybe it was unfair of me, but all I could think of was that he wouldn't even try. 'I'd better go back to the house. It's getting late.'

He reached out to me, laying his hand on my arm. 'Zoe, we're still good, aren't we?'

I hesitated. I loved Rion and always would, but here was yet another hurdle we had to get over. 'I know you mean well, Rion. I thought you could help, but I guess I was wrong. I'm dealing with a lot of stuff at the moment, and maybe I'm not in the best head space. Maybe we should take a break, just for now.'

'I don't want to take a break. I want to be with you, Zoe. I know I've messed up big and this is one more thing that's upsetting you. I'll make it up to you in any way I can. But, please, let's face all this together.'

I almost relented because I wanted to be with him, but, and it was a big but, I realised everything in my world had shifted. I had lost two things, my belief that nothing could happen to my mother and my belief in Rion.

'You should go, Rion. It's late, and we've both got school in the morning.'

'I'll go, but if you need me, I'll still be there for you, whether we're together or not.'

He left, and I sat in the boat for a moment or two, blinking the tears away. I didn't want to go back in the house and let Mum see me upset. Right now, she was my first priority.

I don't know why I ever thought I was intelligent. When it came to dealing with humans, especially Zoe, I seemed to make one mistake after another. What I told her was the truth. I couldn't help cure her mother of cancer, but I should have said I would try, at least. After all, I had just given her my speech on how I was still an alien. No wonder she thought I had special powers. But I knew I'd only be offering her false hope. Mrs Brennan's best chance was with doctors and the treatments they would offer. All I could offer was sympathy, love, and physical acts like helping with chores or being with them when times were tough. Would it be enough? And even if it was, would Zoe ever come back to me?

I was in no mood to see Pandora that night when she turned up at my place. She didn't even wait to be invited in but barged into the house as soon as I opened the door. I wondered if I had ever been as rude or self-entitled as she was. I didn't think so, but after my performance this afternoon with Zoe, I couldn't be sure.

Closing the door, I followed her into the lounge room where she had already occupied three quarters of the sofa, her feet, in her trademark boots, stretched out on the clean, white cushions. I didn't sit down.

'What do you want, Pandora?'

'My, my, aren't you all sunshine and rainbows. What's up? Did your little human look at you the wrong way?'

That was just too close to the truth. 'She isn't my anything, thanks to you.'

'I just pointed out the truth to you. You're old enough to make your own decisions. More than four times older than me and several thousand times older than Zoe, I might remind you, just in case your maths has slipped as well.'

I clenched my jaw to stop myself from giving a totally inappropriate answer. I waited for her to get to the real point of her visit. One thing about Pandora, she always had an agenda.

'Anyway, I won't stay long. I'm headed over to Chad's. I need a favour. I want you to take Kerri to the high school formal in July.'

She couldn't have said anything that would have astonished me more.

'I thought you told Zoe we were together, not that that was ever going to happen. But Kerri? Why?'

Pandora shrugged. 'Zoe never believed that, especially since you've stayed away from me all week like I've got the plague. But Kerri needs a date, and I don't think anyone else is going to ask her. I know she wants to go.'

'Look, I don't know much about these things, but I do know that it isn't always necessary to have a date. She could go with some of the other girls. She could go with you.'

Pandora nodded. 'I know, and I'd considered it, but Chad Everett has asked me to go with him, and I think I'm going to say yes, if only to annoy Jas. For sure Lou will go with Mike. As for Zoe, well, who knows? Maybe she'll go with Harry. I'm sure he's dying to ask her, and now that you're out of the picture, maybe he will. Kerri doesn't know anyone else, and she won't go on her own. She's too shy.'

A stab of jealousy hit me when she mentioned Harry. Yet he was my friend and a good guy. He was perfect for Zoe, and that's what made it so hard.

I shook my head. 'Sorry, but if I can't go with Zoe, I'm not going at all.'

'Come on, Orion. Do something for someone else for a change. It won't kill you to go with Kerri. All you guys hang out anyway. It'll be just like lunch time at school, except you'll be all dressed up.'

I had nothing against Kerri. In a weird way, she reminded me of some of our own people—smart and painfully truthful—but I couldn't bear the thought of being at a dance, seeing Zoe with someone else and having to pretend it didn't matter. Especially after this afternoon. We had been together for approximately half an hour until I blew it, again. 'Sorry, Pandora. You'll just have to find a date for Kerri somewhere else. Besides, why do you care so much? Thought you believed humans were inferior.'

'Well, of course they are. But Kerri is also my friend. She's kind of sweet when you get to know her. I don't have to explain everything to her twice, like I do with most humans. She gets me, which is rare. I'm too complicated for most people.'

'And so modest as well.'

'Oh, very funny, Orion.' She swung her hair over her shoulder. 'I don't short sell myself, that's true. Unlike you. Have you thought anymore about what I said? You should really consider testing out some of your abilities before you lose them altogether. And, after you've had some fun here, you can return to the mothercloud. They'd take you back. I'll put in a good word for you, if you like.' She gave me a cheeky grin.

'Somehow, I don't think that'd help me much.'

She shrugged and stood up. 'Think about it. Think about the other thing too. Kerri's a good kid and deserves a break.'

'What's going to happen when you're tired of playing with these humans, Pandora? Do you care about the people you'll leave behind, the hearts you might have broken or the feelings you might have hurt? Have you even considered that Kerri might rather go to the formal with you rather than me?'

Pandora looked at me, and for a moment I thought I glimpsed something real in her eyes. 'Sure, I've thought of it. I'm not blind. And you know what, there's a part of me that would also rather go with Kerri than with Chad Everett. But, when I leave here, I won't care about breaking Chad's heart, if he even has one, but I would care about breaking Kerri's. Don't you see? That's why I want you to ask her. I can't risk it. I can't let Kerri become to me what Zoe is to you.' She turned with a whirl of hair that brushed my face and headed out the door, but not before I saw her eyes mist.

Chapter Twenty-Two

School had become unimportant to me. Mum had seen the doctor, and she had had some more tests, including an ultrasound. Now that they knew the lump was cancer, she needed surgery to remove it. She was being positive and upbeat. They had caught it early, she said, so that was a good thing. Dad was all supportive and positive too, on the surface. But sometimes, when he thought no one was looking, I saw the worry etched on his face, and for the first time ever, my father looked old to me.

Mum's surgery was scheduled for the day I had my history exam. It was the last thing I cared about. Studying the past seemed so futile when I was wondering what the future would even hold for Mum, for us as a family. But there was no way Mum or even Dad would let me miss it. This was year twelve, the big one, and my results would decide what degree I would get into at uni. I was so over this and all the pressure. Working at the local IGA didn't seem like such a bad idea at this point. But Mum and Dad went to the hospital, and I went to school.

I couldn't bring myself to tell anyone—not Lou, Kerri, or even Harry, and certainly not Rion. He had tried to talk to me, but I was in no mood to listen. Maybe I was being unfair, but I couldn't help it. I wasn't interested in an explanation; all I was interested in was Mum getting better. There was no room in me for any other feelings. After a few attempts, Rion left me alone, which was fine with me.

So, nobody knew that Mum had gone into hospital, and after the exam, which I could hardly remember even minutes after it was over, everyone chatted on about the most useless, trivial things that seemed completely stupid to me. I half-heartedly picked at my sandwich, wondering if I could skip classes for the rest of the day and go home.

'You're quiet today, Zoe,' Harry said as the others talked about some stupid reality show. 'Anything up?'

'No, nothing.'

'How's your Mum?'

I tried really hard not to show it, but my face started to crumple. Harry grabbed my arm and lifted me to a standing position. 'Come on, let's get out of here.'

As the others looked up, he said, 'Zoe's not feeling well. I'm just walking her to the girls' toilet.'

He started leading me away from everyone as Lou called out, 'Do you want me to come with?'

We rounded the corner of the sports shed, near the trees on the corner of the oval. And then, Harry pulled me 'round the corner, out of sight. I burst into big, shaky sobs as he pulled me into his arms and held me. 'Hey, it's okay,' he said. 'Just let it out. No one can see you here.'

I didn't know how long I stood there, crying all over Harry's school shirt. Finally, my sobs became hiccupy and then turned into just the occasional shaky sniff. When I could talk, I looked up at him and said, 'Thanks, Harry.'

'You okay for the moment?' he asked, his soft brown eyes full of concern.

I nodded. 'Sorry, I didn't mean to break down like that. I've made such a mess of your shirt.'

He shrugged and said, 'It's only my school shirt.' He leaned against the shed. 'You want to tell me about it?'

I closed my eyes, took a deep breath, opened them again, and then said, 'Mum's operation is today. They've confirmed she's got cancer. They're going to remove the lump in her breast.'

'Damn. I'm sorry, Zoe. No wonder you're upset.'

'Mum keeps telling Dad and me that it'll be all right. That they caught it early. But what if they haven't? What if it isn't okay?'

'Your mum's still young, and up till now, she's been healthy. That's got to help. And because they've diagnosed it early, she's got a really good chance of beating it. Lots of people do. The odds are on her side.'

'That's true,' I said. Harry's calm logic made me feel better. 'Thanks, you always seem to know the right thing to say.'

He smiled. 'I guess it comes from knowing you so well. After all, we been friends forever.'

'Yes, we have. You knew I was going to break down, and you got me out of there so quickly because you knew I would hate it if everybody saw it.' I put my hand on his cheek, its warmth feeling so comforting against my cold hand. 'Thanks, friend.'

As I looked into the kind eyes of the boy I had known since I was four years old, I realised how lucky I was to have somebody who would always know how I felt, who would always get me. He raised a hand to cup it over mine. 'I'll always be here if you need me, Zoe. You only have to ask.'

And I knew he meant more than just a friend. But I wasn't ready to go there, and he knew that too. He squeezed my hand and gave it back to me. 'You ready to go back to class. I think the bell went ages ago.'

I shook my head. 'Now that our exam is over, I'm just going to go home. I've had enough of school today.'

'You want me to come with you?'

'No, thanks anyway. I'd rather be alone for a while.'

'Okay, I understand. I'll just head back in then. But text or call if you need me.'

'Yeah, I will.'

He nodded and, giving me another brief smile, turned and went back around the shed towards the school buildings.

I felt totally spent and empty. But, in a way, breaking down like that had also made me feel strangely at peace. I knew, for now at least, I was okay. I could go home and wait for what would happen next. I was as ready for that as I ever would be.

When I got home, Dad wasn't there. He'd decided to stay in the hospital and wait till after the op was over. I couldn't study, so I decided to vacuum and clean the house. At least that was one thing Dad wouldn't have to do on the weekend. Mum was staying in overnight as her doctor wanted to keep an eye on her.

Finally, Dad arrived home bringing pizza. He put the box on the kitchen table and gave me a tired smile.

'How's Mum?'

'She's resting now, but the doctor said the operation went well and they think they've got all the cancer. They'll have the full results in a day or two.'

I gave a deep sigh of relief and then gave Dad a hug. 'I'm so glad.'

He returned my hug and then sat down. 'Me too.'

'And how is Mum feeling?'

'Okay, I think. She says she's fine, but you know Mum. She's a trooper.'

I nodded and smiled and then went to get some plates for the pizza.

As we ate, Dad said, 'How's Rion? I haven't seen him around much lately.'

'Oh, you know, what with school and everything, we've been busy.'

'Everything all right?' Dad looked at me.

I really didn't want to go into the Rion thing at the moment, especially since I was feeling so confused myself, so I just nodded and said, 'Yeah, sure.'

Yet when I was in my room later, I thought about it. I missed Rion, but I still couldn't get over that he had broken up with me, said he was with Pandora—even if he wasn't—and then wouldn't even try to help Mum. That was a bridge too far. Besides Mum wasn't even home from hospital yet, and we hadn't received the full report on her condition. Even though it seemed good at this point, cancer could always come back. And I just wasn't ready to forgive Rion yet.

The next day Mum was home, and I was so glad to see her. 'Mum,' I said, rushing into her arms. She winced a little, and then I remembered her surgery. I let her go and stood back. 'I'm sorry, I didn't think. I'm such a klutz at times.'

'That's okay, darling. I'm a little sore, but I'm not made of glass. I won't break.'

'I'll get you a cup of tea,' Dad said. 'You just go and sit down with Zoe.'

We went into the lounge room, and Mum sat down on the sofa. I sat next to her, waiting for her to tell me what happened but not wanting to bombard her with questions.

'The operation seemed to go well. The doctor spoke to me briefly afterwards and said things were looking good. They removed the lump and some of the breast tissue around it. Now they'll send it to pathology, and I should get the results in a day or two.'

'So, that's it? You're okay now?' I asked, trying not to sound anxious. Even though Dad had told me more or less the same thing yesterday, it was good to hear it again from her.

'Well, I'll probably have to have some radiation treatments, but I'm hoping that's it. I'll know more when the results come back.'

I breathed a cautious sigh of relief as I leaned back on the sofa. Then I said, 'Radiation, that's not so bad, is it? I mean, it's not as bad as chemo where you lose your hair and everything.'

Mum gave me a tired smile. 'No, the side effects are usually not as dramatic. I'll probably be a little red and sore, but hopefully not much more than that.'

'I just want you to get better.' I swallowed the lump in my throat.

'It's what we all want,' Dad said, as he came into the room carrying a tray, the mugs jiggling against each other. He set the tray down and passed Mum a mug and then a plate of Tim Tams, her favourite biscuit.

'Hey, this is pretty good service,' she said as she took one. 'I'll have to get sick more often.'

'Don't even think it,' Dad said as he sat in the chair opposite her.

'You're right, I don't want to think about it. I just want to get back to my life again. Even marking the grade six's history tests has a certain appeal at the moment, compared to being in hospital, that is.' She gave a thin smile.

'You're not going back to school yet, are you?' I looked at her in surprise.

She shook her head. 'I've taken a couple of weeks sick leave, but I'll go back after that. I'll be able to fit any treatments in and around work. And, I'd really rather be active and get on with things. That's the best way, I think.'

We had a quiet evening together and even watched a *Star Wars* movie on Netflix. When I went to bed that evening, I was feeling a whole lot better than the night before. Even though she wasn't out of the woods yet, Mum was getting there. The cancer was gone. Now she just had to get through the radiation treatment, and we could all go back to normal.

That night I got a call from Rion. 'How's your mum?'

'She's okay. She had surgery today, and they removed the lump.'

'You should have told me.' He sounded hurt. 'I wanted to be there for you. I didn't want you to go through this alone.'

I realised I'd asked too much of him when I expected him to magically cure Mum. I'd been unfair because I had been so worried. But there was still a part of me that wished he would at least have tried. And, if I was being totally honest, maybe I still hadn't got over him dumping me. 'That's okay. I wasn't alone. I had Dad, and Harry has been supportive.'

'Oh, Harry,' he said, in a toneless voice. 'He knew about your Mum's surgery then, did he?'

'No, he just knew I was upset, and then I told him.'

We were silent for a few moments. Then he said, 'Zoe, are you ever going to forgive me?'

'There's nothing to forgive, Rion. You haven't done anything wrong. I was just mistaken in thinking you could do anything to cure her. I was disappointed, that's all.'

'Can we at least be friends?'

'Yeah, sure,' I said. 'We'll always be friends.'

'But nothing more?'

'Let's just take it one step at a time for now, Rion. The only thing I'm concerned about at the moment is Mum getting better.'

'Yes, of course. Tell her I'm glad the operation went well and I'm thinking of her.'

'I will, thanks.' I hung up and put the phone down on my bed. I still missed Rion, and maybe when Mum was on the mend, I would reach out to him again. But right now, I needed space.

Chapter Twenty-Three

Mum's doctor rang her to give her the results. The lump was malignant, but the tissue was clear, and it seemed there was nothing else. As Mum had predicted, they were going to give her a short course of radiation treatments to be on the safe side. I finally felt I could relax, and the steel band of worry that seemed to crush my chest was gone. Now, I only had year twelve to worry about—piece of cake really.

Everyone, and I mean everyone, including Kerri, was talking about the year twelve formal that was happening in a month's time. Our school usually had it at midyear so that the year twelve students could concentrate on their studies and exams in semester two. A lot of girls had already bought their dresses and had their dates. I hadn't given it much thought up until now. Earlier in the year, I had taken it for granted I'd be going with Rion, but now that seemed unlikely. Even if he did ask me, I wasn't sure what my answer would be. I wasn't ready to go back to girlfriend/boyfriend status quite yet.

But that left me with a dilemma. What if Harry asked me? Would I say yes? Was I ready to take that step with him? I really didn't know. And the formal was fast approaching. Lou was going with Mike, and she had asked me to go formal shopping with her that Saturday. I had been saving for my dress since the beginning of the year as formal dresses were ridiculously expensive, and Mum and Dad had given me some extra money to help. But, as Lou and I bussed it to the shopping centre, I confided in her. 'I don't know if I really want to go to the formal.'

She looked at me in surprised. 'Of course you have to go. It's a milestone of our high school years.'

I shook my head. 'Things still aren't good between Rion and me. I just don't feel very enthusiastic about the formal at all.'

'You and Kerri can go together, and you can hang out with Mike and me. You don't have to have a date, you know. Lots of girls don't. Just go and have fun, Zoe. You'll always regret it if you don't.'

'Yeah, I guess.'

'And I think Kerri really wants to go. If you don't go with her, who is she going to hang out with?'

'Maybe some guy will ask her out.'

Lou looked at me. 'Kerri is my friend, but the only boys she knows are Harry and Rion. So unless one of them asks her out, I don't think anyone else will.'

I sighed. 'You're laying a guilt trip on me, Lou.'

'Is it working?'

'Oh all right, I'll go to the formal, if only to stop you nagging me.'

Lou sat back in her seat and gave a self-satisfied smile. 'Good.'

When we got to the shops, two things became clear. Not only were formal dresses expensive, they were out-of-this-world expensive and none of them suited me. I was no longer a stick—thank goodness—but I still didn't have enough curves to keep up some of the strapless dresses, and I hated the frills and fussiness of some of the others. I wished we could wear jeans to the formal. That would be so much easier. But if I was fussy, Lou was ten times worse. The afternoon wore on, and I was beginning to think we weren't going to find anything. I decided I was going to get the next dress that a) fit me and b) was in my budget. After all, what did it matter since the formal just wasn't ranking high on my priorities right now? Lou and I went into the last shop that sold formals, and I just grabbed a dark purply dress while Lou decided on a black one. I tried mine on. It was close fitting and had small shoulder straps that kept it up. I twirled in front of the mirrors. I wasn't sure if I liked the cut as it might be hard to dance in, but I was so tired of looking that I decided it would do. When I took a closer look at the price tag and saw it was on sale, it was a done deal for me.

'Hey, Lou, I'm gonna get this one,' I called out to her. She was in the next dressing room.

'Yeah, same,' Lou said. 'Let's have a look at each other.'

We tottered out of the change rooms, nearly banging into each other, and giggled. 'Well, let's see you,' I said, stepping back.

'What do you think?' Lou twirled around in front of me.

Her dress was a strapless black, low cut in the back. It had a slit up the side that showed a red satin lining. Lou definitely had a better figure than mine for such a revealing dress, and she looked good. But I couldn't help feel that it was a bit old for her. Jeez, what was I, forty or something? I was turning into my mother. I smiled at her and said, 'You look awesome, Lou.'

'You think? I hope Mike thinks so too. He didn't really want to go to the formal because he said it wasn't his thing. I had to persuade him to go. I want to make sure I look really good for him, so he'll feel it was worthwhile.'

'As long as you like it, Lou, that's the main thing. And I'm sure he'll think you look beautiful.'

'Yeah, maybe,' Lou said, sounding doubtful. 'Sometimes, I'm not so sure.'

'What do you mean?'

She shrugged. 'Oh nothing, just my overactive imagination…. Hey, stand back and let me see your dress. Yeah, it looks great, Zoe. That colour really suits your dark hair.'

'Thanks. We're done then. Let's get out of these things and go for a burger. All this shopping has made me work up an appetite.'

We'd just ordered and were heading towards a booth with our number when I heard a small but familiar voice say, 'Hey, Zoe.'

I looked down and there was Emerson with his Dad. Emerson had a huge hamburger in front of him along with a chocolate milkshake. I could just imagine what his mum would say if she could see him now. I stopped and said, 'Hi, Emerson, Mr Stewart.'

'I'll just go on and grab us a table,' Lou said.

'Zoe, this is a happy coincidence,' Mr Stewart said. 'I have to go to a work function tonight and my babysitter just called a short while ago and cancelled on me. I've been in touch with Emerson's mother, but she has to go out as well. I don't suppose you're free tonight to babysit?'

It was never a hardship to look after Emerson, and I could do with the extra money as there were still other expenses for the formal, like hair, make-up, and shoes. 'Sure, I can do that. It'll be fun, won't it, Emerson?'

He beamed up at me. 'It sure will. We can continue our chess lessons. You're getting better.'

I laughed. 'Must be because I have such a good teacher.'

'You should get Rion to teach you. He's even better than I am, and not many people are.'

I said nothing to that.

'And you're so modest too,' Mr Emerson said, ruffling his son's hair. 'You know where I live, don't you, Zoe?'

I nodded. I'd been there once before to babysit Emerson and, of course, Tiberius, who seemed bigger every time I saw him.

'Great. We'll see you about six thirty? I can pick you up if your dad is busy.'

'No, it's okay. Dad can do it.'

'How's your mum, by the way? Your dad mentioned she'd had her operation.'

Mr Stewart worked with my dad, which was how I got to babysit Emerson in the first place. 'She's good, thanks. She's going to start radiation soon, but the doctor is happy with her progress.'

Mr Emerson nodded. 'I'm glad to hear that. Please give her my best.'

'Will do. See you tonight, Emerson.'

'Awesome,' he said before picking up his hamburger and taking a bite. It was funny, but I'd never seen him so happy since his parents split. Maybe that was because his dad, who was actually a nice man, treated him more like a normal boy than a fragile boy genius. I headed towards Lou, who had found us a table in the corner.

She put her phone down as I sat across from her and said, 'So that's Emerson Einstein, hey?'

I nodded. 'I'm going to babysit him tonight, which will be good for my finances. The Stewarts pay well.'

'Mike's coming to meet us. He's just finished his shift. That okay with you?'

'No problem, Lou, you know that.'

Mike, unlike Lou and I, was actually allowed to have a part-time job, and he worked in one of the fast food places in the food court downstairs. He seemed nice enough, though I never really felt I knew him well. He arrived a few minutes later. After giving Lou a quick kiss and saying hi to me, he slid back into his seat and played with the paper serviette on the table. I wondered sometimes what he and Lou had to talk about, since he never seemed to have much to say. But she seemed really into him, and that was good enough for me. I didn't stay long, as I wanted to grab a shower and a change of clothes before I headed over to Mr Stewart's place.

Later that evening, Dad dropped me off. Emerson and I were soon huddled over the chessboard. 'Zoe, are you and Rion back together yet?' Emerson looked at me with his clear, blue eyes.

'I don't really think that's any of your concern,' I said in my best grown-up voice. I was not going to discuss my love life with a six-year-old, no matter how smart he was.

'Now you sound just like my mother,' he said, shaking his head at me.

I sighed. 'Seriously, Emerson, I just don't want to talk about it at the moment. Let's just get on with our chess game.'

He raised an eyebrow and then looked down at the board again. Studying it for a moment, he moved a piece on the board and said, 'Checkmate.'

'How did you do that? I really would like to win at least one game against you, or at least have a game that lasted more than seven moves.'

'You just need a bit more practise,' he said kindly.

There was a knock on the apartment door, and a little smile appeared his face.

'Who's that, I wonder? Maybe your dad forgot his key or something.'

Another knock, a little louder this time. Tiberius started to bark and wave his tail.

'You'd better answer it,' Emerson said.

I scrambled to my feet and went to answer the front door, which opened up onto the small lounge area of the unit. Tiberius beat me to the door, barking joyously. I opened the door and saw... Rion.

'What are you doing here?' I said, totally surprised.

'I'm here to babysit Emerson. And obviously so are you.' He looked as surprised as me.

I opened the door wider to let him in. 'Did his dad call you too?'

'No, Mrs Stewart did. She said the babysitter cancelled on him.'

As he closed the door behind him, the familiar aroma of his aftershave hit me, and I tried not to notice how good he looked in his brown leather jacket and well-fitting jeans. His taste had certainly improved from the first day when I'd taken him shopping, and he had tried to buy a Hawaiian shirt three sizes too big for him.

Tiberius danced around us, tail wagging, and Emerson beamed at us both.

'But Mr Stewart asked me to come over when I saw him and Emerson this afternoon. He never knew you were coming. What happened?' I said.

I heard a giggle behind us, and we both looked over at Emerson. I studied him suspiciously.

'Emerson, what's going on here?'

'Tricked you!' he said and laughed again. Tiberius started to bark.

'Tiberius, sit,' Rion commanded, and to my complete surprise, he did, and he also stopped barking. Obviously, Rion could add dog whisperer to his many other talents.

'Now, Emerson, perhaps you can explain what's going on,' Rion said in a patient voice.

Emerson stopped laughing and looked up at us. 'It was really easy. Mum asked me to tell Dad that Rion was going to babysit tonight. She doesn't like talking to Dad anymore. That's why she gave me a mobile phone. I meant to tell Dad, but then we saw Zoe, and Dad asked *her*. So, I thought it would be great if you were both here.' He shrugged his little shoulders. 'I know you love each other and everything. It's not like it is between Mum and Dad.' He gave a sigh.

Rion and I looked at each other, and I wondered if my face was as red as it felt. Talk about awkward. He looked like he wanted to say something, but instead he sat down on the sofa next to Emerson. I sat on the other side of our small, determined Cupid.

'Emerson, I know you think you were doing the right thing, but you have to leave decisions like that to Zoe and me. It's up to us to work things out.'

'But, Orion, you told me you really loved Zoe and missed her.'

Our eyes met over his head. He had never actually said those words to me. I wondered why he found it easier to say them to Emerson. As his steady, dark eyes looked into mine, I couldn't help wishing that all the stupid stuff that had happened to us could be erased, like a pencil erases a mistake.

'Yes, but it's not just up to me, Emerson. It's Zoe's decision too. And, as she once told me, I don't have the right to make decisions for her.' Rion kept looking at me, and I knew he was waiting for me to say something.

I wanted to say it was okay, that I wanted us back together the way we were, but there was something stubborn inside me. I wasn't sure if it was the Irish or the Italian in me, but I needed him to say that not only did he love me but that, of course, he would try anything to make sure Mum stayed well, even using those magic powers he said he didn't have. I needed that commitment.

I lowered my eyes, not sure if I was making the biggest mistake of my life or not. 'Emerson, sometimes things are not as easy as they look. Sometimes, they are complicated. You can't always fix things just by wishing for it.'

Rion said nothing, but I could feel his disappointment.

Emerson looked up at me, blinking away tears. 'Let me fix it then. I couldn't fix Mum and Dad, but maybe I can fix you.'

'Oh, Emerson,' I said, not knowing what to say. I hated that he felt this rift between us so much. He'd had enough disappointment in his life.

Rion stood up. 'I should go. Your dad doesn't need both of us here.'

'But I do, Orion,' Emerson said.

'Sorry, mate, another time. You two have a nice evening.'

'You don't have to go,' I said, feeling a lump in my throat. I felt so guilty. If I had just said the right thing, he would be staying. But I couldn't.

'Yes, I do,' he said quietly. He was at the door in two strides. Then he opened it and closed it behind him with a click.

Emerson burst into tears, and between his sobs, he said, 'I hate you, Zoe.' Then he ran into his room and banged the door shut behind him. I didn't think

I ever felt so miserable. Even Tiberius looked at me reproachfully, and went to lie down outside Emerson's bedroom door. Rion was gone again, and this time it would be for good.

Chapter Twenty-Four

She was never going to forgive me. And I didn't blame her. I acted like a jerk when I broke up with her. I had good reasons, or so I thought. The trouble was I couldn't stick to them. I was selfish enough to still want to be with her. And then, to make matters worse, I told her I couldn't cure her mum. If I could, I would have done it in a heartbeat. But I couldn't lie to Zoe or give her false hope, even though I wanted to. And I should have told her I loved her long ago. I always felt it. I thought she should know. But I realised now it didn't work like that. You had to tell someone how you felt. My people had never considered feelings all that important. And yet, I realised, they were the most important things of all. I had made a total mess of everything.

I decided to walk home the longer way to give me time to think, and I found myself walking past the modest house Pandora shared with the woman she'd mind controlled. She was just coming out the door when she saw me.

'Rion,' she called, 'come on in.'

I shook my head. It was only by accident that I walked past and bad luck she was coming out at the exact same time. 'I'm headed home.'

'Then wait for me. I was about to leave for Chelsea's, and it's in the same direction. We can walk together.'

I was in no mood to be with other people at the moment, especially not Pandora, but I didn't want to be rude. I stopped by the gate.

She called over her shoulder, 'Hey, Maude, I'm off now. Don't wait up, and make sure you take your medication.' Then she closed the door and came down the front path to join me.

'Tell me you're not drugging her or anything?' Mind control was bad enough, but that would be even worse.

Pandora gave me a scornful look. 'You really have a great opinion of me, Orion. Maude has a heart condition and she takes blood thinners, but sometimes forgets. I keep an eye on her and, surprise, surprise, I actually do care about her.'

I felt instant shame. It seemed I was making one mistake after another these days, especially where girls were concerned. 'I'm sorry. I shouldn't have said that.'

'No, you shouldn't,' she said as we swung into step and headed down the street. 'But what are doing walking here at night?'

I gave a heavy sigh.

'Let me guess. Oh yeah, one word, Zoe.'

I nodded. 'She just hasn't forgiven me.'

'For breaking up with her? Well, it was for her own good. You did the right thing. Although, you weren't very convincing when you said we were together. Don't think she believed that for a New York minute.'

'We were about to get back together, but then I said the wrong thing, again. Her mum has cancer, and Zoe asked me to use my "super alien powers" to cure her. Somehow, she got the idea that because you've used your powers, I could use mine. She wasn't too happy when I told her, not only did I not have any powers, but that I couldn't heal her mother.'

We came to a cross road, and Pandora pointed left. 'This way.'

'Chelsea certainly has a lot of parties.'

'No, it's just a few of us girls getting together. We might go out later. Jas has a car.'

'And she lets you in it?'

'Yeah well, if she cuts me out of things, she's worried the others might take my side. And she wants to keep me

close so she can keep an eye on me.' Pandora laughed.
'She can try.'

I wasn't too interested in what was going on between
those two, so I said nothing.

Then Pandora said, 'How do you know?'

I was puzzled. 'How do I know what?'

'That you can't cure her mum.'

'Don't be ridiculous, Pandora. You know we can't do that.'

'Actually, no I don't and neither do you. We've never
really tested what we are capable of before. So few of us
have ever materialised, and besides, we have this whole
"not interfering with the human species" kind of code.'

'And for a good reason. But that's not it. I told you,
when I became human, I lost everything about me that
was alien. I will age, get sick, and all of those things that
humans experience. If I were able to cure people, then
I would be able to cure myself and wouldn't be mortal.'

Pandora turned her head and looked at me, her
shrewd eyes making me feel vulnerable and exposed. 'I
don't buy it, and you know it. As I've told you, you're
always going to be an alien, Orion. Sure, you may age
a bit, but deep inside you know who you are, and that's
why you broke up with Zoe, remember? And now, when
she's asking for your alien help, you say no. I'm not
surprised she's annoyed at you. I bet you didn't even try.'

'I didn't try because it's not possible,' I snapped at her. 'And I'm not going to lie about it. That would be worse. Besides, her mum has had an operation and the cancer has been removed. She'll be okay now.'

'I don't know how you could have lived so long and have learnt so little, seriously. First of all, cancer can always come back and often does. Secondly, it's about showing that you'd do anything for the person you love. My recent host, he even went clean for six months because his partner at the time asked him to. It didn't last, but at least he tried. It meant something to her.'

I had no answer to that. As we walked together, our feet hitting the pavement, the only sound in the dark still night of that quiet suburban street, I thought about what she said. The longer we walked, the more the realisation came to me that maybe Pandora had a point. Zoe, who had hardly ever asked me for anything, had asked me to do this, and I had said no. I should have said I would try, even if I didn't think it would work.

'I'm an idiot, Pandora.'

She cracked a smile and said, 'Tell me something I didn't already know.'

'Do you think it's too late, to try that is?' I suppose I sounded desperate because Pandora gave me a sympathetic look for once.

'You're really totally hooked on this girl, aren't you?'

'Totally and completely. There was never anyone else, and there never will be.'

'Yeah, well it's pretty hard to have a love life when you haven't got a body. But I kind of get it, now.'

'You mean Chad Evertt?'

'Puleeese! He's just a distraction for when I'm bored, and also to annoy Jas. She's had things her own way for far too long. No, I mean Kerri. I get that people think she's a bit different, but I think that's one of the reasons I like her. She's blunt, honest, and pretty smart for a human. And I'm going to miss her when I go.'

'You're going? When?'

'Don't get excited, buddy. Not yet, not for a while. I'm having too much fun. But eventually I will have to go, and I don't want Kerri hurt. That's why I'm not going to let her get too close. There's no way I want to be a human for life. I've got more sense than you in that regard. Hey, we turn here.'

We turned into a street and were soon in front of Chelsea's house.

'You want to come in? Chelsea won't mind.'

I shook my head. 'Not in the mood. But thanks, Pandora, for the advice, though I never thought you wanted Zoe and I to be together.'

'Maybe I just understand it more now, and I'm getting to understand humans, especially girls, better now.'

'Very occasionally, you might just be a little smarter than me.'

'Newsflash, buddy, I'm a *lot* smarter *all* the time. And, to answer your question, no, it's not too late to show Zoe you're not a complete jerk.' She turned and headed up the concrete path.

Maybe I'd head back to Emerson's house, and if I was lucky, she wouldn't slam the door in my face. I went down the street, eyes on my phone, thinking I'd text her to let her know I was coming. Suddenly, I ran into someone, my head crashing into his.

'Sorry,' I said as I took a step back.

'That, my boy, is what they call an understatement. I'm surprised you've even lasted this long as a human.'

I looked at the one person I never expected to see again. 'Archimedes!'

It was hard after Rion left and Emerson was so upset, but finally, Emerson decided he would talk to me. He even agreed to have the cookies and milk his dad had left for a snack, and we watched *Despicable Me* together.

Mr Stewart had bought some DVDs for Emerson, unlike Mrs Stewart who wouldn't let him watch TV, let alone movies. After that, he let me put him to bed, and even allowed me to give him a hug. It seemed I had been forgiven. But he said, 'Zoe, are you ever going to get back with Rion?'

I thought for a moment. I was already regretting letting him walk out that door. I was being stupid and stubborn. I missed him so much. If I could have that moment back again when our eyes met over Emerson's head and he waited for me to say I was ready to take him back, I would have. And now… maybe he wouldn't want to come back anymore. I'd seen the hurt look in his eyes.

I sighed. 'I don't know, Emerson. I want to.'

His eyes brightened up. 'Then tell him. Text him right now. He could come back here. I'm going to sleep now, so you can have some alone time.' He gave me a little smile.

Jeez, even a six-year-old could make me blush. 'Not tonight, Emerson. It's late. But I will think about it.'

'Tomorrow then,' he said, falling back on his pillow and giving a yawn.

I pulled the blankets up and tucked him in. 'You'd better get to sleep. I let you stay up to finish the movie, but it's way past your bedtime.'

He turned on his side and closed his eyes. 'That's okay. Dad doesn't mind.' But within seconds his breathing became regular, and I knew he had already fallen asleep. I tiptoed out and turned off the light, then closed the door gently.

Back in the lounge room, I opened my chemistry book. Chemistry wasn't my strongest subject, and I'd need to study if I had any hope of passing that exam on Monday. But somehow, the words were making even less sense than usual. Rion was good at chemistry and even better at explaining it. If he were here right now… I put the book down. I had to stop thinking about him. I leaned my head against the sofa and closed my eyes. I had never felt so connected to anyone in my whole life as I had to Rion. It was true that Harry and I shared a history together, but it was different. Yes, we got each other, and I would always care about Harry. With Rion, it went deeper. Once we had shared each other's thoughts, but it was only when he materialised that I realised how close we were. I used to laugh when people talked about soul mates. And yet, that's exactly what Rion was to me. I realised that I had forgiven him, and more importantly, somehow, I needed to get him back.

Chapter Twenty-Five

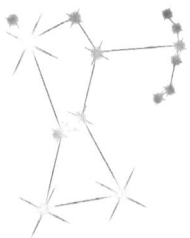

'Archimedes, what are you doing here?'

I looked at the being who had once been my guardian. His sandy hair, blue eyes, and middle-aged looks did not indicate that, far from being human, he was a nearly 5000-year-old alien. He had not approved of my decision to be human, and we had parted on cool terms. As he hated materialising in physical form, I couldn't imagine why he was here.

'Because, yet again, my superior abilities have been called on to sort out another problem, and it is all your fault.'

I hadn't expected a warm or cordial greeting, but this was too much. 'What are you talking about?'

'You made the foolish decision to materialise and then, when our indulgent supervisor gave you the choice, you turned against your own people and became human.'

I felt my face turn warm and my body tense. I didn't experience anger often, but maybe it was because he was saying one of the very things that had caused me to break up with Zoe, I was feeling it now. 'You have no right to criticise my decision and even less to criticise our supervisor, who has shown a lot more wisdom than you. If that's all you came to say, you can leave. Or better still, I will.' I turned on my heel and started to walk away from him.

'Stop!'

I hated that my steps slowed, and I turned around.

He was standing under the street light, and I could see he was struggling to compose his facial expression.

'That was discourteous of me. I am sorry.'

An apology from Archimedes—that was a first.

'I need your help.'

Another first. I waited for him to continue, curious as to what this self-professed 'superior being' could possibly need my help for.

'It's about the rogue being who calls herself Pandora. Following your example, she has decided to materialise, but unlike you, she has ignored our communications. She has also broken several of our most important rules, including her influence over the human, Maude Butterfield. It cannot be allowed to continue. She is jeopardising our entire space mission with her foolish and reckless behaviour.'

Of course. Pandora. I should've realised she would attract the attention of our people sooner or later. She hadn't exactly kept a low profile.

'I don't see how I can help. I've already asked her to return, but she refused. Perhaps you should try, Archimedes. She might listen to you.' I walked back a few steps to stand in front of him.

Archimedes gave a heavy sigh. 'I've tried, several times. She is the most irritating, self-centred, and stubborn creature I have ever encountered, and that includes humans.'

'I didn't know you had contacted her. She never said.'

'No, she wouldn't, would she? She doesn't want you to know that she has been commanded to return to the mothercloud at once. It's only a matter of time before she tells people who she is, and someone might actually believe her. I've always thought newbies should not be allowed to leave the mothercloud until they are at least 1000 years old. But no one listens to me.' His face had a martyred look. 'I was endeavouring to contact her yet again this evening, when I saw you. It was one of the few times the sight of you has given me pleasure.'

Archimedes didn't even realise he was insulting people most times, so I decided to let that one go. 'What do you want me to do?'

'Try talking to her again. Tell her it is imperative she return. Use whatever means are at your disposal. You might even tell her human life is a disappointment and you're sorry you made the choice to become human.'

'Except I'm not.' I decided not to mention I recently thought I might return to the mothercloud. After Zoe's words about the 'gift' of choice my supervisor had given me, I realised that I would not throw it back at him. I would remain in my human state, whether I was with Zoe or not.

'Then convince her she's made a mistake. Surely you must have some influence over her?'

I shook my head. 'Pandora has gone rogue, and she will only return when she's ready. She doesn't really want to be human, Archimedes. She's just playing at it and having fun. Eventually, she'll go back to the mothercloud.'

'Having fun? Since when did our people ever consider that important. I really think letting her into the space mission was an error of judgement. She is a bad influence, not only on humans, but on the younger souls of our kind.'

'She's not a bad entity. Maybe misguided at times, but essentially she cares, and sometimes she can be kind.' I realised that more and more as I had gotten to know her.

'Kind? Caring? What have those emotions to do with our purpose and mission to further our knowledge of this errant planet? Dear oh dear, things are worse than I imagined. We must rectify this at once. Go to that house and talk to her. Tell her our supervisor's patience is wearing out. If she doesn't return soon, he will prevent her from returning at all and she will be stuck in this human form forever.'

'Have you told her that?'

'Of course, but she doesn't believe me. It is for her own good, especially if she doesn't really want to become human.'

I thought for a moment. I knew, more than Pandora, that if our supervisor commanded us to do something, we had to do it or suffer the consequences. He was wise and understanding, but he would not put up with disobedience. I had met him only once, and I had felt his power. I had to make Pandora realise she must do as she was told or risk never returning to her own people.

'Okay, I'll try. Will you come with me?'

Archimedes shook his head. 'My presence seems to disturb her. But I will be close by if you need me.' Slowly his physical presence dissolved in front of me and I was left alone. I looked along the street where Chelsea's house was.

I didn't want to go inside, so I closed my eyes and tried to reach her with my thoughts. It had worked once before, although I had been a lot nearer to her then.

Pandora, I need to speak with you. Come outside.

I waited for about a minute and was about to give it up and go to the front door, when I heard her answer whispering in my mind.

What is it now, Orion?

You didn't tell me that Archimedes had been in contact with you.

Is that old windbag with you now?

Close by. We need to talk.

Silence, then a few moments later the front door opened and she came striding down the path, not looking pleased.

'I don't know how you put up with him when he was your guardian. Of course I didn't tell you. Nothing to tell. I'm not ready to go back yet.' She stopped in front of me and folded her arms.

'It's not just him. You've been ordered back by our supervisor. You know how serious that is.'

'Yeah, but when he says immediately, he could mean anything up to a year or two. You know our people's concept of time is different to what it is here.'

I shook my head. 'No, he means right now. You're breaking all the rules, and that has certainly got his attention. If you don't go back now, then you won't be able to go back at all, ever.'

She looked up at the sky. 'See the Orion constellation up there. That's where our planet is. I think I made a mistake when I joined our space mission. I was too young. I didn't know what I was giving up. I've missed being an organic and having senses. You know I've never even been kissed by a boy before I came here.'

'Do you want to stay then? To become human like me?'

She lowered her head and looked at me. 'No, I don't. I still want to be around in a couple thousand years, in one form or another. But I also want to experience human life from time to time. I guess I want it all.' She gave me a small smile.

'I understand, but I don't think that's possible, Pandora. If you don't go back now, you won't have that choice.'

'But they let you stay. They gave you a choice.'

'And I made it. I can't go back now. You haven't met our supervisor. He is more powerful, wise, and superior to us in every way possible. But he isn't weak, and he won't put up with disobedience. Once he's made his mind up to let you go, there will be nothing you can do to change it. Believe me, Pandora. I've met him. It was an incredible experience, but I wouldn't want to cross him, ever. He's not like Archimedes. Look at me. You know I'm telling the truth.'

We stared into each other's eyes for a moment. Pandora was rebellious, but she wasn't stupid. She saw the truth of my words.

She closed her eyes for a moment, and I sensed the turmoil that was going on in her mind. Then she opened them again and said, 'Okay, I believe you. I'll go back, but not right away. I need to stay until the formal. At least that way I'll be able to say goodbye to all the things and people I've learnt to care about. It's not that long.'

'That's not my choice. But maybe Archimedes can help.'

As if he had been listening to our conversation, which he probably had, he materialised in front of us. Luckily, Pandora and I had walked down the street away from Chelsea's house and there was no one to see him.

'At last you've seen sense,' he said.

Pandora turned to look at him. 'Oh, it's you again.'

Archimedes ignored her lacklustre response. 'Are you ready to go? The sooner, the better.'

'Since you've obviously been eavesdropping, you would also have heard I want to stay until the formal. Then I'll be ready to go.'

His forehead wrinkled. 'The formal? What is that? Some primitive ritual I suppose? And when is it?'

Pandora unfolded her arms and put them on her hips. 'Seriously, Archimedes, how can you not know what a formal is? It's the year twelve dance, and I want to say goodbye to my friends. If I just disappear, they'll wonder what happened to me. And what about Maude? She'll probably call the police out to look for me. I have to finish things here properly, you know.'

'Yes, well it will be the only thing you've done properly. When is this event?'

Pandora rolled her eyes. 'It's in two weeks. That's a nanosecond in our time.'

Archimedes looked at her, considering. 'I suppose we might let you stay for that short period of time, providing of course that you promise to come back after that immediately. And that you don't get yourself into trouble.'

Her arms folded again, and she gave another eye roll. 'Yeah, yeah, I promise. And now that's sorted, I'm going back inside with the girls. We might go out later.'

'Is that wise? It's getting late.'

'No lectures, right? I'll be good, but you need to back off. In two weeks, I'll return to the mothercloud. See you then.' She turned, her hair flying across his face, and then she headed back to the house, hips swinging and boots ringing on the pavement.

Archimedes gave her a look of distaste as he wiped his face with a hand. 'How she ever made it into the space mission, I'll never know.' He turned back to me. 'Thank you,

Orion, for your help. I'm grateful. And if I can ever be of assistance, you may call upon me. I realise that I may have underestimated your qualities in the past.'

I nodded and was about to say goodbye, when a thought occurred to me. 'Actually, Archimedes, there is something you can help me with. It concerns Zoe's mother.'

Chapter Twenty-Six

ou?' I looked at her tear-stained face as she stood on my doorstep. 'What's up?' It was Sunday morning, and Mum and Dad had gone out to the markets.

'Mike broke up with me,' she said, and her face crumpled.

I pulled her inside and closed the door. Then I gave her a hug as she burst into tears. 'Come on. Let's go to my room and you can tell me all about it.'

We sat on my bed, cross-legged, and, in her still shaky voice, she told me what happened.

'He's met someone else on one of those stupid online games he plays. They met up at that arcade where Mike and I had our first date…' She stopped for a moment, then taking a deep breath, continued. 'Anyway, he's met up with her a few times now, even while we were still going out, the… the…' Lou couldn't bring herself to say a rude word, even when she was angry. Instead she said, 'The jerk!'

I hid a smile. That was Lou, sweet to the core. 'You're better off without him.'

'Yes, I am. He texted me last night. He didn't even call me. He said he couldn't hide his true feelings anymore and that he felt we weren't suited. But I tried so hard, Zoe, to do the things he liked. I even learnt how to play some of those arcade and online games.'

I took her hand and tried to choose my next words carefully. 'The thing is, Lou, you shouldn't have to try so hard to be with someone. It should be easier.'

'But things haven't been easy for you and Rion,' she pointed out.

'That's true, and I'd be the first person to admit it. But you shouldn't have to change who you are, and you shouldn't expect someone else to do that either.'

And then it hit me like a lightning bolt, that's exactly what I'd expected from Rion. I wanted him to use his alien powers and, whether he had them or not, was beside the question. He didn't want to do it. It went against what he believed, and I should have respected that.

Lou gave a heavy sigh. 'I think you're probably right, Zoe. I was trying to make myself into someone Mike would like rather than finding out if he liked me for who I was. How did you get so wise?'

I shook my head. 'Not wise at all. Still dateless for the formal.'

'That makes the two of us now, and so is Kerri. Hey, we can all go together now. It'll be fun.'

'Correction—it'll be awesome!'

'Rion!' I opened the door to my second visitor of the morning. Lou had just left and was, I thought, a little happier than when she arrived.

'I hated the way things ended between us last night, and I just wondered, do you want to…' He hesitated.

'Come in.'

He came inside, closing the door behind him. We stood staring silently at each other for a moment. There was so much to say, yet it was so hard to speak.

'I'm sorry,' we said at the exact same moment, and then we both laughed nervously.

'I didn't want you to leave last night. I regretted it as soon as you left. It was just my stupid pride that got in the way,' I said.

'No, you weren't to blame. It was all my fault, everything was. I don't care what happens. I never want to leave you again.'

I looked up into his dark eyes and touched the face that I loved so much. He took a step closer to me, and before I knew it, we were in each other's arms, his warm lips on mine.

It was only the sound of the key turning in the door that caused us to pull apart.

Rion looked at me and blushed, brushing the hair out of his eyes.

Mum came in first. 'Hi, Rion. It's good to see you.'

Dad was close behind, carrying bags. 'Glad to see you two have patched things up. About time.'

'Dad,' I said, feeling my face go red.

'Come on in through to the kitchen,' Mum said.

'Actually, I was just about to ask Zoe if she'd like to go for a coffee.'

'I can't go like this!' I said. 'Give me five minutes to change.'

I helped Mr Brennan carry the bags into the kitchen. He started to unpack the fruit and vegetables and motioned Mrs Brennan to sit down. I sat down across from her.

'I can manage to unpack a few groceries,' she said to her husband. 'You said you had a bit of work to catch up on. Why don't you do it now?'

'You're still recovering, and I'm nearly finished.'

'I can help,' I offered.

He tumbled the apples into the fridge crisper and said, 'Thanks, but I'm done.'

'Then go do your work.'

He smiled at me ruefully and said, 'She's an awfully bossy woman. I'll see you later, Rion.'

As he left the kitchen, Mrs Brennan said, 'So, what have you been up to, Rion? Is your uncle still travelling a lot?'

The Brennans still thought Archimedes, my supposed guardian, was looking after me but, because he was a photo journalist, went away a lot. I was glad she brought him up though, because it fit into my plan.

'He's here in Brisbane at the moment. But how are you, Mrs Brennan? Zoe said your operation went well. I'm sorry I haven't been to see you, but things have been… busy.'

She gave me an understanding smile. 'I'm all right, thank you. I start radiation treatment in a few days. The doctor has removed the lump and, so far, knock on wood and all that, there doesn't seem to be any signs of it anywhere else.'

'I'm so glad. Archimedes sends his regards too. I think he would like to visit, for coffee that is, not a meal.' I hastened to add that last bit because the previous time Archimedes had come over, it had been a disaster. I just hoped she would overlook that.

Mrs Brennan gave a determined smile. 'Of course, we'd be glad to see him, if he isn't too busy.' And that, I think, was the biggest lie she had ever told. But her manners were impeccable.

'Great. He said we might come over tomorrow afternoon after school, if that's convenient.' Archimedes had actually suggested today, but I wanted to make sure things were okay with Zoe before that happened.

'That would be lovely. I'm still on sick leave for the next week, so I'll be home. Unfortunately, I don't think Greg will be able to make it as he'll be working.'

I smiled with relief. Zoe's dad and Archimedes were not exactly on the best of terms. Things might go a lot more smoothly if he wasn't there.

I heard Zoe's feet on the stairs, and then she burst into the kitchen, like a blast of sunshine and warmth and everything that made me feel happy. How had we stayed apart for so long?

'I'm ready,' she said. 'Let's go.'

'You look beautiful,' I said as we held hands walking down the street. She was wearing a yellow top and jeans, and her long, dark hair fell over her shoulders in waves.

'You don't look so bad yourself,' she said, 'although there is a spot on that white tee shirt of yours.'

'Where,' I said, looking down in a panic. I had tried really hard to look my best before I left the house this morning.

'Just kidding. You're immaculate, as usual.'

We walked in silence for a while, each of us not quite knowing what to say.

'Rion, I—'

'Zoe—'

We both spoke at the same time and laughed. 'You go first,' I said.

'Okay.' She took a deep breath. 'I realised how wrong I was to ask you to do something you were uncomfortable about, like using your alien powers. No,' she said, as I started to speak, 'let me finish. You shouldn't have to change who you are for me. Whether or not you even could have helped Mum is beside the point. It went against everything in you to try. I should have respected that. I only realised that this morning when I was giving advice to Lou, advice I should have followed myself. I don't care what stupid stuff has been happening in the past, let's get over it. I want you back again, Rion.'

What could I do but kiss her right there and then? I touched her soft lips and then, even though I didn't want to, I pulled back and said, 'My turn to talk now.'

'Sometimes talking is highly overrated, Rion.'

'And sometimes, it's necessary. I've been so stubborn, convinced I couldn't do anything that I wouldn't even try. You've hardly asked anything from me, and this was so important. I love you, and not only should I have said that, but I should have showed it by trying to do what you asked. I can't change who I am. A part of me will always be alien. What that means for the future, I don't know. But I do know, I don't want a future without you in it. And whatever you want me to do, I'm going to do it. I've talked to Archimedes.'

'Archimedes, is he here?'

'Long story and it has to do with Pandora. But I've asked him about your mum. He is older than me, and whatever powers he has are much stronger than mine. He wants to meet your mum to see if he can help in any way. He isn't guaranteeing anything, but he might be able to tell if the cancer is completely gone. He's coming over for coffee to your place tomorrow afternoon.'

'He's willing to do that?'

I couldn't blame her for being surprised. He wasn't known for his helpfulness or consideration for others. 'I did him a little favour with Pandora, and he wants to pay me back,' I explained. 'Besides, you know he's always been fond of your mum. I think he has a bit of a crush on her.'

Zoe laughed, and then she said, 'Yeah, I remember when he tried to kiss her after that dinner he had with us. He would have succeeded too, if you hadn't pulled him back.'

I shook my head at the memory of it. 'He's impossible at times, but he can do the right thing on occasion.'

'With a little persuasion from you. Thanks, Rion. I really appreciate it.'

'I should have done something before this, even if it came to nothing. I'm s—'

She put a finger to my mouth. 'No more sorries. We're good.'

I took her hand. 'So, do you really feel like coffee?'

'Well, I have had a large milkshake with Lou, and it sort of filled me up. Why, what are you suggesting?' She looked at me, head tilted to the side.

'I was thinking that it isn't that far a walk to my place, and that it might be fun to curl up on that sofa of mine and watch a movie or something.'

A smile formed on her face. Then she said, 'A movie or something? What's something?'

'Well, we have a lot of catching up to do.' I put my arms around her. 'And I don't think the middle of the street is the best place to do it.'

'I agree,' she said, resting her head against my chest. 'How long do you think it will take us to get there?'

I raised my arm and looked at my watch. 'Six minutes and thirty-five seconds, if we hurry.'

She moved away and grabbed my hand. 'Let's go.'

We made it in five.

'How lovely,' Mum said as she looked at the large bouquet of yellow daisies that Archimedes presented her the next day.

'Beautiful and bright, like you, dear lady.'

I coughed to cover the laugh that wanted to escape. Archimedes hadn't changed since I'd seen him last.

'Come in and sit down. The coffee is on and the brownies have just come out of the oven,' Mum said, playing the gracious host. I'd tried to persuade her from baking anything, but nothing, not even an operation, prevented her from trying her best. I'd rescued them before they were burnt.

Mum and Archimedes sat in the armchairs while Rion and I sat on the sofa. I was so glad Dad wasn't here. It was awkward enough as it was, and everyone felt it, except for Archimedes. We sat drinking coffee and eating brownies, trying to make small talk.

Finally, Archimedes put down his cup and said, 'So, how are you, my dear?' he asked. 'I heard you hadn't been too well.'

Mum gave a shrug. 'That's true, but things are better now since the operation. I start radiation treatment soon. Thank you for asking, Archimedes.'

He leant over and took her hand in his, looking into her eyes intently. Mum looked uncomfortable, and I could tell she wanted to pull her hand from his, but she didn't. I didn't know how long he held her hand like that, but for a moment it seemed like time stood still and nobody moved, or even breathed. Then he let her hand go, and she sat back in her chair as if dazed.

'You will be all right,' he said. 'And you have your family around you, which is, I think, the most important thing for you. But don't work too hard, dear lady. Humans have too little time on this earth as it is. You should enjoy it, in moderation of course.'

'Thank you,' Mum said, looking confused and uncertain how to answer him.

Archimedes rose. 'And now I must say goodbye. It has been lovely seeing you again. No, don't get up. Zoe will see us to the door.'

With a little bow to her, he left the lounge room and went out the door, while Rion and I followed. I closed the door behind us as we stepped out on the path.

I looked at Archimedes expectantly. 'Well?'

He looked down at me, his face expressionless. 'She has no cancer that I can detect. She will recover her strength and health in time.'

I breathed a sigh of relief. 'Thank you, Archimedes. That is so good to know.'

'But, Zoe, you need to understand this. While I might be able to detect an abnormality in the body, I cannot cure it. If she had had cancer, I would have been able to do nothing. Orion was right. Our powers do not extend to that. We have enhanced perception, honed by centuries of training, but we cannot perform miracles or magic or whatever nonsense Pandora may have persuaded you to believe.'

I looked at Rion, feeling slightly ashamed. I should have believed him. I had been wrong on so many levels to blame him.

'I know,' I said. 'I should never have asked.'

He nodded in agreement. 'You should go back inside. She won't remember much of what happened, except that I'm a little strange, which is what I am used to from humans. But she might be feeling confused. I put her in a trance while I scanned her.'

'Thank you again,' I said before going back inside, leaving Rion to say goodbye to him. It's funny, but when you got to know some people, they weren't so bad after all. Although, I thought, as I closed the front door behind me, I don't know if you could exactly call Archimedes a person.

Chapter Twenty-Seven

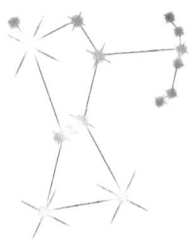

I twirled in front of the mirror on my cupboard door, the purple and indigo skirt of my dress swishing slightly.

'Wow, you look great,' Lou said as she pulled the bodice of her dress up. 'I wish now I'd got something different. What was I thinking? This just isn't me.'

I went over and grabbed her hand. 'You look really beautiful, Lou. And you know what's even better? You're just as nice on the inside as you are on the outside.'

She gave me a hug, and then we both said at the same time, 'Make-up! Hair!' We bounced away from each other. We had both spent a small fortune on getting our hair and make-up professionally done, and we weren't about to mess it up now. Lou had an updo, which really suited her, and mine had every kink and curl straightened, hanging like I wished it always would.

'You could have gone with Rion to the formal, you know,' Lou said as she checked her make-up in the mirror.

I fingered the small silver necklace with the heart that Rion had given me back. We were back together, and that was all that mattered. But we'd both decided that being with friends was important too. 'I think it will be more fun if we go as a group. That way no one gets left out. I wonder where Kerri is. She was supposed to be here by now.' But just as I spoke, I heard a knock on the door downstairs.

And then I heard Mum's voice. 'Kerri, darling, you look so lovely!'

I went out and leaned over the railing. 'Come on up, Kerri. We're just about ready.'

I saw her red head coming up and a sea of green around her. When she got to the landing, I looked at her. 'Wow, you look amazing!' And she did. One side of her bobbed hair was held back with a flower clip, and make-up toned down her freckles and made her wide grey eyes seem larger. Her dress, a sea green, had a full skirt that floated around her, and the lacy short sleeves of the top were perfect. Because Kerri had never, ever bothered about her appearance, I hadn't realised that she actually was so attractive—not that it mattered, I thought. Lou and I still loved her and her quirky personality.

Lou came out the bedroom door and was just as surprised as me. 'Gee, Kerri, you look great. Where are your glasses?'

'Mum persuaded me to try contact lens, and I've been putting them in for a few hours every day to get used to them. I thought I'd take a chance and try them out tonight. They're not much good for studying, but I thought I probably wouldn't need a book tonight. Besides, my handbag is too small for one.'

She was totally serious.

'Are you belles of the ball ready,' Dad called up, jingling his car keys. 'I think it's time to go.'

We grabbed our things and headed downstairs.

Dad looked at us and said, 'You look dazzling, ladies. Do those poor boys at East Valley High know what they're in for? You'll have them lining up for dances.'

'Dad,' I said, with only a slight eye roll, 'you're such a dork. We don't need to wait for guys to dance with us. We'll dance with each other, and if they want to join in, fine.'

Mum looked at us, a suspicious moisture welling in her eyes. 'Photos before you go, I insist.'

'We'll have photos taken there, you know.'

'That's fine, but I would also like photos now,' she said, holding up the camera.

So, we spent the next five minutes in various groupings. The last one was just Mum and me. 'You look so beautiful, darling,' she whispered in my ear. 'I'm proud of you, and I love you.'

I felt a lump in my throat, and I suddenly felt grateful to know Mum was okay and would be with us for many years to come. 'Love you too, Mum.'

Then, with a flurry of skirts, hugs, kisses, and goodbyes, we were off.

The school had hired the function room of the River Bend Inn for a formal, and we were all just a little bit excited to go to such a fancy venue. The place was buzzing when we got there, with parents dropping off their kids and even a few limos that some students had hired. Of course, Jas and her group had hired a white limo. No real surprise there. I wondered if Pandora was with them, though, considering everything that went down between her and Jas, I doubted it. I had heard that Pandora was going with Chad. No accounting for taste. I couldn't believe that I had a crush on him when he first came to our school last year. So much had happened in those twelve months. Soon I would be seventeen, and I felt so different to that annoying, attiude-y teen I was back then.

When we got inside and saw the tables with white linen tablecloths and the smooth dance floor, I had to pinch myself to believe I was here. In a few short months, year twelve and high school would be behind me. I only just realised I was one step away from starting the next phase of my life, and I was so glad that Rion would be there to share it with me.

'I wonder if the boys are here yet?' Lou said, looking around.

Then I heard his voice saying my name. I turned around and my heart dropped right to my feet. I had heard the word 'swoon' before, but I never understood it. Now, I did. Rion in a tux was drop-dead gorgeous and smokin'. He had tried to slick his dark hair off his forehead, but some of it still managed to escape and drift over his dark, intense eyes that were looking straight at me. His hands found mine, and he pulled me towards him.

'You look so beautiful,' he whispered in my ear.

'So do you,' was my dumb answer. But he did.

After a few moments, I became aware of everyone else. Harry was looking pretty good himself, and I wasn't the only one who noticed. Lou seemed all breathy and definitely flustered when she said, 'Hi, Harry.' And with those two words, I realised she just might be getting over Mike.

And it was by no means one sided, because he was looking at Lou like he'd never really seen her before. 'Wow, Lou,' he said. 'Wow.'

And then we started to notice each other, and everyone told Kerri she looked great, and for once she just accepted the compliment gracefully, looking quietly pleased with herself.

'Well, we scrub up well,' I said, 'for the nerds of the school, that is.'

'Not bad, guys,' said a familiar voice. Pandora sashayed up to us in a tight red dress with ruffles and a slit down the side. She would not have looked out of place as a flamenco dancer. Her straight black hair was held back on one side with a red flower, and her mouth creased in a wide scarlet smile. 'Do you mind if I join you?'

We were too surprised to object. 'Where's Chad?' I asked, hoping we wouldn't have to put up with him too.

She gave a dismissive wave of her hand. 'Oh him, I dumped him. He was getting too boring for words. I thought I'd rather hang out with my peeps.'

Kerri looked at her, open mouthed.

'Hey, is this band ever going to start?' Pandora looked impatiently to where the band was setting up.

'I think we're going to eat first,' Harry said, his eyes still on Lou.

'Eating? What a waste of good dancing time.'

'And have photos taken,' Kerri said.

Pandora looked at her, and her eyes softened. 'Hey, you look really pretty tonight.'

Kerri blushed. 'Thanks. You look awesome.'

'You know what? We should get our photos taken together. That would be great fun.' Pandora put her arm around Kerri, who gave her an enthusiastic nod.

It seemed the right time. We all moved over to the line where photos were being taken. And, as naturally as if it had been planned, I went with Rion, Lou went with Harry, and Pandora and Kerri followed.

As Rion stood next to me, I felt a surge of happiness. This was our first proper photo together, but I hoped it wouldn't be the last.

The meal seemed long with speeches and toasts, but luckily our group, so used to eating lunch together and hanging out, managed to have a good time in spite of it.

During a break in the speeches, I went to the ladies room, and then I went outside to catch a quick breath of air. So much had happened in the last few months, and I had so much to be grateful for, it was overwhelming.

I slipped outside to the terrace and stopped when I saw two figures. When I looked closer, I saw, to my surprise, that it was Kerri and Pandora. They were facing each other and holding hands. I didn't want to intrude, and I was about to go inside when I heard Pandora say, 'Kerri, I don't want you to ever forget what a special person you are, especially to me.'

'Pandora, I've never met anyone like you.'

'Same. We're binary stars, remember.'

'I'll never forget.'

Then Pandora bent her head and kissed Kerri. I felt how special it was, even from where I was standing. Tears, but happy ones, sprang to my eyes, and I realised in that moment, Pandora had become one of us.

'But, Kerri, one day you will forget.'

'No, never.'

'Yes, you will. I want you to. But for now, you'll remember. We had an awesome night, and then I had to go away. And that's okay.'

I slipped inside again, feeling it was wrong to stay any longer. It seemed to me we had all grown this year in ways we never expected.

Finally, it was time to dance, and that was the most fun of all. Of course, I danced with Rion and Harry, but we girls danced together too. Pandora got up and whispered in the ear of the lead guitarist, and then I heard an old song that my parents, total dorks, sometimes sang.

'Come on, girls. This one's for us,' Pandora said. We all got up, Lou, Kerri, Pandora, and me, and we totally owned that dance floor. It was the best fun I'd had in a long time.

Then I was in Rion's arms again. It was a slow one, and I was happy to lean my head on his broad chest and sink into his arms. 'I'm so glad we're together again. I never want to be apart from you again.'

'Me either, and we have all next year to look forward to when we go to university. I can't wait to start the next phase of our life together. I really love you, Zoe.'

I didn't think I could be happier.

When this wonderful night drew to a close, Pandora came over to us. 'It's time,' she said.

Rion looked at her. 'You're ready then?'

She nodded. 'I thought I'd be able to say goodbye, but I don't seem to be able to.'

'What's happening?' I asked.

'I'm leaving, Zoe. Going back to where I belong. I've been ordered back, and this time, I really have no choice.'

This was the first time I'd ever seen her look sad. She'd been larger than life and had blown into our lives like an unexpected cyclone, and somehow it seemed strange that she would no longer be there. I reached out my hand and touched hers. 'I'm sorry, Pandora. We will miss you. Kerri most of all. Have you told her?'

Pandora shook her head and looked over the dance floor to where Kerri was talking to Lou and Harry. 'I can't. It would be too hard on both of us. But at least we've had tonight. Tell her goodbye for me?' Pandora's eyes misted over.

I nodded, feeling a lump in my throat.

Pandora looked at Rion. 'Will you walk me out? I think Archimedes is going to materialise just to make sure I keep my word.' She gave a little laugh. 'He doesn't trust me.'

Rion nodded. 'You're doing the right thing, Pandora. You know that, don't you?'

She nodded. 'Sure, but it doesn't make it any easier. Come on, let's us two aliens get out of here. See you, Zoe. You know what? I never said this before, but Orion's lucky to have you.'

Rion put his arm around her. 'Let's go,' he said. They walked out the door, those two beautiful aliens that managed to turn everyone's lives topsy-turvy. Thank goodness one of them would be coming back to me.

Pandora shivered in the cold night air. I pulled her in a little closer. 'It's okay,' she said. 'It soon won't matter.'

We walked to the river, which was not far from our venue. The winter sky was studded with stars, and the black water rippled gently under a nearly full moon. Pandora breathed in deeply and moved away from me. 'I'll miss this, Orion. To smell, to see, to touch, and even to feel cold. She raised her arms towards the sky and turned around. 'But I've had such fun. It's been a blast.' She lifted her head, her dark hair tumbling down her back, and laughed in her carefree way.

Then I saw the shimmering form of Archimedes take shape beside her. 'Are you ready?' he said.

'Come on then.' She lowered her arms, linking one of them with his. 'Let's get on with the next adventure.'

I watched them slowly dissolve until there was nothing left but grassy bank and the river beyond. I wondered if I would ever see any of my people again.

I went back to the formal, where the band members were slowly packing up their instruments. Most people had left. Zoe had her arm around Kerri, whose eyes were red. 'So, she's gone?'

I nodded, wondering what Zoe had told her.

'Do you think she will ever come back?'

I looked at Zoe, who said, 'I don't think so, Kerri. France is a long way from here, and she was only ever going to stay here a short while.'

'But why did her aunt have to take her now? Tonight?' Kerri asked. 'She never even said goodbye.'

'She only stayed for the formal. She was supposed to go earlier. She wanted to say goodbye, but she couldn't.'

'I really cared about her.' Kerri's voice was sad, heartbroken.

Zoe said softly, 'And she cared about you. She told me that. She'll never forget you, and you'll always have this night to remember.'

'Yes, we had an awesome night. I know she had to go away, just not so soon. But she told me it would be okay, and Pandora never lies.'

We took Kerri home in a cab, while Harry took Lou home. It had been one of those nights where both good and sad things had happened. I was surprised how Pandora's departure had even affected me. I had wanted her to go. I knew it was the best thing. Yet, I would miss her more than I realised. Maybe it was because of her total honesty and her determination to live life on her own terms. That took courage, and I admired her for that.

Finally, there was just Zoe and me at her door saying goodnight. She put her arms around my neck. 'This night has been more… more of everything. I can't describe it.' She sighed and leaned her head against my chest.

'I know what you mean,' I said, holding her close.

I looked down at her, wondering if I could ever love her more, want her more than I did right now. 'I love you, Zoe.'

She smiled. 'That wasn't so hard, was it?'

I put my hand under her chin and lifted it, looking at her so trusting and loving. 'I think I've loved you from the first moment when I fell on you on that beach nearly a year ago, even though I was a conceited, self-important little bubble of alien consciousness.'

'You did not. You were forever giving me lectures day and night about my unhealthy lifestyle, and poor choices about friends, school — just about everything.'

I laughed. 'I don't know how you put up with me. But I only did that because you drove me crazy — none of my other hosts had ever done that. Then, I realised it was because I cared about you. That had never happened to me before.'

'Well, you sure had a strange way of showing it,' she said. But she smiled. 'You loved me from the start eh? I have to tell you it wasn't mutual.'

I dropped my hand. 'I know. I've made a lot of mistakes.'

'And you'll probably make a lot more.'

I gave a heavy sigh.

'But, you have improved.'

'Really?' I looked down at her.

'And, I think you could improve even more.'

'How?'

'You are slow tonight, aren't you? Hurry up and kiss me already.'

I didn't need any more encouragement.

A while, maybe a long while, later, she moved away from me. 'This is lovely, but I'm freezing.'

'You'd better go in, then,' I said, reluctantly.

I gave her a last kiss goodnight, and she slipped inside, calling out softly before she went inside, 'Good night, my alien.'

I'd let the cab go, happy to walk home tonight with my thoughts. I never realised when I was a bodiless, cerebral entity for thousands of years what it meant to be human. But in the last twelve months, I had experienced more life than I had in the previous four thousand. There was heartache, disappointment, and sometimes even despair, but there was also joy, love, and unending hope. I knew that a part of me would always be alien, and I accepted that finally. As I had told Emerson, it was okay to be different. But I didn't regret my decision to be human either, no matter what it meant for the future. And I knew, with a sudden sobering thought, that Zoe would need me as much as I would need her in the future. For Archimedes hadn't told her everything about her mother. 'She's clear... for now. But of the future...' He shook his head. All he would say was, 'Be there for her.'

I would never tell Zoe that. It may not even come true, but whatever happened, I had every intention of being there. The ups and the downs we'd face together, because that was what being human was all about.

Acknowledgements

Books are never solo efforts, and mine is no exception. There are several people who have helped in so many ways to make this third book of *The Alien Chronicles* a reality. The support and critiques of my fellow writers from Write Links has been invaluable. In particular, I'd like to thank my critique partner, Tyrion Perkins, who gave such detailed and valuable feedback. Also, being part of that wonderful organisation, The Romance Writers of Australia, has helped me enormously in the journey of being a writer. Another big thank-you goes to Anthony Puttee and the crew at the Self-Publishing Lab for making my book look its best. Finally, I would like to thank my cheer squad, Rob, Ruth, and Richard, whose very existence makes it so much easier to write. Ruth's insightful critiques have helped me avoid many pitfalls, and now, as a fellow writer, she has made my journey less lonely and certainly more fun. Richard's encouragement and support is always there for my writing, and for building my writing business. Last but not least, my appreciation and love goes to Rob, who shares the ups and downs, not only of the creative life, but life itself. You guys are my anchor.

About the Author

Robin Martin has been a writer and a teacher for many years. Originally from Canada, she has lived and worked in several countries, but now lives just outside Brisbane, Australia. Writing has always been her passion, and in recent years she has written several novels for adults and young adults, including *The Alien Chronicles* series.

When she is not plotting stories, she loves reading everything from cereal boxes to long books that she can get lost in. She finds her inspiration in beach walks along the beautiful Queensland coast; an eclectic music collection that ranges from The Rolling Stones to Chet Atkins to Bach; and good coffee, without which she wouldn't be able to function. She and her family are also *Star Trek* fans.

Visit Robin at www.robinmartinthomas.com to find out about her other works and to sign up for her newsletter to receive free stories and the latest updates on her next books.